^ADEATH_{IN} REMBRANDT SQUARE

ANJA DE JAGER

CONSTABLE

CONSTABLE

First published in Great Britain in 2018 by Constable
This paperback edition published in 2019 by Constable

1 3 5 7 9 10 8 6 4 2

Copyright © Anja de Jager, 2018

The moral right of the author has been asserted.

A CIP catalogue record for this book
is available from the British Library.

ISBN: 978-1-47212-631-3

Typeset in Bembo by Photoprint, Torquay
Printed and bound in Great Britain by Clays Ltd, Elcograf S.p.A.

Papers used by Constable are from well-managed forests and other
responsible sources.

Constable
An imprint of
Little, Brown Book Group
Carmelite House
50 Victoria Embankment
London EC4Y 0DZ

An Hachette UK Company
www.hachette.co.uk

www.littlebrown.co.uk

A DEATH IN REMBRANDT SQUARE

Chapter 1

It was 13.35 on an autumnal Wednesday, and the woman standing at the desk in the police station on the Elandsgracht was making the indoors almost as stormy as the outdoors.

'For fuck's sake,' she shouted, as if the loudness of her voice would make up for her lack of stature. Her Asian heritage made her look minuscule in this country where almost everybody was tall. 'When are you going to get off your lazy arses and do something?' she swore in flawless Dutch. She was so petite it looked like a schoolgirl had dressed up in her big brother's corduroy jacket. Her black hair was tied back in a topknot and shaved at the sides as if to showcase her ears, which had a row of small rings running all along the rim. Her eyes were protected by black-framed glasses.

Her entire appearance demanded the attention that her height wasn't going to get her.

Every police station in Amsterdam had its fair share of angry people, crazy people, drug-fuelled people and drunk people, or any combination of those four, and normally I would just have thrown a quick glance at the duty officer to see if he needed a hand, and then ignored it if everything was under control.

But now I paused, because I could see the woman's face properly, and even though it was red and contorted, I recognised her. Of course I did. Most police officers here would.

'Please calm down,' my colleague said. He leaned on the desk as if he needed to have a closer look, and loomed over her. 'We've said that someone will come to see you.'

She continued to rant. 'I was burgled yesterday and nobody's been round. I've called and called.'

The public entrance was separated from the rest of the police station by glass walls. It was for security reasons, but it made it seem as if the woman was by herself in a glass cage, cordoned off or locked away like an animal in the zoo. It was this that tempted me to take a quick photo, until I realised how inappropriate that would be and put my phone back in my pocket.

'Someone went through my papers,' she said. 'Yesterday afternoon. And still nobody's talked to me.'

'I understand,' the duty officer said with a small smirk around his lips, as though he was enjoying the woman's powerless rage. 'But in your statement you said that nothing was missing, nobody was injured and nothing had been damaged.'

She took the elastic band from her topknot, shook her hair loose and tied it back again. The redness slowly receded from her face. 'Was it you guys? Did you do this?'

'Please stop making these groundless accusations.' My colleague sounded like a disappointed schoolteacher talking to a misbehaving pupil.

Sandra Ngo having a complete meltdown in the police station on the Elandsgracht was something that a lot of police officers would appreciate. Even though she was no longer on TV, her true-crime podcast still had a huge following. Trying to prove that we were doing a lousy job made for interesting listening for the general public, but it obviously didn't endear her to anybody here. She might have to wait for a long time before anybody came to take the details of the burglary in which nothing had been stolen.

Suddenly she looked up and saw me. 'Detective Meerman, would you care to give a comment for our podcast?' She spoke more loudly, but I could hear her clearly through the glass anyway.

I shook my head, as I'd done the dozens of times that she'd asked me the same question before. 'He did it.' The window didn't seem like strong enough protection any more.

Sandra gave me a rueful smile, as if she'd been hoping for something else. I walked away.

'You're not going to help me?' she called out after me. 'I'm keeping your name out of it.'

I stopped and turned back towards the window. 'Is that a threat?'

'No, of course not. I'm just saying: one good deed and all that. I only try to get to the truth. I give a voice to the vulnerable party.' She sounded as if she almost believed it herself. 'Haven't you listened to yesterday's episode? He's innocent.'

At least she hadn't said his name, because for me, that would have to come with a trigger warning.

I didn't respond, but escaped and made for the stairs: it was already late for lunch.

I did not want to think about Sandra Ngo. I only wanted to think about food. My stomach rumbled as if in agreement with my brain. Having a late lunch put me in a slightly cranky mood, and the fact that it was caused by an excruciatingly long internal briefing only made it worse. It was mitigated by being greeted by a sea of empty tables, including the one by the window that was my favourite.

But as I was carrying my lunch over to my usual spot, five minutes after the encounter with Sandra and lulled into a false sense of security, I heard someone else say the name. Instead of continuing to where I was going to sit, I had to drop my tray on the table closest to the two men who were talking. The words had caught me like a fish hooked through the lip, the stab of the memories as sharp as ever.

'I couldn't believe it was him at first,' the man nearer to me said. The oversized fluorescent yellow jackets hanging over the backs of the chairs and the motorcycle helmets on the table made it pretty clear that they were traffic cops. Maybe the guy had given him a speeding ticket. If I'd sat by the window, I could have looked out and pretended I wasn't listening to them. Now I just had to hope they were too deep in conversation to notice my odd seat choice.

'I'd just listened to the latest episode,' the guy continued, 'so it was weird to see Ruud Klaver in person.'

I couldn't breathe for a second. I took a gulp of milk and it washed some of the lump from my throat to my stomach. I had hoped the memory's jagged edges would have been smoothed, because over the past six weeks I'd heard more people talk about him than I had in the entire ten years before. Maybe if I heard his name dozens more times, I would slowly become immune to it.

That would be the only upside of this trial by public opinion, even if the public never knew who I was. Sandra Ngo's *Right to Justice* podcast was careful to talk about 'the police' instead of using individual officers' names. Maybe the two men having their lunch didn't know that I'd been one of the investigating officers on the case, or maybe they hadn't noticed that I was sitting here at the table next to them.

It was also possible that they knew both these things and simply didn't understand how terrible it was to have this particular case discussed over and over again.

'It's ironic, isn't it?' the guy said. 'That this happened just now.'

'I don't know if it's ironic.' The man facing me rubbed his eyes. He was the one more likely to spot that I was surreptitiously eavesdropping. He was dressed more for a holiday in France than police work in Amsterdam, in a long-sleeved white top with horizontal blue stripes. He was in his mid thirties and had light brown hair that he wore with a side parting. My mother would describe him as a 'nice guy'. 'I think it's sad,' he said.

Sad? So they weren't talking about a speeding ticket.

I hadn't really kept tabs on him since he'd come out of prison, but I'd looked in the database as soon as the *Right to Justice* podcasts had started airing. He'd been clean. Had something changed? What had he done?

'What did Forensics say?' the man with his back towards me said.

'Still waiting. Checking the car's trajectory. Not sure it will help us much.'

I gave up any pretence of eating. He'd been in an accident?

'I'll go to the Slotervaart hospital later,' Stripy Top continued. 'It's not looking good. As a pedestrian, you don't stand a chance against a car.'

He'd hit someone with a car? Before I could muster up the courage to ask what was going on, Stripy Top tapped his helmet, pushed his chair back and got up. He looked at me, and I got the impression that he'd known I'd been listening all along.

I took a couple of bites from my sandwich, then went back up to the office that I normally shared with two of my colleagues. At the moment, it was empty. It was the autumn school break, and Thomas Jansen was on holiday with his family, while Ingrid Ries was having lunch with her boyfriend.

Since I was alone, I woke my PC and pulled up a file from the archives. It was the same one I'd been furtively looking at every day since the current series of *Right to Justice* had started to air. At least I'd stopped reading the comments on their website.

I opened the transcript of the interview with the murderer. The interrogation during which he'd admitted killing Carlo Sondervelt. In the back of my mind a little voice whispered that just because a man had confessed, it didn't mean he was definitely guilty. Other innocent people had confessed to crimes they hadn't committed. A woman had walked into the police station and announced she'd murdered her husband and her son. They had both, luckily, turned out to be completely unharmed. The woman had ended up in psychiatric care. A man had confessed to a rape until forensic evidence exonerated him. So yes, my experience told me that it was possible this man was innocent.

Only he wasn't. He'd done it.

As I read, the afternoon slipped away unnoticed until the darkness came. That was earlier each day anyway, and I switched on my desk light with a click that resonated in the space. Ingrid had come back and gone home at some point. I think she knew what I was doing but had left me to it.

When I was by myself, I didn't like sitting with my back to the door, and I thought about using Thomas's desk instead of my own. Our office contained four L-shaped desks, pushed together to form a plus sign. Ingrid's was to my left, by the window. Thomas had the ideal spot: facing the door and also by the window. My old case being discussed made my desire to see who was coming up behind me even stronger. It was ridiculous, of course, because not many people knew that I'd been one of the investigating officers. Plus nothing was going to happen inside the police station.

I stared at my computer screen for a few minutes without reading and then hit the x in the top corner to kill the file, because what I really wanted to know couldn't be found in this ten-year-old transcript. As I grabbed my coat and shut the door to our office, I wondered what the quickest way to the Slotervaart hospital was. I walked down the corridor and then took the stairs two at a time. That was definitely faster than waiting for the elevator.

I left the police station through the door at the side without looking back, and passed the little courtyard garden where the metal statue was visible now that the plants had been stripped by the wind of most of their leaves. My bicycle was parked just around the corner. I unchained it. The Slotervaart was a twenty-minute cycle ride from here. The blustery northerly wind would be behind me on my way there, so I might even make it in less time.

I set off along the road towards the canal. Details of my old case occupied my mind. Sandra Ngo's question about whether I'd listened to the latest episode made me wonder if she had discovered new information. Surely there was nothing.

Still, just to be sure, I stopped by the side of the road, put my earphones in and pressed play to listen to the latest instalment of *Right to Justice*. Sandra's voice in my ears was mellow, as if talking about past crimes was as soothing as an easy-listening music programme. It was very different from the angry shrieks and shouts at the duty officer earlier.

It was dark, but the street lights were on and their glow accompanied my journey. My front lamp threw a dim circle onto the street ahead of me. The cycle path was empty apart from a scooter that overtook me noisily. I went over the wide bridge that signalled the end of the canal ring and came to the newer part of town. The road dissected a park, with statues on either side that might have been memorials to something, or maybe were just art. One day I really should stop and check. The streets were deserted. No more tourists here, no late-evening shoppers.

In my ears, there was no explosive new material. Sandra

didn't talk about anything I didn't already know. Whenever she said his name, I blocked it out by imagining her loud shrieks in the police station. She and her team still hadn't unearthed a single thread of evidence that corroborated the murderer's story. Nothing to imply that justice hadn't been done. Of course, she didn't say so openly. It wouldn't make for interesting listening to say: yup, the police were right, this man is guilty. Instead she did her best to keep the possibility of innocence alive, but I wasn't convinced, and I didn't think many of her audience would be either.

I shouldn't have followed the podcast series as closely as I had done. The police had initially been portrayed as incompetent fools. That meant that I had been.

The road widened out as it came to the roundabout at the bottom of the park. I glanced to my right, but there were no cars coming. The wind was starting to pick up, as had been forecast, and the tops of the young trees that separated the cycle path from the street were bending under the force.

Back into a built-up area, the cycle path disappeared, but the road was empty anyway. Here it was lined on both sides by ordinary blocks of flats with shops on the ground floor. A nail bar had five treatments for the price of four as a special offer. The Indonesian toko next door flashed red and green lights, as if buying takeaway food needed to come with a warning sign. It understood how I felt.

I sat up straight on my bike, taking one hand from the handlebars and stuffing it deep into my pocket. I exhaled deeply, and tension I hadn't even been aware of spread from my shoulders through the rest of my body. A sudden blast of wind blew my hair in front of my face, and the material of my jacket flapped around me with the sound of a sail cut loose in a storm.

'But more of that next time. We're on the trail of some interesting information that we think proves Ruud Klaver's innocence,' Sandra said.

I cycled past cars parked nose to tail that looked more depressing than they had done before I'd started listening. I was certain of this conviction. What was Sandra talking about? In the back of my mind I was worried about what she was going to dig up on the case.

When I reached the hospital, I put my bike in the covered bike racks.

'Thanks for listening to us,' Sandra concluded. 'You can of course continue to post any information on our website.'

I took my iPod out of my pocket to switch off the podcast, and was just locking my bike when three people left the hospital through the revolving doors. The first was the traffic cop from the canteen. The zip of his thick fluorescent jacket was undone and I could see the striped top he was wearing underneath. He paused and exchanged a few words with the two people who followed: a woman maybe ten years older than me and a man in his early twenties. I took a quick step back towards the bike racks so that my colleague wouldn't notice me. He got on his motorbike and left.

The woman started to cry. It surprised me. She hadn't cried last time.

It was as if listening to Sandra Ngo's voice had conjured these two people up. The woman now had grey hair, spiked up, and wore tight trousers and Doc Marten boots. The young man wrapped an arm around her shoulders. He was built like a bear, with a beard and glasses. I didn't want to acknowledge who he was. He could be a young friend, or the older woman's neighbour.

The woman's tears shook me up enough to wake me and make me wonder what the hell I was doing. I shouldn't be here. Before anybody could see me, I recovered my bike and left.

I hadn't seen her since I'd given my testimony in the court case. Then, as I'd answered the prosecutor's questions, I'd had a clear view of her. She'd been sitting motionless in the row behind the murderer, like a gorgon, with hatred blazing out of her eyes.

Chapter 2

It was pitch dark by the time I got back to the police station. I could have gone straight home, but I knew that without the rest of my team in the office, I could get the couple of minutes by myself that I needed. I wanted to know why that woman had been in tears, but I also knew that I'd be better off not looking into it tonight. I sat at my desk, pushed the palms of my hands against my eyes and slowly counted to ten as I conjured up a picture of a cardboard box full of fluffy kittens. Just as I was putting the finishing touches to my mental calming exercise by adding a red bow to an imaginary white ball of cuteness, I heard footsteps coming up behind me and turned quickly.

Standing in the doorway was the one person I didn't want to speak to.

The fluorescent yellow of the traffic police uniform was extremely bright, and it made me blink after the self-created darkness. The man carried his motorcycle helmet under his arm. He smiled, but seemed uneasy.

'Can I talk to you for a minute?' He was solid enough to keep a motorbike upright.

'You're traffic police, right?' I said.

'Sorry, yes. I'm Charlie,' he said. 'Charlie Schippers.'

The parents of my first boyfriend had had a cocker spaniel called Charlie. Apart from giving my boyfriend and me a great excuse to be together by taking the creature for a walk, my main memory of that dog was its endless ability to fetch the same stick from the same place over and over again without ever getting bored.

'Lotte Meerman,' I said.

'I know.' Charlie did his best to look serious, but a grin kept creeping onto his face. I could tell he was delighted to be here. 'Can I ask you something?'

'Sure.'

'Ruud Klaver's been in an accident. He's in a bad way. He got hit by a car.'

I couldn't say anything for a second. The fluffy kittens were running away really quickly.

'We're still treating it as a hit-and-run for now, but there are some doubts. It looks like he was targeted on purpose. Have you kept tabs on him at all since he was released from prison?'

I could understand why he was here, because when a murderer is hit in a traffic accident, you do get curious. 'I haven't followed him since his release, but I checked his record earlier today, and he's been clean. No incidents, no contact with the police. A couple of traffic tickets.'

'Any threats against him? Anybody saying they wanted to kill him as soon as he came out?'

'The victim's parents were pretty upset at the time, of course. They were angry with him, but they didn't seem the killing type. Still, you never know.'

ANJA DE JAGER

My phone rang. It was my mother.

'Where are you?' she said. 'You haven't forgotten, have you?'

'No, I'm on my way now.' I looked at my watch. It was later than I'd thought. 'I'll be there in five minutes.' I was grateful to her for giving me an excuse to cut short my conversation with Charlie.

As I reached the canal where my flat was, I could see my mother standing outside my front door. We used to play cards together once a week, but we'd now changed that to having dinner every Wednesday night. I wanted to keep an eye on how much she was eating. She was too skinny for a woman in her mid seventies. Her cheekbones were so sharp that they looked as if they could cut through the loose skin that covered them. Her white hair was so short that even the storm outside hadn't managed to disturb it.

She'd come bearing food: she was carrying a white plastic bag filled with boxes. It probably came from the toko on the corner. I didn't hold out much hope that she'd ordered my usual, but at least she'd saved me from having to cook. Luckily it wasn't raining, because then I would have felt even guiltier.

'I'm sorry,' I said. 'I got held up.' I chained up my bike and opened the communal door. My flat was the top floor of a seventeenth-century canal house. When it was built, the tax on houses was decided by the size of the footprint of a building, so like many of the others along the canal, it was high and narrow. The stairs were steep. My mother followed me up the three flights. She looked petite and fragile but

14

I knew she was strong underneath, and she wasn't even out of breath when she got to the top. It was probably all that cycling she did.

I could hear my cat meowing from the other side of the front door, but as soon as she saw my mother, she froze in silence, then ran away to hide in the study.

'How are you?' my mother said.

'I'm fine. Come in.' I held out a hand for the food. 'I was going to cook for you.'

'I got a set meal for one, but that should be plenty for both of us.'

I wasn't going to argue. She had a bird-like appetite, and however often I urged her to eat more, she never did. The portions from the toko were always on the generous side, and buying one meal would have saved her money as well.

I tidied up the table and removed the papers that always seemed to congregate at one end of it, then closed the curtains, blocking the view of the canal. I loved my flat. The walls were painted pale blue and soft grey, colours that were picked out again in the curtains. I had bought the place from an interior decorator in financial difficulties. I had been a cash buyer and she had needed the money. The deal, which included most of the furnishings, was done quickly. She'd had great taste and I'd had a lot of sense when I changed as little as possible.

I told my mother to take a seat at the table and went into the kitchen to get plates and cutlery. The rest of the country might eat Indonesian food with a spoon, but my mother liked chopsticks, Chinese style. It was more of a challenge and made a meal last longer. I also filled Pippi's food bowl, so that she'd have something to eat once she'd got over the shock of seeing her arch-enemy on her territory.

In the meantime, my mother opened the plastic boxes. Boiled white rice, chicken satay, prawn crackers and beef rendang. Even though she knew what my favourite was, she'd actually got hers. Well, she'd paid for it, she was entitled to. She bowed her head and said a quick silent prayer, meeting my eyes again when she said 'Amen.'

'*Bon appetit*,' I responded.

'I've been listening to that podcast.' She spooned a helping of rice onto her plate.

'*Right to Justice*?' I said, taking the smaller of the two skewers of satay. 'I didn't think podcasts were your kind of thing.'

If anything, I would have expected my father to get in touch and talk to me about it. He was always interested in my cases. Maybe he didn't listen to *Right to Justice* – as an ex-policeman he probably wasn't a fan – or maybe he didn't know that I had been the lead detective on that case. My parents had got divorced when I was five years old and I had lost touch with my father. We'd only started to get close again about a year ago.

My mother looked at me with her duck-egg-blue eyes. 'Wasn't that the case you were working on when—'

'Don't,' I interrupted her sharply. I didn't want to hear it.

'But it was, wasn't it?' She looked at the plastic boxes as she said it, as if she was fully concentrating on the food and this was just a throwaway comment.

Of course she knew exactly when the Carlo Sondervelt case had been. She never liked that I was a police detective, thought there was something wrong about me wanting to follow in my estranged father's footsteps, but during that particular case it seemed as if she was waging an all-out war against my profession. Every time she saw me, she would tell me that I had my priorities all wrong, that I should be thinking about my health and not chasing after criminals. I'd laughed at her concerns.

She helped herself to the beef rendang – three pieces of beef, with the tiniest amount of sauce possible.

'That's not a proper meal.' I took the spoon from her and scooped some more onto her plate.

'In yesterday's episode they said that maybe he was innocent.' She frowned at the food, as if that would make it disappear. 'I know you like to think you're always right, but that time,' her voice was hesitant, 'maybe you weren't thinking as clearly as you normally do?'

At least she made it sound like a question. 'The guy did it,' I said. 'There was a witness.' I gripped a piece of chicken between my chopsticks and twisted the wooden skewer with my other hand to loosen it. When the meat was free, I pulled it from the stick. It was good. The sauce was rich and peanutty.

'The witness was the victim's girlfriend.' My mother locked eyes with me. She didn't even have to say it.

'Yes. Nancy.' I spooned rendang onto my plate.

'Wasn't she pregnant at the time?' She used her chopsticks to mix rice and sauce together on her plate.

'Yes, and that was great for us because she hadn't been drinking.'

She must have finally been happy with how well mixed

the food was, because she scooped up a mouthful of it, sticking out her tongue as she brought the chopsticks to her lips to stop any rice falling on the table. She chewed slowly and I was pleased at the respite in the questioning.

Eventually she swallowed. 'I don't know why they were even there if she was pregnant.'

'Mum, it's where students go on Thursday nights.' I knew that well, because when I'd been at university I'd often gone clubbing around Rembrandt Square with my friends. I grabbed a prawn cracker. Pippi reappeared in the room. She glowered at my mother, then fled to safety behind my legs. She wasn't a fan. The feeling was entirely mutual.

'Don't give any to that cat,' my mother said.

'I wasn't going to.' Pippi didn't like spicy food. I reached down and scratched her behind her ear.

'Have that other satay skewer too.' She pointed at the one I'd left behind.

'No, that one's yours. I've had mine.'

She took it reluctantly. She shouldn't have ordered it if she didn't want it, I thought. She grabbed the meat with her teeth and pulled on the skewer. I grimaced, because that always seemed a precarious way of eating it. I was concerned that her teeth could give way at any minute.

'What a waste of a life,' she said.

And now the murderer had been in a car accident. I thought of what his family had looked like when they'd come out of the hospital: the woman with the young man following the traffic cop. He'd come to see me afterwards, hopefully just to get some background information on the initial case.

Both my mother and I stopped eating.

'Do you think,' my mother finally said, 'that it's possible he didn't do it? That he was innocent? That's what they said on that podcast.'

'I really don't think so.' I pushed my plate away.

'But if there's evidence . . . It's possible, right?'

'Do you doubt me too?' I got up from my chair. Instead of becoming annoyed, I focused on clearing the table.

'I wouldn't normally, you know that, but I know when this case was. And with that girl being pregnant—'

'Don't go there. Don't say it.' I pushed a plastic lid hard onto one of the boxes until it snapped shut.

'You would have automatically believed her whatever she said.' My mother got up from her chair to stack the plates, because that way she could avoid my eyes.

'Leave it,' I said. 'I'll do it.'

She put the plates back down on the table. 'How's Mark?' Her hands dangled by her sides now that they didn't have anything to carry or clear.

'He's well.'

'Does he know?'

I shoved the boxes in the fridge and closed the door so that they were out of sight. If only I could store my memories away as easily.

'You should tell him.' She grabbed her coat as though she'd decided that if we weren't going to talk about it, she had better things to do.

After she'd left, I tried not to think about what she'd said. As I wiped the table clean to remove the last bits of food, I decided I was going to stop listening to the podcasts.

Thinking about the case felt like picking at the scab of a recently recovered wound until you made it bleed all over again. I no longer wanted to remember it. I felt good about being sensible at last.

I opened my laptop and Skyped Mark. We chatted about his new project for a bit and discussed the colour scheme for the house he was working on. I mentioned that my mother had bought me food. I didn't mention anything else.

I went to the bookshelves and dug out my scrapbook. It contained clippings of all the cases I'd worked on. I opened it and turned to the two blank pages near the front: the pages where the photos of that trial used to be.

Chapter 3

The next morning, I walked to the police station through rain that came down so hard it was practically a curtain of water. I'd abandoned the idea of cycling, as I'd only get to the office looking like a drowned rat. The wind pulled at my umbrella, fighting me for control, and I had to hold on with both hands. Keeping it as low as possible above my head gave me better odds. My feet and the lower half of my legs getting soaked was the price I had to pay for keeping my hair dry. It hadn't stopped raining all night and I had to jump over a puddle that was the size of a lake.

As I got to the final bridge before the police station, I sped up to a jog. The entrance was a welcome sight, as I would finally be protected from the rain. I stopped under the overhang and folded up my umbrella. But before I could swipe my card through the reader and push open the gate, I heard footsteps behind me.

I turned and saw Charlie Schippers holding a large golf umbrella. 'Do you have a few minutes?' he said. 'There's something I need to talk to you about.'

I checked my watch. It was still early. I had half an hour

21

before my official starting time. Not that anybody stuck to that. 'How about a coffee?'

'Sure.' He seemed relieved.

'Canteen?'

'No.' He looked around him. 'Let's go somewhere else.'

The protection of the police station was so near. 'Only if it's close.' I was fine with canteen coffee if that meant not getting drenched further.

Charlie pointed to the little café by the bridge behind the police station.

I nodded. That was close enough. I slipped my swipe card back into my pocket and put my umbrella up again. The wind was strengthening. I turned up the collar of my coat to keep the gusts from driving the air down my neck.

We crossed the bridge to the café together. The wind whipped up the surface of the canal until there were little foam-capped waves on the normally languid water. The trees on the canal's edge swayed in the storm. A lone cyclist had to work hard against the wind; one gust was so strong that he almost came to a complete standstill.

The green circular beer-sponsored advertising hung over the doorway. I'd had coffee a few times here before. It was good. I took a seat by the window and watched Charlie order our cappuccinos at the bar. The place was almost empty. I played with one of the beer mats that covered the round wooden table, spinning it on its edge. A gust of wind drove the rain against the window; it sounded as if someone was throwing a bucketful of water against it. The rivers flowing down the glass distorted the outside world, alternately obscuring it and revealing it again. The houseboats moored along the canal wall were shaken by the storm, moving as if they were chomping at the bit to leave, eager as horses at the start of a race.

I knew how they felt. I checked my watch just as Charlie put both coffees on the table and pulled back his chair. The metal legs scraped on the wooden floor. He slid a sachet of sugar in front of me.

'How's the guy doing?' I asked. I didn't even need to say his name. We both knew why we were here.

'He's still in a coma in intensive care.'

He'd mentioned last night that it was serious, but I hadn't realised that the injuries were that severe. 'And you said he was hit by a car?'

'Yes.'

'Have you found it?'

'Not yet. It may well turn up.' He gave me a nervous smile, as if he was reporting to a rather demanding boss. 'Whoever did this is hiding it well. Often we find the car crashed into something else later on, but not in this case.'

'Nothing from garages? No repairs?'

'There might not be much wrong with it. Maybe it's only got a broken headlight. Then it would be like looking for a needle in a haystack. It really depends on what kind of vehicle it was, and how it hit him. A pedestrian was killed by a car last year and it only had a few scratches.'

I nodded. I'd seen something similar myself. 'Where was the accident?' I took a sip of my coffee. It tasted as if it was made from proper coffee beans and with real milk, not like the instant stuff they served in some other places.

'The corner of the Johan Huizingalaan and Comenius-straat. He was on foot. The car must have hit him at speed.'

'Is there CCTV on that junction?'

'No, unfortunately not.'

'Have you got any witnesses?' I scooped up some foam with my spoon and licked it off.

'Two people saw the accident. One was an elderly lady who lives in the flat above the takeaway place. She said the car was dark blue but had no idea of the make or the shape. A "nice car", she called it. The other was a guy who was walking along the pavement opposite when it happened. He called the ambulance – that's how they got to Klaver so quickly. He said it was a dark-grey car: an Audi or maybe a BMW, but he wasn't sure. He didn't see a number plate.'

'Did he see the driver?'

'No. It was already dark and things happened quickly.' He glanced down at his notepad.

'Dark? Wasn't it yesterday morning?' I had assumed the accident had happened just before I saw Charlie and his colleague in the canteen the previous lunchtime.

'No, it was on Tuesday night, around eight p.m.'

A day before I found out about it. 'Sorry,' I said. 'I shouldn't be asking all these questions. You wanted to talk to me about something?'

'I can give you information about the accident.' He smiled as if to pretend it wasn't a serious offer.

'And why would I want that?' I needed to stay far away from that guy, and especially his family. I looked out over the canal and watched the trees bend this way and that in the storm.

'I thought you might be curious. It's possible that it wasn't an accident.'

A couple dashed towards the café and took refuge under the awning. They obscured my view of a woman with a red umbrella that provided such a small circle of shelter that her legs and feet got wet with every step she took.

'Why do you think it wasn't an accident?' I asked. It was what he'd hinted at last night. 'Is there any specific reason?'

'It wasn't a normal hit-and-run. I don't like the car's trajectory. It's suspicious. Do you want to see?' Charlie asked.

A large gust of wind grabbed hold of the red umbrella. The woman lost her grip on it and for a second it floated on the air, dancing this way and that until it was pummelled by the rain and crashed to the ground.

'I can take you to the site of the accident, give you all the reports. I just want something in return.' He leaned forward on the table and looked at me with the same pleading look that cocker spaniel had had when it had wanted me to throw its favourite stick. 'I want to get into CID.'

I shook my head. 'I can't help you with that.'

'I've been a traffic cop for almost ten years now. I just need a chance. A break.'

'That isn't up to me.'

'You know that if this wasn't an accident, it will go to CID. All you need to do is keep me involved. Let me work with you. Then I can learn, and that will help me with my next application. I'll help you prove it was a murder attempt,' he said.

That was very much not what I had in mind. I wasn't going to touch this with a bargepole.

'Let's not,' I said. It was probably just an accident.

He sat back on his chair. 'Not? I thought you would want to know everything about Ruud Klaver.'

'Don't say his name.' The words came out involuntarily. 'Keep me out of this.'

Charlie narrowed his eyes and looked at me over the rim of his coffee cup as if that was the most interesting thing I'd said so far.

I didn't say anything else; just drank my coffee slowly and looked out over the storm-churned water of the canal. Eventually he pushed back his chair and left.

He had been right about one thing: if this hadn't been an accident but a murder attempt, then the case would come to CID. I just had to make sure that it didn't come to me. I'd already been thinking about that investigation of ten years ago far too much. Too much for my own sanity.

I walked along the corridor to our office behind a man who wasn't familiar to me. Young, with ginger hair, he wore jeans with large holes in them, and his white T-shirt showed off a pair of brawny, muscular arms. I was surprised when he went into our office.

Detective Ingrid Ries looked up from her PC screen. Her eyes darted from me to the guy who'd gone in before me. Ingrid and I had worked together now for over six months, and were comfortable with each other, so it was a shame that she was moving on next week to work in the serious crime unit. I'd only been half joking when I'd told her it was a mistake to work in the same team as your boyfriend. I'd seen it go horribly wrong with other work couples. I hadn't convinced her. She would find out for herself.

Next to her keyboard was a half-eaten chocolate bar. I was always surprised how she could eat so much junk and manage to stay so skinny. The knots of her wrists were visible where her jacket sleeves didn't cover them. It was hard to find clothes that fitted, she'd once told me, because her arms and legs were so long. When the third member of our team, Thomas, was annoyed with her, he compared her behind her back to a stick insect. When she was annoyed with him, she told him to his face that he looked as if he should be in a middle-aged boy band. She also made fun of his fake tan and perfect haircut.

'Sorry to disturb,' the brawny guy said, 'but we're swapping the paintings today.'

'Oh fantastic. Best news all day,' Ingrid said.

Dutch art subsidies were turned into pieces from so-called promising new artists to hang in government buildings. Every so often new pieces were added to the collection and old pieces removed. Probably to be sold, but nobody knew that for certain. The painting that was on our wall at the moment was mainly red and blue squiggles, equally as likely to depict the inside of an electricity cabinet as someone's guts.

'Can we have something good?' Ingrid asked.

'I'll settle for something not awful,' I said.

'You'll love your new one.' The man lifted the despised painting off the wall, leaving a peaceful blank space behind. 'Even I can tell what it's meant to be.' He winked at me.

'We can just have nothing. That's fine too,' I said. I dropped my soaked umbrella on the floor and hung my coat on the rack behind me.

'No can do, I'm afraid. I'll be back this afternoon with the new artwork.' He hooked his fingers in the metal string that had been used to hang the painting up, and carried it out of the door.

'Don't be like that,' I said to his back. 'Just tell us what it is.'

The man turned and winked again, then walked away.

'It's going to be bad, isn't it?' Ingrid said when he was out of earshot.

'Judging by the look on his face,' I said, 'I reckon so.'

'A naked woman?'

'A dead body?'

It was disconcerting that we weren't entirely joking.

'Either way,' Ingrid said, 'I bet it's going to be a car crash.'

Suddenly a picture of an electricity cabinet seemed rather good.

Chapter 4

An hour later, my phone rang. It was the boss, who told me that he wanted to see both Ingrid and me in his office. The timing gave me a hint as to what this was about. I wished I'd had more time to think about how to play it. I would just have to go with the flow. I was nervous.

Chief Inspector Moerdijk had recently returned to indulging his love of extreme exercise after an enforced break because he'd done his knee in. It was a testament to his addiction to training that he'd run into work this morning through weather that was so bad, even the ducks complained it was a little bit wet. Ingrid and I paused in the doorway to his office.

'Good morning, boss,' I said.

'Sit down, guys, I just need to finish this.'

I had no idea what 'this' was, but it was clearly taking place on his computer. We took a seat at the other side of his large dark-wood desk and I rested my notepad on my lap. Moerdijk's head was bent in full concentration over his keyboard, and he was half hidden by the screen. This could all blow up in my face. I stared at the wall of the office, which was covered by rows of law books.

The window behind the boss was getting washed from the outside by the rain that showed no sign of abating. If the weather stayed like this, he might have to swim home. Raindrops were hitting the glass so close together that they no longer made an individual impression, and instead combined to form a river as soon as they struck the window. I wanted to see one drop by itself, because that would give me the confidence to stand up against what I knew the boss wanted. Instead, every drop that crashed into the window was immediately swallowed up by the ones that had gone before it.

Ingrid scribbled something on her notepad and passed it to me. *What's this about?*

I took the notepad from her without saying anything and wrote: *Car crash.*

She looked at me and raised her eyebrows. She held the notepad up for me to read. *Art?* she'd written.

I had to work hard not to burst out laughing, and just managed to stifle an amused snort. I shook my head. I should have filled her in on the way here. There'd been time. Keeping quiet wasn't always the best policy. I drew some circles on my notepad and filled them in with diagonal lines.

'Right.' The boss glanced up. 'Sorry about that. There's something I need you guys to look at.'

I drew another circle.

'I'm sure you're both aware that an old case of yours, Lotte,' he looked at me over the top of his reading glasses, 'has been covered in that *Right to Justice* podcast.'

'Yes, we know,' Ingrid said.

'And now the guy who was in prison for the murder

of Carlo Sondervelt has been hit by a car, a couple of hours after the episode claiming that he was innocent was broadcast.'

Ingrid looked at me, suddenly realising that I'd been serious when I'd written *Car crash* on the notepad.

The boss also stared at me. 'I have just been informed that forensic evidence has shown it's likely this was a murder attempt, and therefore the case has been moved to CID.'

'I understand, but I'd prefer that someone else handled it,' I said. 'There's no reason to involve me.'

'If someone tried to kill this guy over something that happened ten years ago, I can't think of a team better suited to investigating it than us,' the boss said. 'You know all the parties involved, so it will make it all a lot quicker.'

'I'd prefer it wasn't me,' I repeated. 'Why do you think it has something to do with the old murder case?'

From the corner of my eye I could see that Ingrid was studying me. She knew me well enough to realise that it was unlike me to walk away from a case, or ask not to work on something.

'That podcast, the questioning, it could have brought a lot of feelings back to the forefront,' Moerdijk said.

I wanted to nod in agreement but had to argue the other side. 'It could be something more recent. Who knows what the guy has done since he came out of prison.'

The boss smiled at me. It worried me. 'It sounds to me as if you're unwilling to take this case. As if you're not interested.'

'I would really prefer not to get involved.'

He frowned at me. 'If you hadn't wanted to get involved, you should have stayed away. You had a meeting with the traffic police to discuss the case.'

I swallowed. I hadn't thought Charlie would tell anybody that he'd talked to me. 'I only had a chat with the guy. He said he wanted to ask me some questions. I didn't visit the scene or anything like that.'

'Still, given your involvement with the traffic department, I naturally assumed you were already working on the case. Without telling me, I have to add. So I'm curious as to why you don't want it now.'

I drew another circle on my notepad and linked it with the others. Surrounded by small versions of itself, it was caught with nowhere to run. 'It's not that I don't want it . . .'

'Oh good,' the boss said. 'For a second there, I wondered. All yours now. Talk to Traffic. Officially, this time.'

As we walked back to our office, I could only hope that Ruud Klaver had done something illegal after he'd come out of prison and that I had missed it the last time I checked. If he'd been involved in another criminal activity, that would make it possible that this wasn't about the murder of Carlo Sondervelt.

I opened up the police database on my PC. There really was nothing recent on Ruud Klaver. For the last year he had been a law-abiding citizen.

Chapter 5

'Hey, Lotte,' a voice behind me said in what would best be described as a stage whisper.

I saved the notes I had been typing up and turned around. Charlie Schippers was looking over his shoulder as if checking his escape route.

'Sorry, is this a bad time?' His face turned an even darker red. He was hiding a cardboard folder behind his back. He was probably worried that I was angry with him. He should have learned by now that it wasn't a good strategy to annoy someone you wanted a favour from.

'Hi, Charlie, how are you?' Ingrid had just popped out and I wondered if he'd been waiting around the corner until she'd gone. He looked as though he might bolt out of the office if I was too openly irritated with him.

'I'm fine.'

I gestured towards Ingrid's desk next to me. 'Have a seat.' I made sure my tone was friendly. If I kept him on my good side, there might be some wriggle room to get out of this case. I had to make him understand that you couldn't turn a traffic accident into an attempted murder just because you wanted to get into CID.

'Shall I close the door?'

That made me pause. 'Why? Is there something you didn't tell your boss?'

'No. Of course not. I borrowed his files for a bit. I thought we could have a look at the forensic evidence.'

'Are you trying to convince me? My boss has told me to work on this, so I will.' I smiled to take the sting out of the words.

He rubbed a hand through his hair. 'I know. Sorry.' He skirted the back of my chair to get to Ingrid's desk and sat down.

'Remind me never to ask you to do anything politically delicate. You're really bad at this.'

He looked like a dog unsure if the treat being held out in front of him was going to be taken away. 'I guess that's not a bad thing?' he said.

I moved my chair next to his so that we could look at the file together. 'Show me what Forensics found.'

He opened the cardboard cover. Inside I could see a pile of photos. He closed it again and looked at me. 'This was a bad idea. It doesn't seem . . .' he scratched the back of his head, 'it doesn't seem the right way round.'

'If you don't want to show me, then don't.' I normally liked looking at the photos first – it was how I worked on old cases anyway – but I had no wish to look at the pictures of this particular victim.

'Okay. All right then.' He turned to a drawing of the cross-roads. 'Forensics talked me through Ruud Klaver's accident this morning.'

I blinked at the pain that hooked in my heart. 'Don't use his name,' I said.

'No? Is that a CID thing?' He looked at me with enthusiasm over this titbit of insider knowledge. More than ever, the cocker spaniel came to mind.

'Yes,' I said. 'It's a CID thing.'

'What should I use instead? Oh, a code name? Like Operation Car Crash?'

I glared at him. 'No.' This was going to be a long day.

'Not a code name? Then what?' He tapped his fingers on the desk as if that would get his brain into gear. 'Oh, of course. The victim. Sorry.'

The victim? The murderer, he meant. But that wasn't the point right now. 'Yes, call him the victim.'

'Thanks! This is so helpful. I would just have done it wrong. Right. We know where the victim was found.' He looked at me for approval.

'Well done.' I managed to keep myself from saying *good boy*. 'Go on.'

'Forensics concentrated on the point of impact of the car. When the ambulance crew arrived, the victim's body was here.' He pushed the drawing over to me and pointed at a red cross. 'From the blood splatter on the road, we also know that he didn't move after the accident, so he probably lost consciousness straight away.' His voice relaxed as he talked about things he was comfortable with. He clearly had expertise in dealing with traffic accidents. More than I had, that was for sure.

He took out a photo and put it next to the drawing, even though I'd told him I was okay with not seeing them. The picture was of a bloodstain on tarmac. I made myself imagine it was someone else's. He picked up a pen from Ingrid's desk and tapped on the edges of the spot. 'Where

35

he was found was where he hit the ground. There is no sign of dragging. The victim was stationary.'

'Okay, so he didn't move. Why is that important?'

'Because he was in the wrong place. He crossed the road from east to west, right to left on the drawing if you like, but he was struck on his left-hand side.'

'The car went through a red light? Is that the issue?'

'Not just that.' Charlie's voice was strong. 'From the victim's wounds, from where we can see the point of impact was, and his position on the ground, we know that he was hit from the side. But he was almost across. The car wouldn't have been coming from that direction on that side of the road, so it must have swerved. It deviated from a straight line to hit the victim.'

This pulled me up, but I reminded myself that he had only brought me this case because he wanted to get into CID. 'You're not suggesting the car came for him on purpose?'

Charlie shrugged. 'I don't know. What I can tell you for certain is that it veered out of its lane. That's what these photos tell us.' He closed the folder and I pushed my chair back to return to my own desk.

'What are you up to?' Ingrid said behind me.

Charlie started as if he'd been caught doing something naughty.

'We were looking at the photos from the accident.' I turned to him. 'Thanks for showing me these.'

'No problem.'

I would have liked him to leave, but he hung around. I had no choice but to make the introductions.

'Now that Ingrid's back,' I said, 'shall we have a look at where it actually happened?'

36

The three of us took the lift down to the basement car park.

'You can drive,' I said to Charlie. 'You know where it is.'

Ingrid beeped the doors of her red car open, then lobbed him her keys. She climbed into the back, obviously assuming I was going to take the front seat. On a whim, I walked round and got in next to her. It was a petty revenge, but it gave me an enormous sense of satisfaction to have Charlie function as our driver. Ingrid and I checked through the contents of the file and ignored him.

I could see that he was disappointed, but if he wanted to get into my good books, he needed to do more than just bring me some photos.

It was the utter normality of the location that made it a strange place for an accident. A minor road dissected a major traffic artery at a broad crossing. In its boring mundanity, this crossroads could be a poster child for 1970s Dutch traffic design. My mother would often tell me of the campaign to make cycling safer, called Stop Child Murder, after more than a dozen kids cycling to school had been killed by cars in a number of accidents. But it was probably expedited by the fuel crisis of the early seventies, with its now legendary Car-Free Sundays, when people rode their bicycles on the motorways.

That focus on equal rights for all road users had created crossings like the one we were standing by, with separate cycle lanes and wide pavements, all divided from each other by knee-high shrubs. The plants were kept low to provide good visibility at any time of the day, and the crossing point for pedestrians and cyclists was controlled by traffic lights. The Comeniusstraat ran due east–west and the Johan Huizingalaan north to south, and the extreme centimetre-perfect right angles of the roads should have provided further safety and security. High poplars were planted close to the houses to break the flat monotony of the roads and shield the people living there from the uninspiring view of a continuous stream of cars.

Today the leaves of those trees whispered in the storm. They whispered of pain and suffering; of blood soaked into the tarmac. They hummed of a life damaged. I wouldn't have been able to hear it if it hadn't been so close to the humming of the blood in my veins, as though we were linked via an umbilical cord. The storm gusted down the main road, where it had free rein. It made my jacket flap, and I did up the zip to stop the noise. An empty plastic water bottle came barrelling down the pavement, accelerated by the wind, until its bid for speed was thwarted by a tree trunk.

The road had returned to cleanliness now. Two nights of heavy rain and a street-cleaning team had made sure there was no trace of blood left on the tarmac. But of course there was still evidence of the accident. Not just in the sound of the poplars or the voice of the wind, but in more concrete terms, because Charlie had brought the photos with him, and I could now match up what he had tried to show me in the office with the reality of this crossroads. Ingrid looked over my shoulder.

A car came past. I instinctively took a step back, further onto the safety of the pavement. We were standing in the shadow of a row of three-storey apartment blocks, in front of a florist.

'Was it here?' I looked at the gutter in case some shards from a shattered headlight had landed there.

On the other side of the crossing was a carpet shop. Rolls of carpet were stacked up in the window. Even if my flat hadn't had wooden floors in all the rooms, I wouldn't have been interested in the rolls in fifty shades of beige. It made me wonder if these blocks of flats were actually an old people's home or sheltered accommodation, and the shop across the road was purely here to service their needs and cater for their tastes.

'I think it was on the opposite side,' Ingrid said.

'He was walking east to west along the Comeniusstraat,' Charlie said, eager to help out, 'and he crossed the Johan Huizingalaan.'

I knew that he'd crossed the main road, because I knew exactly where he'd been going.

'Forensics swiped the area,' Charlie continued. 'We're still hoping to find some paint fragments from the car. Work out what colour it was, analyse the paint and – if we're lucky – identify the make of the vehicle.'

'Sure.' I pressed the button for the pedestrian light. Even though there were no cars coming, I waited for the little man to turn green. While I waited, I looked at the next photo. More blood. A pair of broken spectacles. He'd crossed at the lights. I looked up at the crossing. It had been dark when these photos had been taken. The road looked different in broad daylight. Not the patchy light from the street lamps, but the scattered light of beams bouncing off clouds. The main road, the Johan Huizingalaan, widened out as it approached the crossing, with an extra lane for cars turning left. Between the two streams of traffic there was a slim raised central reservation of grass, like the world's narrowest lawn, not even a metre wide.

The lights changed and we crossed the first lane of the road. As I walked, I threw a glance at the photo I was still holding. I could hear a car coming from my left.

'The second part of this crossing is where Ruud Klaver was hit,' Charlie said.

I froze. All my muscles tensed. Charlie and Ingrid walked on as if nothing had happened, but I turned to look at the car. It was dark blue. The woman driving it had stopped for the red light. Of course she had stopped.

'Sorry, the victim, I mean,' Charlie corrected himself.

The driver and I made eye contact for a second. I didn't know her. I hurried to catch up with the others to cross the second half of the road. I looked at the photo again and walked to the safety of the pavement as if nothing had happened.

'He was on this section of the crossing, walking east to west.'

East to west. He'd come from the florist side and crossed to the carpet-shop side. 'He was walking home, wasn't he?' I said.

Charlie looked at me but didn't ask me how I knew.

'That can't be right,' Ingrid said. 'The injuries are on his left-hand side?'

Charlie nodded.

'But if he was here, they should have been on his right. It must have been a car coming from the other direction.' She took the photo from my hands.

'No, the witnesses said that the car came from there.' He pointed towards the viaduct where the S106 crossed high above the Johan Huizingalaan south of where we were. 'And hit the victim here.'

In my mind, I could see the route the car had taken. It must have formed an arc to the left. He had been hit whilst he was on the leftmost strip of tarmac. That wasn't where the car should have been. It should have been driving on the right-hand side of the road. I understood why Charlie thought this was a suspicious accident.

'The car was on the wrong side of the road,' Ingrid said.

'Or it swerved to hit him,' I added. 'Unless the body was flung up and landed further to the left.'

'No, that's why Forensics examined this so closely.'

I looked at the raised central reservation. Unless the car had taken the wrong lane after the roundabout, it must have driven over the grass. Had Forensics checked this? There were no cars coming, so I crossed back to the middle and balanced on the concrete edge of the reservation, careful not to add any footprints to the soft ground. The wind grabbed my hair and whipped it around my face. It tried to push me over. I crouched down and checked the ground. There were faint tyre marks.

'Look at these,' I said.

'Exactly. They're not as clear as we'd like because of the weather,' Charlie said. 'But we recorded the tracks. As soon as we find the car, we'll be able to match them up.'

This should have been the first thing he showed me. This was the crucial point. The tracks were about two metres away from the crossing. Someone had made a sudden decision to drive over the central reservation and into the oncoming traffic. They had cut across the grass specifically to hit the guy on the crossing.

'Were there any robberies in the vicinity?' Ingrid asked. 'Was this a getaway car? Have you checked?'

'We checked,' Charlie replied, 'but we haven't found anything. Nothing big happened that night.'

I pulled my hair away from my face.

'Is there anything else you want to look at?' he asked me.

'No,' I said. 'I've seen all I need to see for now. We can always come back later.'

It felt as if a ton of weight had landed on my shoulders. I could picture in my head how this had happened. The car would have slowed down as it approached the red light, and the driver would have seen the guy walk across in front of it, just as I had walked in front of the car driven by that woman just now. He'd recognised him, floored the accelerator, bumped over the central reservation and struck him at speed just as he was crossing the second lane.

Charlie was right. This hadn't been an accident. 'You guys go ahead and I'll catch you later,' I said. 'There's something I need to do.'

I had no choice. I had to go to the hospital and see the victim.

Not the murderer, I repeated in my mind, the victim.

I had to do this by myself because I was the only one who couldn't think of him like that.

Chapter 6

I wasn't a big fan of hospitals. You could argue that they were places where doctors made you better, but to be made better you always had to be ill or injured in the first place. Large sections of this part of Amsterdam had been built in the late sixties and early seventies, all in that architectural no-man's-land between historic and modern. The buildings of the Slotervaart hospital were blocks of the kind of grey cement that had been the height of fashion in those days, and there'd been uproar some years ago when someone pointed out that from the air their shape formed a swastika. The best that could be said for it was that it was extremely functional.

Nobody stopped me or asked me who I was as I followed the signs leading to the intensive care unit and went up in the lift. As soon as I got out, I noticed a small group of people: two men in their twenties accompanied by an older woman. The older of the two men was dressed in a suit and tie with a long dark-blue overcoat. He had slicked-back blond hair and a suntan. He stood a couple of paces away from the others and was looking down at his phone. The younger was dressed in jeans and a jumper and had small round glasses and a beard. His jeans were dirty and his

43

jumper was unravelling at the cuffs. He was the bear-shaped man I'd seen yesterday with his arm around the woman's shoulders. The woman was today dressed entirely in black, and her grey hair was smoothed down, as if her outward appearance needed to reflect how serious her husband's condition was.

I could no longer pretend I didn't know who these people were. I rubbed my hand over my eyes as if that would wipe away my anger. This was the last moment I had before I became involved in the case.

'You can't do this,' the guy in the glasses was saying.

Suntan stopped looking at his phone for just a second.

'Seriously, Remco, this is wrong!' Glasses turned to the woman. 'Mum? Say something.'

The guy with the suntan was Remco Klaver. I'd only briefly spoken to him at the time. He'd been a teenager then, just about to start university.

'Dennis,' Remco said, 'we've got to do the right thing for Dad.'

I felt nauseous. The bearded man with the glasses was Dennis Klaver. I hadn't wanted to acknowledge it, but really I'd known from the first time I saw him outside the hospital. I had just hoped he was someone else. A second cousin once removed, for example.

I had wanted to keep that possibility alive.

The two men didn't look like brothers at all: one of them so well groomed and the other an obvious mess.

If Dennis had been anybody else, I would have assumed he hadn't paid attention to what he had put on this morning because his father was in a coma. I would have thought that the bleary look in his eyes was due to worry and lack of sleep. Instead, I wondered if he was homeless. His hair was long and his beard was overly bushy. I wondered if he had been drinking.

I wondered what the last ten years had been like for him.

'You can't do this. Not now. Why not wait?' He grabbed Remco's arm. 'You just fly in and make these decisions.'

'We had a vote.'

'You're killing him. You don't have the right. I know why you're doing this! You hate him. You've always hated him.'

'Dennis, it isn't just me. Mum thinks it's the right thing too.' Remco looked up, but didn't really pay attention to me. He only noticed that there was another person listening. 'And this isn't the time or the place to be having this conversation.'

'Oh, there's a right time and place for deciding to kill your father?'

'Dennis, that's enough.' The mother's voice was sharp, like a whiplash.

Dennis took off his glasses and rubbed his eyes. 'He can't decide this.'

His mother put her arm around his shoulders. 'It's what Dad would want. He wouldn't want to suffer.' Suddenly Angela Klaver looked at me. 'You look familiar,' she said. She paused. 'Oh my God, you're that policewoman.'

I only nodded. I shouldn't have been surprised that she'd recognised me. After all, I'd recognised her immediately as well.

Dennis's face turned ashen. He took a step towards me and then stopped. 'Have you come to have a look?' he said.

45

Anger made his voice shoot up so that it sounded like it was on the verge of breaking. Like that of a teenager.

Like that of the kid he'd been at the time.

Remco was momentarily distracted from his phone screen. Now he really looked at me. His eyes were very pale blue against his suntan. He put the phone in his pocket as if he was on autopilot, as if my presence had hypnotised him.

'What are you doing here?' Angela glared. 'This is crazy.'

As if I didn't know that. I put a hand against the wall to keep myself steady.

'God, you people really are useless,' she said.

The two sons were four or five years apart, if I remembered correctly. Ten years ago, Remco had been one of those tall, lanky kids who would grow into their body later. Dennis had just started middle school, was twelve or thirteen, with a spotty face and greasy hair. I tried not to see those kids in the grown-up men in front of me now. They were no longer a murderer's family. They were a victim's family. But I remembered that they'd both been at home when we'd arrested their father. Dennis had been a bullet of anger. Remco had reacted differently. If anything, he'd seemed to hang back. He hadn't got involved. Even when I'd interviewed him later, with his mother present, of course, he hadn't said much.

He didn't seem to want to get involved even now. After a ten-second pause, he got his phone out of his pocket again, and turned to it as though what was on the screen was all-important, a life-saver to distract him from the reality of what was going on around him.

Over his shoulder, I saw someone else walking towards us.

She was wearing the same coat as yesterday. Her hair was no longer tied in a topknot but hung loose and floppy.

'Sandra, good to have you here,' Dennis said. 'Thanks for coming.'

'Of course I was going to come.' Sandra Ngo shook Dennis's hand, her other hand grabbing his elbow as if she was a vote-winning politician. Then she held out her hand to the man in the suit. 'Remco, I heard you were here. It's been a while.'

Remco seemed to pause before he accepted the handshake.

The mother got a hug.

Sandra saw me, but it took her a couple of seconds before she recognised me. 'Detective Meerman? What are you doing here?'

'Don't mind her,' Dennis said. He pushed open the door to the nearest room. The rest of the family followed him in.

'I hope your father recovers,' I said. I was talking to their backs.

Only Sandra threw a glance at me over her shoulder, but even she didn't say anything.

Through the open door, I could see that a doctor had been waiting at the man's bedside. Now he was talking to the family. He was speaking softly and I couldn't catch his words. I did see that the wife was nodding and the younger son bit his lower lip.

When the doctor left the room, I followed him down the corridor. 'Excuse me.' I showed my badge. 'Can I ask you a question?'

The man paused and looked at his watch. 'If you're quick.'

'Of course.'

'Your patient,' I said. 'What's the prognosis?'

'He's in a vegetative state. His brain is damaged from the impact and his heart had stopped for too long. Even though they got it going again in the ambulance, he was oxygen-deprived. He's also got a broken neck and is paralysed from the neck down.'

Paralysed. If anything was crazy, as Angela had said, it was that. 'The family . . .'

'Are going to have to make a decision.'

I nodded. 'Thank you.'

The doctor rushed away. There was a hushed silence in the intensive care unit that was only interrupted by the beeping of a heart monitor. I peered into the room. Nobody was looking in my direction.

Angela sat at her husband's side on a small red stool, holding his hand. The only thing that betrayed that she was going through a hard time was the make-up smudged beneath her eyes.

A phone buzzed. At the sound, she looked up.

'Sorry,' Remco said, and silenced it.

'Oh Remco,' his mother whispered. 'You didn't have to come.'

'Of course I did.'

'I was going to call you when he woke up. Then he would have known that you were here.'

'Mum.' Remco stayed standing at the foot of his father's bed. 'We need to talk about what we're going to do.'

I knew I was intruding on their privacy, on their moment together, but I couldn't tear myself away.

Angela Klaver shook her head. 'He wouldn't want to be like this.' Her voice wobbled. 'He's locked up all over again.'

Dennis walked up to her and put an arm around her shoulders. He put his other hand on his father's, careful not to disturb the drip.

With his face largely hidden by the oxygen mask, the man in the bed didn't look like Ruud Klaver any more. He looked like a stranger. The heart monitor showed a steady beat, and the ventilator making him breathe was moving his ribcage up and down.

He no longer looked like a murderer but like a patient.

Maybe even like a victim.

I left the hospital slowly, pausing under the glass awning. I could wait here, or I could find the nearest tram stop and take line 2 to the Leidseplein, and walk back to the police station from there. The rain was coming down in streams again. It pummelled the awning with the sound of drums, forming a waterfall where there was a dip in the glass.

Instead of going to the Louwesweg to get on the 2, I walked to the Johan Huizingalaan. My umbrella wasn't big enough to keep me dry, and I felt the rain seeping into the hems of my trousers. The wide road was busy with traffic. I came past the shopping mall with the Albert Heijn supermarket. Cars were speeding in either direction. How come only two people had seen the accident? The car had crashed into the man around 8 p.m. The shops closed at 6 p.m. on Tuesdays, so traffic would have died down quite a bit by then. Most people would have been at home. My left arm was getting soaked where the umbrella didn't cover me. An elderly man coming in the opposite direction stared at me.

I reached the elevated section of the tram rail, and went up the stairs to the stop. From there, I could just about see the traffic lights at the intersection of the Johan Huizingalaan and the Comeniusstraat. The intersection that I now thought of as 'the accident crossing'. Two people were standing under umbrellas, looking at it. The man pointed at something.

The tram turned up and I got on. It was full. There were no seats available. A young man wearing headphones took one look at me and stood up. I considered refusing the offer of a seat, just for one second, but then thanked him and sat down. I didn't know why he'd got up. Did I look tired? Ill? Heaven forbid I looked old. It was better not to speculate about that too much. As I watched Amsterdam go by through the rain-streaked windows, I thought that sometimes making assumptions was a lot better than knowing the truth.

Chapter 7

'Shall we go for lunch?' I said to Ingrid as soon as I got back to the police station. My caffeine withdrawal was showing itself as a niggling headache. It seemed to be positioned just behind my forehead and made it hard to focus. I hadn't had breakfast either.

'When is this storm going to stop?' I collapsed my umbrella and leaned it against the wall of our office.

'Two more days, apparently,' Ingrid said without taking her eyes from the screen. 'They're forecasting force ten winds for tonight.'

That was just what I needed. My flat was on the top floor of the building and the storm would make the roof rattle even more than usual. I could forget any kind of peaceful sleep. 'Coming?' I asked, but she wanted to finish whatever she was typing up before she lost her train of thought, so I went down to the canteen first.

I'd just fetched a coffee in a brown plastic cup when she turned up with a guy I didn't know.

'It isn't often that I get to have coffee with a high-profile member of CID,' he said, smiling as if to indicate that this

51

was meant as a joke. It was the guy who'd been sitting with Charlie in the canteen yesterday.

I opened the small tub of coffee creamer and poured it into my cup.

'Sorry,' he said. 'I'm the traffic cop who investigated Ruud Klaver's accident.' He shrugged. 'Before the powers that be decided it wasn't an accident.' He stuck out his hand. 'Arnaud Groot.'

'Lotte Meerman.'

'I know,' he said. 'How are you?'

I took a sip of my coffee and felt the first hit of caffeine course through my veins. 'Much better now,' I said.

'I'll take that as a compliment.'

I'd meant the coffee, of course. I would have been even better if I'd had that without any company.

'We were looking at the footage from other traffic cameras further down the road,' Ingrid said, 'to see if we could pick up the car.'

'Any luck?' I asked.

'None,' Arnaud said. 'Where the car veered across, at the intersection, there are no cameras. Then it turned into a side street, so nothing there either. There are no shops or anything like that. And it's hard because all we know is that we're looking for a dark-blue or dark-grey vehicle.'

'It's close to Ruud Klaver's house. And very close to the Sloterplas,' Ingrid said.

'You think someone dumped the car there?' I asked.

'No,' Arnaud said. 'I reckon it's gone. Someone's got it out of the country, to Eastern Europe or the Middle East. Like that one last year.'

I remembered that a car had been stolen and traced to Iran. Not that the owner ever recovered it, but he'd had some satisfaction from finding out where it had ended up.

'I wonder how badly damaged it was,' Ingrid said.

'It really depends,' Arnaud said. 'If it had a bull bar or outsized bumpers, it would have been surprisingly intact. Or at least nothing so severe that it would have shown on a traffic camera. It's probably just got a small dent.'

I drank some more coffee. It took the edge off my headache but didn't clear it totally. That surprised me. Over Ingrid's shoulder, I saw Charlie Schippers cross the canteen. He was carrying a plastic bag. Arnaud turned round to see who I was looking at, then leaned forward across the table, closer to me and Ingrid, and lowered his voice.

'Do you see that guy? He's got the desk next to me.'

Ingrid turned to check out who he meant.

I picked up my coffee cup to hide my face.

'He's desperate to get into CID,' Arnaud said.

It was just my bad luck that the guy with the desk next to Charlie seemed to be the office gossip.

Ingrid turned to me with a tight smile and raised eyebrows. 'Is that right?' I knew what conclusion she would draw from that.

'I know, right?' I said, like we were in on the joke together.

I was saved by my mobile ringing. I had a visitor.

I wasn't surprised to see Sandra Ngo here; I had expected her to get in touch ever since I'd seen her in the hospital. If anybody was surprised, it was probably her, because I was keen to talk to her. It just went to show that there was a first time for everything. She was standing in almost the same spot as when she'd been yelling at the duty officer on Wednesday. I wondered if she remembered that too.

'Why were you at the hospital?' she asked.

'Let me take you to an interview room,' I said. I didn't want to talk to her out here in the open.

'Is this official?'

'I don't know what you've got to say. You came to see me. If you want to talk out here, that's all right by me.'

'No, okay. Fine.'

I checked the system. Interview Room 2 was empty. I texted Ingrid surreptitiously that we were going there. She could watch us from the observation area.

Sandra sat down at the table. She looked relaxed. Her hair wasn't tied back today but hung loose, and the front skirted the edge of her jaw. It was straight and swept sideways. She took her jacket off and hung it over the back of her chair, then leaned back in her seat, crossed her legs and rested her ankle on her knee.

'I heard you suspect Ruud Klaver's accident wasn't an accident.' She looked as if she thought she was in control. These interview rooms could intimidate some people, or make them more nervous. It had no such effect on Sandra. Or maybe if you were as tiny as she was, everything was intimidating and you had to get used to it.

'Where did you hear that?' I said.

'Someone called the family. They told me.' She looked around her as if it was fascinating to be here. As if the recording equipment hanging from the ceiling and the microphone in the centre of the table were details that she had always been keen to see. Maybe she was trying to memorise the room so that in her next podcast she could talk about this meeting and describe the surroundings in detail. I had to watch what I said.

'The accident appears suspicious, so we're having another look at it,' I said.

'That's why I thought I'd come and see you; we might be able to help each other.'

'I appreciate that,' I said. Cooperation would make a nice change from shouting in the police station. 'In your podcast, you mentioned something that would prove Ruud's innocence. Is there anything you want to share with me?'

'Ah, so you are one of the many people who download our podcast every week. That's nice to know. I'm broadcasting a special one tonight.' She tipped her head sideways. 'Share, you say. That depends. Is there anything you're willing to share with *me*?'

'You've been investigating him for a month at least.'

'Try two. None of this is quick, you know that. It's been two months since Dennis got in touch.'

'Dennis did?' I wondered how much he had told her. There were many things that weren't in the case files, things that had never come up during the trial. I was sure the family hadn't shared any of them with Sandra Ngo. 'I'd assumed it must have been Angela.'

'No, Dennis called me after the first series of *Right to Justice*. Quite a few people did, in fact.' Her voice was smug.

'I can imagine,' I said. 'There are quite a few people in prison who claim that they are innocent.'

'Maybe some of them are.'

I didn't even bother to react to that. Even though we could always close more investigations, the Dutch police solved 80 per cent of murder cases. To imply that we were often wrong was just ridiculous. 'So, Dennis Klaver contacted you. To say what? That his father was innocent?'

Sandra nodded.

'What made you look into this one, especially as so many people contact you?'

'I was at university when Ruud was on trial. That's where I first met Remco. So I was intrigued.'

'You were at university with Remco? Did he tell you anything about his father's case?' I remembered overhearing Dennis say in the hospital that Remco hated his father.

'No, he didn't talk much about his family. He'd moved out of his parents' house and lived in student accommodation.'

'In Amsterdam?'

'No, Maastricht.'

That was about as far away from Amsterdam as he could get without leaving the country. He really must have wanted to put distance between himself and his family. 'That's quite a way.'

'He went even further after he graduated. He lives in Dubai now.'

That explained the tan. 'But at university he told you who his father was?'

Sandra shrugged. 'No, not really. I think he wanted to hide it, but I found out. It was easy enough.'

Remco had been a student himself when his father had gone to prison for shooting a student. That couldn't have been easy for him. It was often hard on the kids. I wondered how much he had enjoyed having to talk to Sandra about it. When she'd greeted him in the hospital, he'd hesitated before shaking her hand. Their past was probably the reason for the animosity I'd sensed between them.

'Isn't this nice,' Sandra said, 'the two of us having this chat.'

She fished an elastic band out of the pocket of her jacket, turned round to check her face in the two-way mirror that hid the observation area, and then tightened her hair back into the topknot that was her trademark look. I hoped Ingrid was watching from behind the glass.

'If only you'd been willing to talk to me over these past months,' she said once she was happy with her hair. 'There's so much we could have discussed.'

There was no way I would have talked to her about this case if I hadn't had to. It was only because someone had tried to kill the guy, and had tried to make it look like an accident, that I had no choice. 'You can't use any of this in your podcast.'

'I'm going to talk about the accident. The family asked me to.'

'You think the family are really open with you?'

'Dennis has shared all his information with me.' Her smile was complacent.

I could have said something that would have wiped that smile from her face, because I very much doubted that he'd shared everything. There were many facts about this case that were in a closed file. If Sandra knew about them, she would have mentioned them in her podcast, so that meant the family had kept quiet about them.

It didn't surprise me. Dennis would only have talked about facts that he thought would prove his father's innocence. That was his sole aim. He would not have mentioned anything else. That's human nature. People tend to voluntarily share only the information that makes them look good or that supports opinions they already have.

I felt sorry for Remco. He'd been trying to be an anonymous student whilst his father was on trial for murder, and then this girl had found out the truth about him anyway. 'So even when you were a student, you liked digging up secrets,' I said.

'It interests me. Doesn't it interest you? Those things that people don't want to tell you, isn't it fun finding them out?'

'Have you found out anything now? Anything that might give some insight into why someone might have wanted to kill him?'

'I think we're really alike, you and I. From what I've seen of your cases, you want to get to the truth too.' From behind her black-rimmed glasses, her dark eyes stared at me intently.

She was silent for a bit as if to gauge my reaction. I kept my face neutral. Sure, we might both like to find out the truth, but I had a feeling we had very different motives for it. I shook my head.

She seemed disappointed that I wasn't agreeing with her, because her voice was harder when she said, 'Anyway, I found out something. I believe Ruud is innocent.'

I tipped my head sideways this way and that to release some of the tension in my neck. The only result was that the headache shifted from my forehead to my temples. I sat back upright again. 'You believe? Or do you have evidence?'

'What will you do for me if I tell you?'

'If you don't tell me, and you're obstructing the course of justice, you'll be in a lot of trouble.'

She sat back in her chair and folded her arms. 'Such a shame,' she said. 'You're going with the threats. I'd thought you might be willing to make a deal.'

'Threats?' My headache started to throb. 'I'm not going with threats, I'm going with the law.'

'Going with the law. Interesting.' She nodded slowly.

Sandra's needling had made my headache so bad that I had trouble focusing. When the witness is a stone-cold-sober pregnant woman and there are traces of the victim's blood on the suspect's clothes, you have a solid case.

It had been as simple as that.

'Anyway,' she said, 'if you're interested in talking to me further, if you want to know what I've found out, for example, give me a buzz. You've got my number.'

'Yes, I've got it. You've given it to me often enough.'

'You know the family won't talk to you. Ruud Klaver's family, I mean.' She pushed her chair back. 'So maybe you need to call me this time. Hopefully we'll talk later.'

I rubbed my head but the pain wasn't shifting. I got up and showed Sandra out. I felt like a giant next to her. She didn't even reach my shoulder.

She paused on the threshold of the interview room. 'You know what first interested me in you?' She rested her hand on the door handle.

I shrugged. 'Probably nothing.'

'It was how Remco talked about you.'

'Talked about me?' I could only imagine what kind of names Ruud Klaver's son had used for me.

'I'll tell you some other time. Actually, I'll make a deal.' She grinned. 'I'll tell you if you tell me something about yourself that you don't want me to know.'

I frowned. 'Something I don't want you to know about me?'

She nodded.

'Why would I do that?'

She smiled. 'You don't have to. That's fine by me too. Then you'll just have to ask Remco. Maybe he'll tell you. But I'm guessing not.'

I knew what she was implying. She seemed very keen to rub my nose in it. But her words rang true. It was likely that the family would refuse to cooperate with me even though someone had tried to kill Ruud. They might well have given Sandra something that they would withhold from me. Seeing them in the hospital this morning had definitely given me the impression that they were capable of that. But if they wanted to find out who had tried to kill their husband, their father, they might change their minds. I would have to have a proper talk with Angela and her sons, then I would know much more about their position.

It could be bad.

I sat down on the sofa at reception and rubbed my forehead. I'd got off to a terrible start. I had been too preoccupied with my memories of that family to actually do my job. The sofa was normally occupied by people coming in to tell us about burglaries and robberies. That thought reminded me that Sandra Ngo had been here yesterday to report that someone had broken into her house the previous day but hadn't stolen anything. That had been on Tuesday, the same day that someone had tried to kill Ruud Klaver. As I watched her leave the police station, talking on her phone and looking up to the sky, probably to gauge the need for an umbrella, I felt uneasy.

If the family wouldn't talk to me, it could be hard to get the crucial information that Sandra seemed to have. Once again, it struck me that I was the wrong person to work on this case. It surprised me that the boss hadn't understood that. It wasn't purely about my own preferences, but those of the victim's family too.

What must they have thought when they'd seen me? I hadn't even had a chance to clarify that I was there to investigate the accident; to ask if they knew of anybody who might have wanted to kill their husband and father. I hadn't told them that it wasn't about me, it was about them. That I was there to help them.

I checked my watch. I could get back to the hospital in time for the afternoon visiting hours. If I was going to do this, I was going to do it right.

And if it all blew up, that would be okay too. It would be the perfect excuse to prove to the boss that he had to take me off the case.

Chapter 8

I walked down the hospital corridor, following the blue stripe to the lifts. If only I'd done it right the first time round, I wouldn't have had to come back. As the lift doors opened, I saw an elderly woman standing in the corner furthest away from the door. She was looking down at the bunch of flowers that she was holding in both hands. She resembled my mother, equally skinny and delicate, but there was something in her eyes that was very different from my mother's focused, intelligent gaze.

'Are you okay?' I said.

'Hospitals are confusing, don't you think?' She smiled, but I could tell that she was trying not to cry.

I thought hospitals were distressing, depressing and thoroughly unpleasant, with an overpowering disinfectant smell that didn't hide the odour of illness. I decided it was best not to share that opinion with her. 'Where are you trying to get to?' I asked.

'My husband's in intensive care.'

I stepped into the lift. 'I know where that is. Come with me, I'll take you there.'

She nodded gratefully. 'I've been up and down twice

now. It's good that he's here. They'll look after him. I really couldn't.'

'I'm sure they will.' To ask her what was wrong with him seemed an intrusion.

It was only one floor up to the ICU. I was going to point the woman in the right direction, but when the lift doors opened, instead of the normal hushed silence, I heard shouting.

'You're a murderer!' a man yelled.

I took the woman by the elbow and guided her out of the lift. 'The ICU is just through there, but you'd better stay here for a moment,' I said. 'Have a seat. I'll go and check it out.' It was safe here, where a double set of doors separated her from whatever was happening on the other side.

'Be careful,' she said.

'I'll be okay.' I gave her arm a reassuring squeeze. 'I'm a police detective.'

As soon as I had pushed the button to open the doors, I saw Dennis Klaver, standing toe to toe with his brother. A girl at the nurses' station was on the phone. I guessed she was calling security. There was no time to wait for them.

Dennis had his back to me as I rushed down the corridor. Remco didn't make eye contact with his brother but stared at the wall over his shoulder. 'It's what he would have wanted,' he said.

'What he wanted? It's what *you* wanted! I know you hated him.'

Things had escalated severely in the three hours since I'd last been here.

'Dennis, calm down,' his mother said. 'It wasn't just Remco. We agreed.'

'So what? We killed him because the majority of the family wanted it? Murder by democracy? This is crazy!'

Killed him? Had Angela and Remco decided to switch off Ruud's life-support machine? That seemed too fast.

'He wasn't going to wake up, Dennis.' Remco looked pale but his voice was steady. 'He had already died. He died when the car hit him. He wasn't going to wake up.'

'No! He was going to be fine. And you . . .' Dennis fell silent. His body language changed. His arms tensed and his hands balled into fists. He was much taller and broader than his older brother.

The problems always started when the shouting ended.

'Stop!' I yelled, but he didn't listen. I ran the last couple of steps and managed to catch hold of his wrist before he could punch his brother.

He spun round and pulled his arm up to get it away from my grip. He was on my left-hand side, my weaker side, otherwise I would have had a chance to restrain him. A small chance. But I couldn't contain him, and his hand hit me in the face. It wasn't hard – he wasn't trying to punch me on purpose; it was just the momentum from the upward movement – but pain flared where his knuckles caught my cheekbone. Tears jumped to my eyes.

He didn't look at what he'd done; he just stormed away and didn't turn back. I doubted he even knew he'd made contact. His mother followed him.

He hadn't meant to hurt me; it had been an accident.

Just like last time.

I wondered if he remembered that, because I certainly did.

All these thoughts flashed through my mind as I sank to the floor with my back against the wall. I watched him leave. I didn't try to stop him.

The nurse put the phone down and rushed to me. 'Are you okay?' she said.

'Yeah, I'm fine. Just give me a minute.'

Remco sat down on the floor next to me. He leaned forward to examine my face. There probably wouldn't be a mark; the punch hadn't been that hard. Maybe only a graze.

'I'm sorry,' he said. 'Our father just passed away. My brother's very upset.' He leaned his head against the wall. 'You should have let him hit me. It would have made both of us feel better.'

'What happened?'

'We'd said we didn't want him to be resuscitated,' Remco said. 'But then, when it actually happened, when he went into cardiac arrest right before our eyes, I guess it was different. Reality *is* different, isn't it?'

'Why does Dennis blame you?'

'I told the doctors not to do CPR. Not to shock him. I stopped them.' He hid his face in his hands for a second. 'I told them to let him go. I confirmed that that was what we wanted.'

'Wasn't that in his notes as well?'

'I don't know. Everything happened so fast, it was a bit of a blur. Dennis is only angry with me because that's easier than being angry with the doctors or with our mother.'

'It's hard to make that kind of decision.' My head was

spinning even though it was supported by the cold wall behind me.

'My brother knows it was the right thing to do. We talked about it as soon as I got here. He'd reluctantly agreed until . . . well, until it actually happened.'

At least they hadn't had to switch off the machine. 'I'm sorry for your loss,' I said. If he'd been sitting within arm's reach, I would have patted him on the shoulder.

We stayed on the corridor floor in silence for a minute or so, both working hard to control our emotions, even though I could only imagine that our feelings about his father's death were very different. Eventually I turned to face him. He'd got changed since this morning, and he looked years younger than he'd done when he was wearing his suit and talking into his phone. Maybe it wasn't due to his lack of business attire; maybe you got this lost look when a parent died. Luckily I didn't know that yet.

'Did you fly in this morning?' I said softly. 'I heard you live in Dubai.'

Remco smiled awkwardly. 'Just in case my brother was accusing me of something else?'

'I'm sorry. I didn't mean it like that.'

'It's okay. I understand, especially with Dennis calling me a murderer. I was at home, in Dubai, and came here on the overnight flight after my mother called last night.'

'And there are plenty of witnesses to that?'

'A plane full. And airline personnel as well. Also, my colleagues can confirm that I was at work in Dubai on the day of my father's accident. It's a seven-hour flight.'

'Good. That's good.' I felt bad about asking him that

question, but with Ruud Klaver's death, this had just turned into a murder case. I was pleased that at least someone had an alibi, especially someone whose brother had just accused him of being a murderer. 'Can I ask you something else?'

'Sure.'

'Do you know of anybody who wanted to kill your father? Have there been any threats?'

'I don't really know. You need to ask my mother. I haven't heard of anything, but I haven't been home that much. If there had been, they might not have told me, to be honest.'

I hesitated before asking my final question. 'Sandra Ngo said you talked about me in a certain way.'

Remco's face turned even paler. 'She remembered that? I can't tell you. I really can't.'

'Don't worry, I won't get mad at you.'

Remco looked at me. 'I'm sorry,' he said again, but he didn't answer my question.

Chapter 9

I headed off and cycled over to Mark Visser's house. We'd been together for a little over three months now and had got to that stage where it was becoming difficult to decide how to describe him. Boyfriend sounded like we were teenagers, but partner was a bit too serious, even though he'd met my parents.

I opened the front door with the key I'd now added to the set I carried around with me. Maybe once you'd done the parent thing and had keys to each other's place, you might as well admit that things were serious. I shouted out that I was here, and Mark answered from the kitchen.

I hung my coat over the back of a dining-room chair and walked up to him to give him a hug from behind. He turned his head for a kiss. I loved seeing him busy in the kitchen. I lifted the lid on a pan. It was couscous. I knew I should really cook for him one day, but he was so much better at it than I was. It was embarrassing really.

He ran his thumb carefully over my cheekbone. 'What happened?' There must have been a bruise or a scratch. It didn't hurt much. 'Do you want me to put some cream on that?'

'It's nothing,' I said. 'Just an accident.'

'How was your day otherwise?' he asked. 'Apart from being hit in the face by accident?'

'I met Sandra Ngo.'

'The woman from the podcast?'

'She said she was going to release a special episode of *Right to Justice* tonight. Ruud Klaver died today.'

'Oh.' He paused. He clearly didn't know whether he should say that he felt sorry about it, or that it was a good thing. He chose the smart option and went back to stirring the food.

I smoothed the swirled-up hair at the back of his head.

'Do you want to listen to it?' he said.

'To what?'

'The podcast. If you want to, I can hook up my iPad to the speakers. I'll listen to it with you.'

Even though I wasn't worried about what *Right to Justice* was going to come up with, it would be comforting to listen to it with someone else. It would also be good not to hear Sandra's voice via my headphones, where it often seemed she was talking directly to my mind.

At my nod, Mark gave me another quick kiss and then took his iPad out of its sleeve to find the podcast. 'Do you want to serve up while I do this?' he asked. 'I think it's ready.'

'Sure.' I ladled the stew onto big plates and added some couscous. I wasn't entirely sure how much to dole out, but we could always come back for seconds. I told myself I wasn't nervous, and my hands didn't shake as I carried our plates to the table. The six previous episodes of *Right to Justice* hadn't uncovered anything. They'd gone through every detail of the murder of Carlo Sondervelt, but there hadn't been any new information so far. Or at least nothing that was new to me. There was probably plenty that was new to the listeners, who were glued to their earphones with every broadcast, hoping *Right to Justice* would repeat the success of the previous series and find that someone who'd spent years in prison had actually been innocent.

The theme tune started. I took a forkful of stew as if to prove that I had nothing to worry about. 'Mm, this is nice,' I said.

'Shh. If we're going to listen to this, let's listen.'

'Sure.'

'Welcome to the latest edition of *Right to Justice*.' Sandra's voice came out of the speakers. 'Because Ruud Klaver passed away earlier today, we're broadcasting our last interview with him. Our thoughts are with his family at this tough time.'

I thought back to the two brothers fighting in the hospital. A tough time indeed.

'Last week, we stopped at the point where Ruud Klaver had been arrested. Let's give you a quick recap of what we'd covered so far. Ten years ago, Carlo Sondervelt was shot, and died, in the heart of Amsterdam's nightlife district, just around the corner from Rembrandt Square. He was with his girlfriend, Nancy. She saw the attacker and recognised him as the man Carlo had been in a fight with earlier in the evening. Based on her witness statement, the police were quick to arrest Ruud Klaver.'

I ate some more. Mark looked at me intently, as if he wanted to read my every reaction from my face. He understood how important this was to me.

'Now we'll go to the interview,' Sandra said. 'And I want to thank Ruud Klaver's family for letting us air this.'

The quality of the sound changed. It was no longer as crisp as it had been when it had just been Sandra talking. Instead there was a hum in the background. I thought it was probably traffic, and I wondered where they had recorded this. Then I wondered *when* they had recorded it. Maybe it had been on the day of his accident. I would check that with Sandra later. It seemed important.

'I didn't do it. I didn't kill Carlo.' It was strange to hear the dead man's voice. There had been only fragments of his words in the previous episodes. He sounded exactly the same as he'd done ten years ago. 'I punched him, I hit him, we had a fight, but I left. I was going to go home.'

'But you didn't go home.'

'No. If only I had, because then I would have had an alibi. But I knew my wife would be upset with me for drinking and fighting, and I wanted to clear my head.'

'What did you do?' Sandra's voice wasn't confrontational, but soothing, as if she wanted to coax the whole story from him. I wondered if she'd ever meant for this interview to be broadcast like this, in its entirety.

'I walked around for a while,' he said.

'And you finally got home . . .'

'A couple of hours later.'

That famous I-was-just-walking-around excuse. The truth of the matter was that, after the fight, Ruud had waited for them. Carlo had gone to another bar with his girlfriend and had one more drink. Ruud had waited with a gun for him to come out. Then he'd shot him. And why? Because Carlo had punched him in the face an hour and a half earlier. Because this young kid, this student, had been stronger than the forty-year-old Ruud. Or maybe just because he could. Or maybe he had only been trying to teach him a lesson and had never meant to actually kill him.

But the fact remained that Nancy had seen Ruud, had seen him shoot her boyfriend and had recognised him. She had picked him out of a line-up afterwards too.

'So the police arrested you . . .'

I had to give Sandra credit: she still didn't mention my name. She always referred to 'the police', or 'the detective', or 'a police officer'. I knew that she was talking about me, of course.

'Yes. Even then I thought it was going to be fine. Sure, I'd beaten the kid up earlier, but I hadn't killed him.'

'But you couldn't prove that.'

'No, I couldn't. I didn't see anybody, or at least nobody I knew. Nobody could vouch for me.'

Listening to him now, Ruud sounded like a totally reasonable man. Maybe he had been a totally reasonable man in the last year.

'And you confessed. Is that right?'

'That confession was all lies. The police put so much pressure on me, over and over again, that I didn't know what I was saying any more. I hadn't been sleeping, hadn't been eating, and I just . . . I don't know . . . I wanted it to be over.'

'Would you say they forced your confession?'

'Oh yes. Definitely. It was coerced.'

Memories of that moment overwhelmed me. Waves of emotion rolled over me until I had to stop eating. My ears seemed to fill with a high-pitched squeaking noise that pierced my brain. It was as if my mind knew that I could no longer cope with listening to Ruud Klaver's voice and was providing me with a sound to drown it out.

'Are you okay?' Mark said.

I wanted to reach out and stop the podcast.

'Yes, I'm fine.' At what point in a relationship do you reveal the most painful parts of your past? Just having someone else's key doesn't mean that everything has to be out in the open.

He didn't press me. He knew that whatever there was to tell, I'd talk to him about it when I was ready.

I really should tell him why listening made me so upset. He must think I couldn't listen any more because I was being accused of having coerced a confession. I hadn't, because Ruud Klaver had had his lawyer with him at all times. Maybe Mark thought, like my mother, that I was worried Sandra Ngo would discover something about the case that I'd missed. I wasn't. I was confident that this conviction was solid.

Because whatever Ruud Klaver might have said, he'd done it. He'd murdered Carlo Sondervelt.

The rain tapped incessantly at the window like a memory demanding to be let in. I was warm and protected, wrapped in the duvet with Mark's arm draped over my waist. The weight of his arm actually made me feel grounded. Compared to a year ago, when I'd been a fragile mess, I was solid. I knew that it would take a lot of force to push me over and break me again. It was a very pleasing feeling, this sense that I was strong. Maybe at the age of forty-three I had finally grown up.

Mark moved in his sleep and nestled his face closer into the corner between my shoulder and my neck. His hand was resting on my stomach and I covered it with mine. I knew I'd messed up in this case, but I also knew I'd done everything within my power to make things right.

Or at least as right as I could make them.

In my guilt, had I pushed too hard? That was possible. Because the only way to atone had been to put the murderer in prison, especially when another perpetrator was out of reach.

It was mildly ironic that being happy with someone else made me feel safe enough to think back to the first time I'd met Nancy, at the crime scene, ten years ago. I could picture it all again now.

Even though the police cordon had kept people away from the place where Carlo Sondervelt had died, the noises they made kept streaming over from Rembrandt Square: laughter, shouting and singing. The sound of fun coming from further down the street bumped into the sound of grief in this part of the alley. I'd been in CID for a couple of years and started to recognise the noises of a late-night crime scene: the swishing of the forensic scientists' footsteps like drums played with a brush, the clicking of the cameras and the wail of crying. On the corner of the narrow street was a bar. The shooting had cleared it out. Unfortunately, nobody had seen anything. Now the wind blew a discarded McDonald's wrapper down the alley until it was halted by the wheel of one of the many bikes that were stacked against the wall.

One of my uniformed colleagues approached me.

'You just caught me at the end of my shift,' I said. I looked like a Michelin man in my thick coat, and warmth radiated from my stomach. 'Were you the first officer on the scene?'

'Yes. The guy was already dead when I got here.'

'His name?'

'Carlo Sondervelt.'

Carlo's body was covered by a sheet. He would be taken away as soon as Forensics were done with him.

'Are there any witnesses?'

'Only the girlfriend. Nancy Kluft.' He nodded towards a girl who was sitting on the edge of the pavement. 'She was with him.' He scratched the back of his head. 'She held his hand as he bled out.'

Poor girl. I could hardly see anything of her face: a woollen hat was pulled down low, and she had covered her nose and mouth with the collar of her thick winter coat. Her arms were wrapped around her knees as if she was making herself into as tight a ball as she could.

'It was a single shot to the chest. He was gone before the ambulance had probably even left the hospital.'

I thanked my colleague. I was concerned that I was still the only CID detective here. I hadn't been involved in many murder cases yet and didn't want to make a mistake. I'd called Barry Hoog, the senior detective in the team, and he'd said he'd be on his way, after he'd stopped grumbling about having to get out of bed in the middle of the night.

I liked Barry. He let me do a lot of stuff by myself but was there when I needed help. As a new detective on the team, I could not *have asked for a better mentor. Maybe he'd be here soon, but it could easily take another twenty minutes.*

I was in two minds as to whether I should wait for him. What made up my mind was that, even though a lot of people were now here, the girl looked all alone. She sat around the corner, where she couldn't see Carlo's remains. Everybody avoided making eye contact with her. We did it to give her space in her grief, but it came across as if we were treating her like an outcast.

I went up to her.

Now, as I lay in bed with Mark's hand on my stomach and the storm outside pounding the windows, I was worried about the memory of how excited that previous me had been.

I must have fallen asleep at some point, because I was woken by the sound of silence. I opened my eyes a fraction and noticed that the morning light filtering through the curtains was an unfamiliar colour. Not the blue light that filled my bedroom in the morning, but a more yellow tint. The shapes of shadows on the ceiling were wrong, too. I listened for the sound of traffic rattling along the canal, but all I heard was birdsong.

I opened my eyes fully and saw Mark's face. He was fast asleep. His bare arm lay on top of the duvet. His hair was ruffled up into swirls. I reached out to smooth it out, but I didn't want to wake him, so instead I propped my hand under my head and looked at him. I was content just to watch him sleep. Lying here like this made me feel secure.

He opened his eyes to slits. 'I can feel you looking at me,' he murmured, sleep still thickening his voice.

'I'm sorry, I didn't mean to wake you.'

'It's okay.' He didn't move, but lay there with his gaze touching mine. 'I'm sure it'll be time to get up soon. It's already light.' He reached out and touched my cheekbone with a careful finger. 'How are you feeling?'

'Better for being here.' I suddenly felt self-conscious. 'I'm sorry about getting so drunk last night.'

'You can tell me at some point why you're upset. I'll listen. Or not, if that's better for you.' He pushed a lock of hair away from my forehead. 'It's not fully understanding someone that makes you love them.'

I thought it was a quote from a poem but I didn't know which one. I could think of plenty of flaws in the statement, but it made me smile. I closed my eyes and wished I could hold his words and take them out whenever I needed them.

Because I knew I was going to need them.

I was no longer that optimistic CID detective I'd been ten years ago, but I was also no longer the fragile and broken person I'd been last year. I knew I was strong enough to deal with this case. Even if that meant laying bare all my own mistakes.

Maybe it was time to face up to them.

I got up and cycled to my flat to feed my cat. Then I went to work and asked for my own files to be brought up from the archives.

Chapter 10

With Ruud Klaver's death, the boss called Ingrid and me into his office and declared that this was now a full murder investigation, and we'd get extra resources to help us. They would focus on the traffic cameras and see if they could discover where the car had been before it hit the victim, and maybe find a number plate. Unfortunately it seemed that the tyre tracks over the central reservation had been too shallow to give us anything useful. The heavy rain on the night of the accident had washed most of them away before Forensics had turned up.

The boss told us that we should follow the normal procedures. I agreed, because it would take some time before my old files arrived anyway.

As Ingrid and I walked back to our office, I wondered if that last comment had been a dig at me. I knew I would have behaved differently if Ruud Klaver had been, say, an old-age pensioner rather than a murderer. I wished there was a reset button to my brain and that I could go back to first principles. If he had been anybody else, what would I have done first?

'Did you check if he had any enemies?' Ingrid asked,

as if she'd read my mind and wanted to solve my problem for me.

'Well, he'd murdered someone, so I'm guessing that yes, he did.' This wasn't helping.

'There might have been something after those *Right to Justice* podcasts. We should look into that.'

Remco had told me yesterday that he didn't have much knowledge about it and that I should talk to his mother. She wouldn't be pleased to have to talk to me. I opened the *Right to Justice* website and scrolled through the comments section. There were no obvious threats. Nobody openly saying that they wanted to kill Ruud Klaver. Most comments were very supportive. A number of people wrote that they couldn't wait to hear how Sandra was going to prove Ruud's innocence. Many people had left messages of condolence and said their thoughts were with the family.

Everybody seemed to believe Sandra Ngo when she'd said she had conclusive evidence.

I picked up the phone and called her. At first she stayed silent, but eventually she agreed to give me her evidence. Before I could even be surprised about that, she added that she would only do so if I was willing to be interviewed for her podcast. I flat-out refused and she hung up on me.

I looked out of the window. Yesterday's downpour had turned into drizzle. I had to trust that we would be able to find the same information that Sandra had. All I needed to do was get the family to tell me. I called Angela Klaver to ask if I could come to her house to ask her a few questions. She probably also knew what the normal procedures were, because she didn't refuse.

Ingrid and I went down to the garage to get her car. At the first crossing with a bridge, I looked out of the window to make sure there weren't any cars coming at us from the side. The traffic was still light, there were no delivery vans parked along the canal to hold us up, and we made it out of the canal ring in no time. Most cyclists in the bike lane were going in the opposite direction, from Amsterdam's outskirts into the centre. Students were cycling to classes and kids were cycling to school.

If we kept going straight ahead here, we would cross the exact spot where Ruud Klaver had been hit. Instead, Ingrid took a right. I appreciated the small detour. We drove along the edge of a park. There was only one more turning before we'd be at the house. That turn would lead us onto a road that was a small loop dangling off the main road. As if to make up for that circle, each house was a perfectly square freestanding box.

It wasn't the only thing that I knew about the dwellings in this street. I also knew that the ground floor had no window at the front but instead a garage door. That there was a path leading to the front door on the right-hand side. That the living space was on the first floor of the cube.

I knew all that because I'd been here before.

Then there'd been six of us in a van, all suited up. It was just after 5 a.m. I hadn't been to bed yet. As we drove to the house, the tension was so thick that I could feel it through to my fingertips. It felt as if we were going to war, and there was no way I was going to let the rest of the squad go without me, no matter what Arjen, my husband, would like me to do. I had been the first detective on the scene; I had talked to the witness. It was the first murder case where I had been this instrumental. There was no way I wasn't going to be present as we arrested Ruud Klaver.

But I was going to be careful. It was the least I could do.

Adrenaline coursed through my veins and it would keep me going despite the tiredness. I wanted to put a hand on my stomach, but stopped myself from making that telltale gesture. Instead I mentally hummed a tune to calm myself down and held onto the hand grip as we were going at high speed around a left-hand bend.

The van stopped around the corner from where Ruud Klaver lived. His family would be at home as well: a wife and two sons. We waited for the second van to arrive. It was cold, and I stamped my feet on the ground to get warmth into my body. I blew air into the dead of night and watched my white breath disintegrate in the circle of lamplight.

All the houses were dark. This wasn't a bad area. I was less worried here than I would have been if we'd been in the Bijlmer. It was a false sense of security: we were going to pick up a man we suspected had shot someone dead three hours ago. It meant we were going in with our guns drawn.

I looked at Barry Hoog. His presence made me feel more secure. Close to fifty years old, he was the most senior detective in our team, my mentor, and one of the most easy-going people in our department. He was one of those people who smiled a lot, but now his face wore an expression of total concentration. His blond hair was pale against his dark clothes. The circles under his eyes were picked out by the glow coming from the street lights. My call a few hours earlier had woken him up. He fiddled with the straps on his Kevlar vest. It showed that he was nervous too.

The second van arrived and parked behind ours. Now there were *ten of us in total, all in full gear, all fully armed. We gathered behind the vans.*

'*These houses are all identical: there's a garage on the ground floor and the main entrance is at the side. There is also an entrance at the back.*' *Barry pointed at the house we were standing outside.* '*You two go around the back; you two guard the garage to make sure he doesn't make a run for it that way. The rest come with me.*' *He looked at me.*

*I nodded. '*Yes, boss.*' My heart was pounding but I convinced myself that I wasn't scared.*

Now I was here again because Ruud Klaver had moved back to where he'd lived when we'd arrested him, after he'd served his prison time. As Ingrid parked the car at the side of the road, it struck me that being here in broad daylight made this very different from the time of the arrest. The sound of traffic on the S106 was audible in the distance like a background hum as we walked towards the house.

Angela Klaver opened the door before I had even rung the doorbell. She wore the same skin-tight black trousers as she'd been wearing in the hospital yesterday, but had matched them with a black coat with a fleur-de-lis pattern that skimmed the top of her thighs. Her short grey hair was combed away from her forehead.

She introduced herself to Ingrid, ignoring me. 'Come on in,' she said, but she had one hand on the door frame and one on the handle, as if she was going to bar us from entering. 'My son Remco is here as well.' She turned her back on me and went up the stairs.

So many memories came back as I followed her inside. Barry had warned us about those stairs.

'We'll have to go to the first floor, so there won't be much room for manoeuvre. The living area is above the garage, and that makes it a little trickier.'

It was much easier if we could go straight through a front door into a house. The stairs would be steep and narrow, if the architect had kept to normal Amsterdam building conventions.

'You four are on the search team,' Barry said, pointing to the team that had arrived in the second van. 'Go in after we've secured the premises. Look for the gun.'

For a moment I thought about asking if I could be on the search team too, but I couldn't bring myself to say the words. I would just make sure I wasn't the first one in.

We streamed down the road towards the house. I paused to let three guys go ahead of me up the path, then followed them. Two of my colleagues came behind me, covering my back. I was pleased that I had successfully manoeuvred myself into the safest position. I got my gun out from the holster on my hip.

My boots were solid and secure on the paving slabs of the path between the house and the neighbours' fence. A motion-detection light on the side of the house came on and made our approach easy. The front man had arrived at the door and took up position at the far side of it. The second man paused and looked behind him until the last man in our team nodded that he was in place too. Then the first man banged on the door and shouted to open up, that it was the police.

A light came on on the first floor.

The house next door stayed dark. That was good. Interfering neighbours would only distract.

The front guy banged on the door again. 'Police! Open up.'

The door was opened by a short-haired woman in her pyjamas.

The front guy took her by the arm and pulled her out of the way. The second guy stood on her other side and explained that we had an arrest warrant.

'What's going on?' I heard her say. My colleague's response was drowned out by the sound of my boots clunking on the stairs. With my gun to the ready, I followed the third man in the column, a guy dressed in dark blue, my eyes on the back of his bulletproof vest.

This time I followed Ingrid. I could smell it again, that metallic smell of blood. In my mouth was a bitter taste like coffee, but it wasn't caffeine that had set my pulse racing. I took hold of the handrail by the stairs and gripped it hard. There was a door at the top. I remembered it. We'd stood there.

Third Man and I paused by the closed door to the living area. Guns drawn, we looked each other in the eye. He wasn't part of my immediate team – his group had the office two doors down from ours – but in this moment he seemed closer to me than my husband. My gun felt alien and cold under my fingers, and for a second it flashed through my mind that I had never done anything like this before. I ignored that thought and gave my colleague a single nod to confirm that I was ready.

Then we burst through the door.

The memories of that night threatened to overwhelm me, and kept slipping in front of my vision until reality became like a doubly exposed photograph. On the other side of that door there would be a blue sofa, a leather chair, a table covered with school books, and a wooden floor. A floor that would later be stained with blood.

I blinked to get back to today's reality, focusing on one of the small pictures that lined the stairs. It was a painting of a blood-red starfish. Ingrid pushed the handle and opened the door. I closed my eyes for a second, then opened them to look at the room I could now see. The floor wasn't wood. There was a dove-grey carpet. The sofa was no longer blue but white. No school books, but a bunch of flowers stood in the middle of the table. Angela had redone the whole interior. Maybe before her husband was released from prison. Maybe when her sons had left home.

Maybe immediately after that day.

The inside was so altered that I could push the memories back to the corner of my mind. I could almost fool myself into thinking that this was a different place altogether and that the man who greeted us was not the eighteen-year-old who'd been there that night.

The garage took up the ground floor of the house. The L-shaped layout of the first floor was reversed, with the open kitchen at the front, looking out over the street. The sitting area was at the back, to make the most of the view of the large expanse of water of the Sloterplas. Two sofas were tucked into the corner above the stairs. A dining table with six chairs was positioned in front of a window that took up an entire wall.

On a sunny morning, it would be a great place to have breakfast. Now it wasn't sunny, and the window just told me how grey the world was. The clouds were so thick that the sky seemed lowered. Under the strong wind, they must be racing along, but it wasn't possible to see where one cloud started and the other ended.

To fit in with the outdoor colour scheme, Remco wasn't wearing his suit but a very thick charcoal-grey jumper.

Having flown in from Dubai yesterday morning, he must be feeling the cold. He must also be exhausted, but it didn't show because of the tan. His startling light-blue eyes were so pale, they reminded me of what my mother's eyes had looked like before she'd had her cataracts fixed.

'How are you?' he said.

'I'm fine.' There was only a small bruise on my cheekbone that I'd managed to disguise quite well with make-up. I had hoped Angela would offer me some coffee, but she didn't, and I wasn't going to ask.

Remco pulled a chair out from the dining table. 'Have a seat,' he said. 'Do you mind if I record this?'

Ingrid and I exchanged a glance. At least he'd asked. 'Go ahead,' Ingrid said.

He put his phone in the middle of the table and pressed the record button.

I waited until Angela had sat down next to him. 'This is a great view,' I said to make small talk.

Neither Angela nor her son responded.

'We're looking into your husband's – your father's – accident,' Ingrid said.

Still silence from the other side of the table.

In my decades as a police detective, I'd come to expect certain attitudes towards the police force based on where and how people lived. Yes, they were my own personal stereotypes, but if you go to the different areas of Amsterdam often enough, you come to realise that sometimes stereotypes exist for a reason.

'Actually, we're thinking it may not have been an

86

accident,' Ingrid continued. 'We're concerned it might have been deliberate.'

If someone had shown me pictures of this house and this room beforehand, I would have said that the people who lived here would be the kind to cooperate with the police, especially if they had been the victims of a crime.

I would have been very wrong. Ingrid might as well have been talking to a wall.

'Do you know of anybody who might have wanted to hurt your husband?' She directed this question towards Angela, leaving her no choice but to answer.

'No, not really,' she said.

'Could it have had anything to do with Carlo Sondervelt's murder?' I asked.

'Who knows?' She glared at me. There was no other way to describe it. Part of me understood. If she was convinced that her husband had been innocent of the murder, her previous experience with the police, her previous experience with me, had been very bad, and therefore she wasn't going to help me now.

'Have you received any threats?' Ingrid asked.

'No.'

'And you know Sandra Ngo.'

'Yes.' She looked at her son.

'We went to university together,' Remco said. 'I hadn't seen her since I graduated.'

It was the first time either one of them had volunteered any information. I latched on to it. 'You were no longer in touch?'

'We lost touch when I moved.'

'When was that?'

'What difference does it make?' Angela interrupted me.

'I moved to Dubai after I graduated.' Remco seemed to have no objection to answering my questions.

'You must be cold.' I smiled. 'Was it a shock to the system to get back to this kind of weather?'

'He wouldn't have been here,' his mother said, 'if his father hadn't been killed.'

'Yes, I'm very sorry about your father. I'm sorry for your loss. We'll do anything we can to find out who did this.'

Angela narrowed her eyes at me. 'Nobody has talked to us before now. Even when you came to the hospital, you showed no interest in what had happened.' Her voice had a sharp edge and was getting louder.

'Mum.' Remco put a hand on her arm.

'Until recently, we thought this was a hit-and-run, a very sad accident, of course,' Ingrid said. 'Now that we've found evidence to suggest that that might not have been the case, we're taking a different angle.'

'So that's why you're asking us questions at last.' Angela's tone made it clear that this wasn't a pleasant experience. 'Those traffic cops only talked to us for a minute or so.'

For his family, having me here only seemed to have created more resentment. This was why it was a bad idea for me to investigate this incident.

'You still think he was a murderer who got hit by a car, don't you?' Angela got up from her chair. 'He was innocent. He spent ten years in prison for a crime he didn't commit, because of you. He's lived a completely peaceful life since. But you guys still have him down as a criminal.'

I looked around me. This was a nice house in a respectable area. Sure, it was a bit out of the centre – it would take about twenty minutes to cycle into town – but it was pleasant and it had an impressive view.

Angela glanced at her watch. 'If you have nothing else to ask about the accident, or Ruud, can we finish this?'

There were plenty more questions I wanted to ask, but most of them wouldn't get an answer. There was only one that might. 'Sandra Ngo said there was new information?'

'Sandra believes us,' Angela said.

'Did you get any negative comments after the podcasts? Did anybody post saying they wanted to kill your husband? Anything like that?' Ingrid asked.

'No, the messages have all been supportive.'

I knew of one group of people who must have found it hard to listen to the podcasts. Carlo Sondervelt's family had initially cooperated with Sandra, but had pulled out quickly once they realised the direction she was taking in the first two episodes. She only had one objective, and regardless of what the title of the podcast was, it wasn't to get justice. At least not for the victim. It was definitely worth paying them a visit, if only because they would be happy to see me. Sometimes that was a good enough reason.

Remco looked down and rubbed a finger over the edge of the table, then reached out and picked up his phone, turning it round in his hands. When he realised that he had effectively removed his recording device, he quickly put it back.

If I was going to let Ingrid deal with the family – and Thomas when he was back from holiday next week – I could take the Sandra Ngo angle. I remembered that small pause in the hospital before Remco had shaken Sandra's hand. The mother had received her hug with much more warmth. Clearly not everybody was a fan. Sandra was a prickly personality, but I knew that at least she would be willing to talk to me. She might even share her information.

'The next episode of *Right to Justice* is going to be explosive,' Angela said, as if she knew in which direction my mind was going. 'You won't like what Sandra has found out. It doesn't make the police look good.' She picked up a newspaper. 'But then you hardly need Sandra for that. You guys make yourselves look bad without any help from anyone else.'

The animosity was so thick in the air that I could almost taste it. I bit my lip to keep the words in. She had made up her mind about us and nothing I could do was going to change it. I thanked them for their time. Remco pressed stop on his phone. We left to go back to the police station.

In the meantime, my files had turned up. It was very strange to see Ingrid studying my old paperwork. When I'd worked on this case, I had been the same age as she was now. 'What do you think?' I said.

'There's nothing that immediately jumps out at me,' she said. 'We should go talk to these people.' She held up a file. 'If anybody would have wanted to kill Ruud Klaver, it would be his victim's parents, don't you think?'

I noticed that the pain on hearing his name wasn't as bad as it had been. Maybe working on this case had cauterised the wound. Maybe this was good.

Chapter 11

An hour later, after we'd made sure someone would be there to talk to us, Ingrid and I set off on the two-hour drive to the Sondervelts' farm, with the sat nav guiding us out of my beloved city and towards the heart of Gelderland. The weather had turned to drizzle. The wipers swiped the window at the lowest speed possible.

'Do you think I'm making a mistake?' Ingrid said before we had even reached Amsterdam's ring road.

I couldn't see anything wrong with the route she was taking. 'By doing what?' I asked.

'Leaving the team.'

'Ah, that.' I waited a few swipes of the wipers before I responded. 'How honest do you want me to be?' I adjusted my seat belt and sat up straighter.

She laughed. 'As honest as you want to be, without being mean.'

I nodded. 'I can do that.' We had now left Amsterdam and were on the motorway east. 'In my opinion, there are two things to consider. Moving out of our team and into Bauer's team is one thing, but working with your boyfriend all day is another.'

Large panels had been built along the motorway to protect the houses on either side from the traffic noise. They
formed a truck-high barrier, and it felt as though we were
driving through a corridor.

'This isn't about working with you,' she said. 'You know
that, don't you?'

'I never thought it was. As long as it's not about helping
your boyfriend, then it's all fine. You're a much better detective than he is. I know – I've worked with both of you.' The
sound barrier ended and I glanced back. The landscape was
relentlessly flat.

'You know, I'm going to end up doing it just because
Bauer asked me,' she said. 'After Wouter Poels left, they were
a person short. There's something special about being
approached like that.'

'You felt wanted. I get it.' I turned on the radio. I was sure
she understood that she was now leaving us a person short
instead. We drove without talking.

'Let me know if you want me to drive for a bit,' I said.
It was the windscreen wipers with their hypnotic back-and-
forth swipes that made it hard going.

'No, I'm fine. So do you think I'm making a mistake?'

I thought I'd got away with not answering the question,
but this was why she was good at her job. Unlike her
boyfriend, in my personal opinion.

'I would have liked you to stay in the team longer.' I
smiled. 'But I'm not sure if that's for your benefit or mine.'

'You're a great mentor for me. How long did you stay in
your first team?'

'I didn't move for the first couple of years. Sat at the same
desk, with the same view, just different cases.'

'Who was the senior detective?'

'Barry Hoog.'

'I don't think I know him. Is he still there?'

'No, he left years ago.' I sometimes wondered who, apart from me, still remembered Barry. Even Thomas probably didn't. Did Chief Inspector Moerdijk? If he did, he would have mentioned him to me, surely. I didn't know if it was good or depressing that people's memories were so short.

Traffic was light and we made good progress for the next hour. After a while, we reached the first of the rivers that cut the Netherlands horizontally in half. The rain stopped. The sky was still endless and grey, but at least the wipers could be put to sleep. In the distance, the IJssel calmly flowed west. I looked at my watch.

'Do you want to stop and stretch your legs for a bit? We're close and we're early.'

'Sure.' Ingrid parked in a small car park alongside the motorway. I was grateful for some fresh air. A railway bridge spanned the water, its length twice that of the width of the IJssel. It left plenty of room for the river when it was going to flood, which it inevitably did a few times a year. Even now, the water level was high. The rainfall of the last weeks had raised it, but not yet to the point that it was going to burst its banks.

Three white wind turbines slowly and elegantly milled the air. The clouds tore apart for a second and the unexpected sunlight made the water sparkle, dusting it with glitter. I could follow the bends of the river, edged with grass and the deep grey of the autumn sky.

'Do you cook?' I asked Ingrid.

'Cook?' She frowned. 'Of course I cook.'

'Do you cook for your boyfriend?'

'I do, but he's not a big fan. He says my cooking is too healthy – a bit like rabbit food.'

'Rabbit food?'

'Not enough meat. Why do you ask? Don't you know how to cook?'

'I do. I'm just not very good at it. And he is.'

'That's great, then he can cook for you all the time.'

'He does.' That was exactly the problem.

'Anyway,' she said, 'you still haven't answered my question.'

'And I thought I was dodging it so successfully.' I turned from watching the water. 'Okay, here's my honest opinion. I would personally be worried about spending twenty-four hours a day with the same person, however much I liked them. Or loved them. Working cases together can put a huge strain on a relationship. I've seen it with other people.' The wind gusted my hair in front of my face and I tucked it back behind my ear. 'But even if your relationship blows up, your career will be fine. I guess it just depends on what's important to you.'

'You always say things I don't expect. I thought you were going to say that it would be great for my relationship but damaging for my career.'

'You wanted me to be honest, didn't you?'

She put a hand on my arm. 'Thanks, Lotte,' she said. 'For believing in me.'

I wasn't entirely sure how she had drawn that conclusion, but she seemed happy so I didn't correct her.

'You think my career will survive and I know my relationship will.'

I bit my lower lip and nodded slowly as I stared out over

the river in front of us. People only heard what they wanted to hear anyway, and I could comfort myself with the thought that I'd been honest, and not mean, exactly as she'd asked me to be.

'Thanks for not being annoyed with me too.'

'Annoyed? It just means I don't have to save your life any more. It's all fine by me.'

She laughed.

Obviously Thomas and I had had a discussion about what we were going to do now that we would be another person short. We could do with two replacements, but budget cuts meant that we would be lucky just to get one.

We got back in the car. Once we had left the motorway, we took two more turns until we were driving along a narrow road through kilometres of farmland, passing a house every hundred metres of so. When we got to the right number, I saw an ENTRY STRICTLY FORBIDDEN sign. I checked and double-checked the address. The sign wasn't a handwritten cardboard placard but a proper government-issue street sign in blue and white, with the precise number of the article of law that any trespassers would be breaking printed underneath it. I definitely wasn't going to get out of the car. People who had signs like these might keep big dogs.

'Maybe you can get that traffic cop to replace me.' Ingrid's voice had a teasing edge.

'Don't start. He's got no chance.'

The drive was edged on both sides by tall poplars. There must be a farmhouse somewhere, but we could only follow the path, which was no more than a double track shaped by car tyres, as it bent to the right and disappeared behind the trees.

'Why do you say he's got no chance?' Ingrid asked.

'I've got nothing against people who want to do their job for a long time. I've been in CID for almost a decade myself. It's just that when someone is desperate to move and can't do it for years, there's often a good reason.'

'Aren't you helping him out?'

'He wants to see how we work, and I'm letting him. I'm not helping him.'

'That's mighty altruistic of you.'

'Yeah, well, there you go.'

As soon as we turned the corner, the farmhouse came into view. Its thatched roof was pulled low over the house like a dark woollen hat, coming down as far as the ground-floor windows. The open shutters were freshly painted in white and green. The walls were white. All it needed was some fluffy sheep and it could be on a postcard you'd send to your grandparents from a holiday in Gelderland. There were probably no dogs.

We got out of the car. The leaves of the poplars applauded as the wind rushed past, and the white grit of the path muttered its displeasure at being disturbed.

I rang the doorbell, and when the door opened, there was Carlo Sondervelt's father. It was ten years since I'd seen him last, at Ruud Klaver's trial. He had been grateful at the verdict and I remembered that he'd offered a prayer to the ceiling of the courthouse when the judge ruled Klaver guilty.

Chapter 12

Jelte Sondervelt smiled widely as he invited us in. It was so different from the way Angela Klaver had greeted us that it immediately buoyed my spirits. He wouldn't be this pleased to see us if he'd had anything to do with Ruud Klaver's murder.

Jelte had aged more than I would have thought possible in ten years. He was probably not even sixty yet, but his face was deeply scored with lines. We followed him to the front room, where his wife, Anke, was waiting. Photos of their son, forever frozen in time, and of their granddaughter with her mother, the key witness, lined the walls.

A magazine from the Evangelische Omroep, the main evangelical broadcasting station, lay in the centre of the table, next to a plate of chocolate biscuits. The front cover showed a picture of a prayer leader, dressed casually in a purple shirt, above the quote: *It starts with honesty. You're allowed to complain in life.* I could see a Bible on the bookshelf. I wondered if they'd become more religious after their son had been killed, and had turned to God in their hour of need. I didn't know whether that meant that they had accepted what had happened. After all, the Bible was full of stories about wrath and revenge. My own mother was deeply religious, and she was definitely not one to let bygones be bygones. She'd only forgiven my father for divorcing her about thirty-five years after it had happened, and even then grudgingly.

'I saw that Ruud Klaver had died,' Jelte said, 'and Anke and I wondered how long it would take for you guys to turn up here.' He pushed a glass of water towards the middle of the table. 'Only one day was the answer.'

'I'm sorry, we just need to ask a few questions.'

'Like where I was on the evening of the accident?'

'If you could tell us, that would be great.'

'Of course. It was Nancy's birthday. We were all together. We had a Chinese meal.'

'The whole family?'

'The four of us: me, Anke,' he gestured to his wife, 'Nancy and Wietske.'

'Okay.' I made a note. In the back of my mind, I thought it was rather convenient. If they'd had something to do with Ruud's accident, that would be a tough alibi to discredit.

'You could just have called,' Jelte said. 'You didn't need to drive all the way out here.'

'I also wanted to see how you've been. Since that podcast aired, I mean. Sandra Ngo came here, didn't she?'

'Yes. She came with her assistant a few weeks ago.'

'It was a month ago now,' Anke corrected him.

'Okay. Yes, a month ago.'

'She had an assistant?'

'Dennis or something.'

'Dennis?' Surely Sandra hadn't turned up here with Ruud Klaver's son. 'A young guy? Was he wearing glasses?'

'Glasses? No, he was about fifty and had a bald head.'

That was a relief. 'How did you feel about that? That she was asking all these questions?'

'I felt that it was unnecessary, of course. Carlo's murderer had been locked up, he'd served his time, we'd moved on.'

'And now she was talking about it again.'

'Yes, claiming you guys had the wrong man. I followed the last series and it was fascinating, but I know the police didn't make mistakes like that in this case.' He smiled at me warmly.

'There's no doubt in your mind?'

'None. I'll tell you what I told her,' he said.

I hoped he would tell us things he *hadn't* told her. I hoped there was a difference between talking to the police and talking to a woman who had a podcast. I also hoped that there was a difference between talking to the woman who had locked away the murderer of their son and the woman who had tried to prove that he'd been innocent after all.

'Nancy saw him. She's a smart girl, she doesn't make up stories,' Jelte said. 'Look, I'm sad that the guy was killed. He seemed to have changed his life. Stopped drinking, I heard. If I trust the law, which I think I do, I have to feel that justice was served, that he'd paid the price for his crime and should be allowed to start again. We'll never get our son back, of course, but whatever happened to his murderer wouldn't change that anyway. Don't you agree?'

'I guess so. So you had forgiven the guy?'

'Forgiven? No, not that. But I felt we'd had our revenge. Our revenge through justice.'

* * *

99

'He was lying,' Ingrid said as we drove back. 'There's no way anybody feels like that. So little anger.'

'It's been ten years. I think he believed what he was saying. Or he wanted to believe it.' I pulled the seat belt away from my shoulder. 'I also think there was plenty of anger beneath the surface.'

'It's those ones, the ones who bottle up their feelings and don't accept their anger, who explode. Who press the accelerator instead of the brake and hit pedestrians on zebra crossings.'

I nodded. 'Sure, but that alibi was solid.'

'I love to imagine Sandra Ngo meeting that guy,' Ingrid said. 'Trying to needle him into getting a reaction and hitting a wall of denial instead. What must it have been like for the parents of the victim to have the case gone through again with a fine-tooth comb?'

'It must have been horrendous. To have doubt put back into their minds after they'd come to terms with the identity of the murderer. They'd felt that justice had been done, and then Sandra rocks up and says it might have been a mistake all along and the wrong man had been locked up.' I grimaced. 'I'm just not sure it would make them want to kill Ruud Klaver. If anything, they'd want to take their anger out on Sandra Ngo.'

'Unless they thought he was trying to get something out of it. That he wasn't innocent but was trying to get a payout. Wouldn't they want the acceptance of guilt in return for their forgiveness?'

'But didn't you hear the man? He hadn't forgiven Klaver; he'd felt he had paid the price. That's very different.' It was a feeling I understood. 'He wasn't talking about forgiveness, but about legal retribution.'

'And therefore it was even more upsetting when it was suggested that the verdict had been wrong?'

I had to think about that. If you'd forgiven someone and then it turned out that they'd been innocent all along, that would probably make you feel good about your forgiveness. If the wrong person had been sentenced, that would turn everything upside down. For ten years or so you had believed that the right person had been punished and now you had to accept that that hadn't been the case.

I shook my head at my own thoughts, because of course that wasn't what Jelte had felt. He was certain that Ruud had been the killer, because Nancy had seen him. She'd testified. He must have felt that Ruud was lying. That he'd claimed he was innocent when in fact he was the murderer. It would have made him angry, I was sure of that. Angry enough to get someone to kill Ruud whilst he fabricated an alibi? I thought about the scene of the crash. It didn't look meticulously staged and planned. It looked like a spur-of-the-moment thing.

We got back to Amsterdam and I asked Ingrid to drop me off at the Keizersgracht. Even though it was raining again, I had a coffee at one of the cafés where a bridge met a canal. Cafés and restaurants occupied most of these corners; the bridges worked as funnels that shipped people from one canal to the next, so what better place to have a café? Also, the bridges normally had metal railings, which were perfect for chaining bikes to.

I sat outside at the leftmost of a single row of round tables that were kept dry by a sunshade and looked out over the canal. The water was somewhere between green and brown. The colour of a toad. The houses were different hues from the same palette. Their reflections on the water were disturbed: straight lines rippled as heavy drops created circles that overlapped and disappeared. Sometimes a drop was so big that it splashed up and created a bubble. All the moored boats had their covers up. I drank my cappuccino slowly to the peaceful patter of the rain on the awning. The water streamed down in a minuscule waterfall close to the table's edge. A boat came by. Four people rowing. A soothing, rhythmic noise like the sound of sinking your body in the water of a late-night bath. The murmur of car engines was distant and unable to rise above the high-pitched screeches of a coot.

I called Sandra. I asked her again to share her information with me. Again she said she would do it if I came on the podcast to talk about the original case. Again I refused.

Talk about it. My mind was already flooded with memories of it. Investigating Ruud's death had forced me to think about things I would have preferred to forget. This case that I'd worked on ten years ago had come right back to the foreground of my memory. Now I had to investigate it again.

If Ruud had been innocent, that meant our witness had been wrong.

Could it be possible that Nancy had made a mistake? I really didn't think so.

Of course I had believed her. It wasn't just because I'd felt sympathy for her: her boyfriend had just been killed and she was the only witness. Above all else, there'd been no reason to doubt her. I hadn't treated her any differently just because she was expecting. Her pregnancy had made no difference.

I paid for my coffee and set off home. When I arrived, I went slowly up the three flights of stairs. After I'd fed the cat, I went into my study and put a new sheet of white paper on the architect's table that functioned as my personal white-board. Especially with these old cases, drawing out what we knew helped me focus. I wrote Ruud Klaver's name in large block capitals in the middle of it with a blue marker pen. Seeing his name was no easier than hearing it. I chewed the end of the pen. Had I ever investigated the murder of a mur-derer before? Where should I start? In this drawing, which murder should take priority?

On the top right of the page, I wrote: CARLO SONDERVELT.

Pippi sauntered into the study, having had a little nibble of her food, and weaved her way between my legs. She meowed, and I bent down to scratch her little black-and-white face. Then she jumped up onto the architect's table and stretched out to make herself comfortable on top of the paper. Her tail covered Ruud Klaver's name, as if she too didn't want to see it.

'What are you thinking, Pippi-Puss? That I should stop drawing?' I stroked her, then gave her a longer tickle at that soft spot just behind her ear. 'I shouldn't be working? I should just play with you instead?'

She purred loudly.

It was maybe a mistake to automatically assume that this murder had something to do with Carlo Sondervelt's death. It could well be the case, of course, especially with Sandra

Ngo asking lots of questions, but perhaps it shouldn't be my starting point. Ruud Klaver had been released from prison over a year ago. What had he been doing since? How many people went from prisoner to model citizen? Even if he'd been innocent, he would have met plenty of people in jail. He could have been drawn into something else.

I bit my lower lip. The only thing I had found on Ruud Klaver had been a ticket for speeding two months ago and another one for jumping a red light a week later. I realised I didn't know anything about what he'd done during the last year. I didn't know where he'd worked, how he filled his life or what type of person he was. All I knew was that he'd been hit by a car.

I gave up on my drawing. 'Thanks, puss,' I said. She'd stopped me from focusing on only one direction from the start.

Chapter 13

The next morning, Ingrid had clearly been waiting for me to get to work, because as soon as I came through the door, she said, 'No need to take your coat off, we're going straight out.'

'Okay,' I said. I was slightly surprised, but I liked that she was taking the initiative. She was going to need that attitude once she moved into her new team. 'Where are we going?'

'I just got off the phone with Dennis Klaver. I called him after that pointless meeting with his mother, but he didn't answer. He returned my call this morning and agreed to talk to us.'

'No.' I pulled my chair back, ready to sit down at my desk. 'I'm not going.' I did my best not to sound like a stubborn child, but I didn't think I quite managed it.

'What do you mean, you're not going? Dennis was the one who got Sandra Ngo interested in his father's case. We should ask him why.'

'I know. You should. I shouldn't.'

'Until Thomas comes back, you've got no choice.'

'Just take that traffic cop with you. He'll be so happy.'

'Are you annoyed with me? Is this because I'm moving out of the team?'

'Look, Ingrid, I don't have a good history with this family. I was thinking about it yesterday when we met Angela and Remco. It's best if I don't talk to them any more. I could see how she clammed up as soon as she saw me. Take Charlie, or wait for Thomas to come back and go on Monday.'

'Seriously? We're in the middle of a murder investigation and you're telling me to go on Monday instead? That's stupid. Let's go now, and if we don't get anything, I'll go back with Thomas after the weekend.'

I was tempted to tell her what had happened during Ruud Klaver's arrest, but I knew it had no relevance to his death.

'I'll do the talking,' Ingrid said. 'You can hang back.'

It was only for one more day, I told myself. Thomas would be back on Monday and I could focus on working on Sandra Ngo to give me her information. For today I could follow Ingrid around.

I was quiet as she drove us to Dennis's place.

I was quiet as we walked up the stairs to his flat.

I was quiet as he opened the door and looked at me with unguarded anger.

I would have liked to tell him that I didn't want to be here either. I couldn't even imagine what it must be like for him to have me here on his doorstep. The first time he'd seen me in the hospital, he'd looked as if he was going to throw up. Now he looked as if he could kill me quite easily. My hands were shaking, and I clasped them together behind my back and straightened my spine. I made eye contact and didn't look away, because this feeling was entirely mutual.

He let us in.

I recognised an obsessive when I saw one. I managed to limit my drawing to the architect's table in my office, but Dennis hadn't constrained himself. Everything in this room was small apart from the collection of newspaper clippings behind the bed. They dominated the place. It was as if Dennis had wallpapered his room with newspaper to save money. The stories were all about his father. Ruud Klaver's face stared at me multiple times. I scanned them to see if there were any other faces I recognised. If I was trying to prove that my own father was innocent, I would start by finding another culprit; someone with a motive for shooting Carlo. But the first thing my eyes landed on was the photo from the trial, the one that I'd removed from my scrapbook.

Dennis had cut away the people in the background, so that only I was left. I reached out to grab it.

'Don't touch that.' His voice whipped out.

I retracted my hand.

There had to be something here. I scanned the rest of the wall. It didn't take me long, because I was familiar with most of what Dennis had put up here. At the time, I had cut out many of the same articles. I had followed the newspaper coverage closely to make sure that none of the classified information got out. It hadn't. We'd done a good job of keeping it under wraps.

I found nothing of interest on the wall. There also were no gaps, so it wasn't as if he'd taken any clippings down before we arrived or passed any on to Sandra. Unless he'd quickly stuck up other articles, of course.

Row upon row of binders filled the bookshelves. I didn't have to open one to know that these were about his father as well. It was as if that was all Dennis's life was about. He had dedicated himself to proving his father's innocence.

This one room was his entire flat. His bed took up one end, and a row of bookshelves created a divider between the sleeping area and the eating area and kitchen. There was a single comfortable chair opposite a flat-screen TV hanging on the wall. He must never have visitors, because there really wasn't anywhere for Ingrid and me to sit. We stayed standing until Dennis pointed towards the two bar stools under the tiny table. I pulled mine out and nearly bumped into the fridge.

'Thanks for making the time to speak to us,' Ingrid said.

'Did I have a choice? I could have refused? I didn't know that.'

I didn't think I had ever come across a victim's family so unwilling to talk.

'You were the one who contacted Sandra Ngo?' she continued.

'Yes. I knew she could prove that my father hadn't killed Carlo Sondervelt. I clearly wasn't smart enough.' He pointed at the wall and the binders. 'I tried. But it needed someone like Sandra to actually do it.'

'Do you know of anybody who wanted to kill your father?' Her voice was calm and sympathetic.

'No, nobody.' Dennis's short answers showed that he had

no interest in talking to us, however nice Ingrid was trying to be.

'Any problems you were aware of?'

'No.'

'Money problems? Something at work?'

'Work?'

'Didn't he have a job?'

'No, he didn't. It isn't easy for a man over fifty with a criminal record to get a job.'

'So how was he doing for money?'

'Remco helped. He's got a good job.'

'Were there any threats?'

'Every now and then he'd get a narky email, but nothing serious. Nothing recent.'

'But someone killed him.'

'It could just have been an accident.'

'You were very angry with your brother. You said he hated your father?'

'That was nothing.' He stared at me again. He probably wanted to call me a bitch.

That was what he'd called me that night.

After we burst through the door of Ruud's living room, Dennis was the first person I saw. Then he'd been a spotty teenager with shoulder-length hair, dressed in green pyjamas. He was twelve or thirteen.

I should have got him out of the way first, but before I could reach him, a door to my right opened with a click. I whipped round. A man came out. I recognised him immediately as our guy: Ruud Klaver. He was wearing a pair of jeans and a T-shirt. Maybe he'd planned to make a run for it.

I pointed my gun at his head. 'Freeze!' I shouted. 'Police, don't move!'

He slowly raised his hands. 'What's this about?'

His hands were empty. He wasn't armed. 'I'm arresting you on suspicion of the murder of Carlo Sondervelt. You have the right to remain silent.' I rattled through the rest of his rights as I holstered my gun and clipped the handcuffs around his wrists.

'You bitch,' the kid ranted. 'What are you doing to my father?'

This was as clean an arrest as we could have hoped for. My shoulders lowered a couple of centimetres as I relaxed.

I put my hand on Ruud's arm to lead him towards the door. Then a second door opened. Another teenager came out, this one a bit older, eighteen maybe. He wore jeans and a T-shirt. I wondered if he'd got dressed when he heard us come in, or if he'd still been up. Unlike his younger brother, he didn't scream or shout. He only stared at me, his face immovable as a mask.

'Be quiet, Dennis,' Ruud said to the younger boy. 'I'll be back soon.'

I passed Ruud over to Barry, who was waiting on the other side of the door, at the top of the stairs. The kid started to scream loudly, his words forming an endless stream of profanities.

I turned.

One of my colleagues should have held him back, but, like a football team just after they've scored, our concentration lapsed for a second. Maybe they thought a twelve-year-old kid wasn't a threat. I didn't blame them. I wish I could have. It would have made my life easier. But I only blamed myself.

Now that kid had grown into a man and he was still talking. 'Remco and my dad just didn't get on, that's all.'

'You said that Sandra Ngo had proved that your father was innocent. How did she do that?' Ingrid asked.

'Ask her.' He grinned. 'Or listen to the podcast like everybody else.'

I was starting to get really fed up with this family. Talking to them was like talking to a brick wall. 'Don't you want to know who killed your father?' I said.

'I've been thinking about it and I really think it was just an accident. Nobody wanted to kill him. Is that what I need to say to get you guys off my back?'

'An accident? Someone hit him with a car,' I said.

Out of the corner of my eye, I saw Ingrid flinch.

'But hey, if you want to ignore that,' I continued, 'and just think we're all done here, then be my guest.'

'Yeah, we're all done. Or at least I'm done talking to you lot.'

Ingrid shot me an annoyed glance. I turned and left the flat, pausing outside the front door so that I could hear what was going on inside, in case she needed my help. I fought to get my breathing under control. Getting angry didn't help at all.

Ingrid said a polite goodbye, 'I'm sorry about that,' I heard her say before she joined me. Together we walked towards the stairs.

'That family are impossible,' I said, as soon as Dennis was out of earshot.

'No,' Ingrid said loudly. She stopped. 'What's really impossible is you.'

'Me?'

'Yes. What the hell was that?' Her voice trembled. I could

see the anger in her face. 'You were supposed to be staying quiet. His father's just died and you had to say that he was hit by a car in that tone of voice? Have some consideration for the guy's feelings.'

'I said I didn't want to go.'

'You didn't want to go? What are you? A stroppy teenager? We're in the middle of a murder inquiry and you go and piss off the victim's son.'

'Do you know what he did?'

'I don't care,' she shouted at the top of her voice. 'I don't care what he did ten years ago. I care about solving this case.'

'But Ruud Klaver wasn't innocent.'

'Stop talking about that! I know you really want him to be guilty, but in fact it doesn't matter. No, sorry, it does matter, but only if it's got something to do with why he was murdered.'

'He did it.'

'Lotte, seriously, shut up about it. I've seen you obsessed before, but I've never seen you this blinkered. A man was murdered and you're doing your utmost to piss off his son, who hates the police already anyway. Who hates us so much that he prefers to talk to a journalist rather than speaking to us.' She paused and took a couple of breaths. 'And the way you just behaved, I can't blame him.'

'Wow.' I could understand her reaction, because she hadn't been here ten years ago. 'But—'

'No. Shut up!' She whipped the words at me. 'I'll work on this with Thomas. I shouldn't have brought you here.'

'Well, I did say—'

'I thought you could behave professionally,' she said before

I could finish my sentence. 'This is going to be my last case in this team and I want to do a good job. That means that I don't care if you were right or wrong ten years ago. I care about why someone would have wanted to kill Ruud Klaver. I care about whether there have been threats. I care about anybody he could have met in prison. I care about finding out what he'd got up to since he got out. Those kinds of things. The kind of things his family could probably tell me. If you hadn't pissed them off!' She spat the words at me.

'But Dennis was claiming he was innocent.'

'Yes, and I was interested in that at first because it could have driven the victim's family – Carlo Sondervelt's family, I mean – to do something. But as they have an alibi, a confirmed alibi, we drop it. If it turns out Ruud Klaver was innocent—'

'He wasn't.'

'If it turns out he was,' she continued, as though I hadn't said anything, 'that's interesting because it's possible he knew who really did it. Maybe he blackmailed the real murderer. Maybe that's why he got killed. You see what I'm doing here?' she ranted. 'I'm only interested if it tells me who killed him! And you need to stop thinking of him as a murderer and actually see him as the victim.'

I pushed my hands deep in my pockets and bit my teeth together to stop myself from replying. I slowly counted to ten. 'Fine,' I said when I'd got myself under control. 'Fine, you work on this with Thomas from Monday. Get that idiot traffic cop to go with you if you need anything this afternoon. He'll love that.' My heart was still racing. I could feel it in my throat.

Ingrid slowly shook her head. 'Idiot? Wow, Lotte, you're really something.' She turned and rushed down the stairs, leaving me standing there.

I tried to see her point of view but failed. She might not care if Ruud had been innocent or not, but I definitely did. I couldn't stop myself.

Chapter 14

It was clear to me what I needed to do: I needed to talk to the people who were willing to speak to me. Sometimes there was no point in trying to break down a brick wall; the better option was to go round it. Ingrid might think it was unimportant whether Ruud Klaver was innocent or not, but I was still convinced that this could have been why he was killed. The way the murder had happened, hitting him with a car on that crossing, made it seem such an impulsive act. That meant that there had to have been a trigger for it, and the most obvious trigger was that *Right to Justice* podcast. Ingrid wasn't totally wrong in saying that I really wanted him to have been guilty, but even more than that, I needed to discover what Sandra Ngo had found out so that I'd know what feelings she'd stirred up.

I couldn't talk to Ruud's family, that was pretty clear to me, so I needed to take another angle. I would talk to the people who were friendly towards me and who were on my side. I had to use the connections that I had.

After Ingrid had left me at Dennis Klaver's apartment building, I'd jumped on the bus to get back to the police station.

My mother's words that I would always have believed Nancy Kluft because she'd been pregnant at the time resonated more than I would have liked. I needed to hear straight from Nancy's mouth again what she had seen that night. If my witness had been wrong, then it was possible that Ruud Klaver had been innocent. But she'd been so adamant. She'd never wavered. Surely she couldn't have been mistaken.

I was rummaging through a large cardboard box to find Nancy's original witness statement when the door behind me opened and the guy who'd taken the painting away the day before came in with another large canvas. He smiled at me. 'You guys have won the art lottery,' he said. 'Of all the ones I've hung up today, this is my favourite.'

I was grateful to him for pulling me out of my memories of the past, and therefore I was kinder than I normally would have been and pretended to be interested. 'Show me.'

'I think this guy was inspired by Warhol.'

'You're into art?'

'Not really. I just hang them up. But you know the one I mean? The one with Marilyn Monroe four times in different colours?'

'I know the one. Someone did one of Queen Beatrix as well.'

'Anyway, here's your version.' He turned it over. Robin van Persie's smiling face stared at me in four different colours. 'See what I mean? Just like Warhol.'

'You've got to be fucking kidding me.'

'Don't you like it? Not a fan?' He took a step back to admire it but stopped smiling at the rejection. 'It really is the best of the bunch.'

'How much did this cost the taxpayer?'

'You can't put a price on art. That's what my boss says.'

'Your boss is full of shit. Ask any of the auction houses; they find it very easy to put a price on it. Is your boss a failed artist by any chance?'

'I've seen some of his drawings. They're awful.' The grin was back on his face. 'Anyway, I hope you like football.'

'Hate it.' Robin van Persie in blue, red, yellow and green.

'One of the guys downstairs has a blue and black rectangle.'

'Sounds great. I love rectangles. Maybe we can swap.'

The guy waved away my suggestion and carefully hung the atrocity on the wall. 'Give it a couple of days, you'll love it.' He touched its edge on his way out, as if he was sad to leave it behind.

I was going to have to look at this painting for the next however many months. There was no way I was going to last that long. Well before then I would have brought in a bread knife from home and slashed the thing to pieces.

No, I wouldn't. I would sit here and wait until the day we got something new. In the meantime, I would go back to doing some work. I didn't want to look at my old case any more. It was pointless, I decided. I should look into Ruud's current life. Why was I making the assumption that this definitely had something to do with Carlo's murder? What about Ruud's life after jail? Maybe his wife had got so fed up with having him at home that she'd hit him with her car.

I wasn't serious about that, of course. She'd stood by him all this time. If he'd been tough to live with after he'd got out of prison, she would have just divorced him. It wouldn't be the first time that had happened. I'd worked on another case where someone had been murdered whilst on parole. Hours after he'd been released, in fact. Ruud had been out for over a year when he was killed. Maybe that was weirder.

I knew I was going round in circles. I kept thinking about the same things. I had to get out of the office. I had to actually do something, even if I had no idea what. Often, if you started to dig, something would come to the surface. Without any other leads, I would try to discover what Sandra Ngo had found. I would start with Carlo's murder and work forwards from there.

Looking at my old files made me think about the colleagues I'd worked with at the time. Maybe they had a different memory of the case. I picked up the phone and called my former boss.

I hadn't spoken to Barry Hoog in more than five years. He was surprised to hear from me but said that of course he would love to talk to me and I should come to his house. We'd lost touch since he retired from the police force, and even in the years before that, we'd talked little. He had moved out of CID and into the financial fraud department, where he had been surprisingly successful. Sitting at a desk looking at numbers all day had suited him better than his superiors had anticipated, and they'd ended up very pleased that they'd made the effort.

I cycled to the outskirts of the city. It was such a normal street, this one. A pleasant street with houses made mainly of glass. I was worried before I rang the doorbell. All sorts of thoughts bounced through my mind as I stood there. Guilt over the night of the arrest was still crippling me.

It had always been hard for me to visit him, even though he'd never openly blamed me for anything. Deciding that there was no time like the present, I pressed the doorbell next to the blue front door. I didn't have to wait long. Seconds later, the door swung open.

I made sure I had a sunny smile firmly glued on my face.

He looked up at me and beamed widely. 'Lotte, it's great to see you.'

'You're looking well, Barry,' I said, and I was relieved that I could say it and it wasn't a lie.

His skin was deeply tanned, as if he'd spent every hour since retirement in glorious sunshine. His hair was bleached to an even white, though he wasn't yet sixty. 'Come in, come in,' he said.

He turned deftly and I followed him down the corridor. As soon as he had his back turned towards me, the smile dropped from my face. I caught a glance of myself in the hallway mirror and saw that I looked as sad as I felt.

Because seeing my former mentor in his wheelchair was always a stark reminder of what had gone wrong during Ruud Klaver's arrest.

It had all been going so well until I'd handed Klaver over to Barry.

It was at exactly that moment that I caught sight of movement from the corner of my eye. I saw the knife the kid had in his hand. As he made the movement towards Barry, I could have grabbed his arm. But instead of going forward, I stepped back. I kept myself safe. I kept my unborn child safe. And I saw the knife go into

Barry's back. Even then I didn't move. Even then I stood as if frozen, my arms wrapped around my belly, and watched as my colleague, the guy who'd been next to me as we'd burst through the door, grabbed Dennis tightly in a textbook grip, with one arm bent behind his back and the other held securely. The knife clattered to the floor and Barry crashed to his knees.

Maybe even then I could have stopped his movement. I could have dived after him as he rolled down the stairs and grabbed an arm. But I was stationary. Frozen.

Afterwards they told me that it had all been over in seconds. Nobody blamed me, or if they did, behind my back, they called it inexperience. Everybody in that room had been equally to blame, they said, for taking their eyes off a kid. But when Barry was carried to the ambulance, I didn't go with him. He probably would have wanted me to, but I couldn't. My actions to protect myself and the child in my belly had been instinctive.

And I knew that they had caused this tragedy.

Chapter 15

Barry's house was a mess of books and papers strewn all over the floor, and he deftly whirred past them as though this was a purpose-built obstacle course to test his wheelchair agility. Even though it was Friday, last Saturday's paper still lay open on the sofa. I moved it aside to make some space. 'How's retirement treating you?'

'Egbert keeps telling me not to call it that, but to think of it as my second career.' Egbert was Barry's long-term partner. They'd been together for decades. 'He says hi, by the way. He's sorry he couldn't be here.'

He was probably just giving us space to talk about our old case. 'What have you been up to?'

'Just this and that.' Barry stacked an already precarious pile of library books even higher. 'I was running a campsite outside Amsterdam, but the season's over now.'

'A campsite? How . . .'

'It's fully wheelchair-accessible,' he said before I could even feel embarrassed for having brought it up. 'I've also been doing some consulting work. It's been fun, pays the bills.'

'Do you miss the police force?'

'You've done well for yourself, Lotte. You closed some great cases.'

'I learned it all from you.' I was happy to let him control the conversation and change the subject. 'I'm sure I used to be very annoying.'

'Just really keen.' He smiled at me.

'Yeah, a bit too keen probably.' I'd worked with people who were like that. I could only imagine how irritating I must have been.

'You're here to talk about Ruud Klaver, right?'

'Have you been listening to the podcasts?'

'I like *Right to Justice*. Sandra Ngo is smart, but she's probably wrong this time.'

'I think so.' Whatever else I was going to say was delayed by the clock on the wall telling us noisily that it was ten o'clock.

'Carlo Sondervelt's death was only my second murder case,' I said.

'You did well. Don't worry about it.'

I shook my head at the pride in his voice. It was that of an old mentor, or even a father. 'Ruud Klaver died. It looks like he was murdered.'

'I read about it, but I wasn't sure if it was an accident.'

'I don't like that it happened just when *Right to Justice* was claiming that he was innocent.'

'You think those things are linked?'

'It's a very strange coincidence otherwise.'

'Who knows what he's been up to since he came out of jail.'

'I can't find anything. He looked to be clean. Now I'm wondering if we missed something at the time.'

'You honed in on Klaver quickly and didn't let go.'

I pondered his words for a bit. I remembered that he'd said the same thing at the time. I'd been visiting him in hospital and had talked about the case. Now, ten years later, I was sitting in his front room and he was once more playing the role of devil's advocate. We were having a very similar conversation to the one we'd had that time.

'Are you saying we didn't look into everything?' I asked.

'From day one, even from hour one, we only looked at Klaver.'

'Was that wrong?'

'Not necessarily. There was never any need to spread our net wider.'

I nodded. Sometimes the shortest route was the best one. If you have evidence of guilt, there's no need to dig any further. 'If you think about it now, is there anything that bothers you?'

'The reason for the fight never seemed right. I always found it hard to believe that they fought over Nancy. If there was anything I doubted, it was that. But in the end, it doesn't matter *why* Klaver shot Carlo.'

I frowned. 'It does if we were wrong and he didn't do it.'

'The forensic evidence doesn't lie. I'm sure he did it, and if we've got the motive wrong, then I couldn't care less about that.'

'But if you look at the evidence, what did we really have? Ruud's blood on Carlo's hands and Carlo's blood on a pair of Ruud's jeans.'

Barry sat back and folded his arms. 'Are you doubting that he was guilty after all?'

I pulled my hair away from my face with both hands and groaned. 'I don't know any more. I don't like the fact that Sandra Ngo says she's got evidence that he's innocent.' Plus she refused to give it to me unless I cooperated with her. 'And I don't like that Ruud Klaver was killed the evening after that was broadcast.' I wanted it to be a very bizarre coincidence, but I couldn't get it out of my head that it was all linked.

'We had the right guy, Lotte. But just because he'd killed someone almost a decade ago doesn't mean that you shouldn't investigate his murder properly. Focus on that, and forget about maybe not having discovered the entire truth last time round.'

I shook my head. 'But what if that was exactly the reason for his murder? What if there was more to Carlo's death?'

'Then find that out. But only to solve Ruud's murder. Forget about his innocence or guilt. Forget about anything you might have missed ten years ago and concentrate on getting the guy who murdered Ruud Klaver.'

Ingrid had said the same thing.

I put a hand on Barry's arm. 'You always were wise beyond your years.' I should have visited him sooner. I knew that what he said was right. So why did I find it so hard to accept?

'These days I feel that my years have caught up with your wisdom.'

I smiled and said goodbye.

He saw me out. 'Don't be a stranger, Lotte. If there's anything I can help you with, let me know. Or, you know, if you just want to have dinner with me and Egbert, you're really welcome.' He rubbed a hand through his hair. 'I heard what happened and I've always meant to say that I'm sorry I didn't help you more. In those days, I wasn't very good with the personal stuff.'

'Don't worry. Thanks, Barry.'

'This,' he tapped on the side of his wheelchair, 'wasn't your fault.'

He was only saying that because he didn't know.

Chapter 16

'Detective Meerman,' I heard a woman's voice say. Sandra Ngo was standing on the pavement outside Barry's house. 'I didn't know you were here.' She tipped her head sideways. 'You've come to see the same person as me.'

'You know Barry?'

'I've talked to him once or twice.'

That made me feel uncomfortable. 'What did you talk about?'

Sandra smiled. 'I'll tell you if you tell me something about yourself you don't want me to know.'

Not this again. I didn't even respond this time.

'Can you give me what you have on Ruud Klaver?'

'I've told you what I want in return. Let me interview you, and I'll share my evidence with you. The evidence that proves he was innocent.'

I shook my head. 'I can't.'

'Can't or won't?'

'Did you tell the family that you want me to come on the podcast?'

Sandra narrowed her eyes. 'What do you mean?' She rested her hand on the cement post that anchored the front gate.

'Talk to them. Ask them if they're okay with it.'

'Why wouldn't they be?'

'I'm serious. Ask them if they are okay with me being interviewed, and if there are any subjects that are off limits. Then get back to me.'

With a puzzled look in her eyes, Sandra stepped out of the way and went towards Barry's front door.

I texted him. *Did you tell her?*

The answer came back almost instantaneously. *No.* A second text followed a few seconds later. *I told her I'd been in an accident.*

I watched as the wind blew a mass of leaves down the street. They were maple leaves, red and gold. Further down, yellow leaves floated on the water of a pond. The trees themselves were half bare. Any leaves remaining on the branches were no longer a mass of green but a golden cover, the wood now clearly visible amongst them. A single leaf clung bravely to the end of a spindly branch, as if it was holding on for dear life. It wasn't ready yet to sail away on the wind but wanted to stay rooted to the ground.

If the family agreed, I might talk to Sandra Ngo to get the information she had. It could be a very useful short cut.

The streets were deserted here. The pavement was empty and quiet until a scooter came haring noisily along. I cycled over the wide bridge that signalled the start of the canal ring and got back to the older part of town. I pedalled slowly until I couldn't drag it out any longer, then entered the police station.

I was relieved to find that Ingrid wasn't in. The white-board in our office taunted me. Ruud Klaver stared at me from the centre. There were other names written there, but one stood out: Carlo Sondervelt. However much I tried to focus on Ruud's final year, that name kept drawing me in. Whatever Sandra Ngo might have found out about Ruud Klaver would just have to wait, I told myself sternly. I wasn't investigating Carlo Sondervelt's murder again; I was investigating Ruud Klaver's. What he might or might not have done only mattered so far as it had an impact on that murder investigation. Therefore I should be checking his employment record and known current associates rather than old murder cases.

Some days, being a police detective is really boring. Checking Klaver's employment record was quick: he hadn't had a job since he'd come out of prison. I moved on to looking at number plates, which I knew was pointless. There was an entire team upstairs going through exactly the same footage right now. I was only doing it because I had nothing else to do. I remembered other cases where I'd done this kind of work and been riveted by it, thinking that every detail I checked brought me closer to the solution. Now, not so much.

That was why I was pleased when I was interrupted by Charlie coming to see me. 'Tell me something about yourself that you don't want me to know,' I said.

'Okay.' He paused. 'Do you know why my parents called me Charlie?'

'I have no idea.' Wow, he was actually going to tell me.

'I really don't want you to know this.'

I narrowed my eyes. 'Then don't tell me. I really don't want to know.'

He sighed. 'No, I will. It's because my father was a huge *Charlie's Angels* fan.'

'Ah.' I cringed. 'Really?' I had to stifle my laughter.

'It's so embarrassing. Don't tell anybody.'

'Yeah, that's bad.' I folded my arms and looked at him. 'Just curious: why did you tell me?'

He frowned. 'Because you asked. Now can I be part of this investigation?'

'Why?'

'Wasn't that the deal? I tell you something . . .'

I glared at him until his voice faded away.

'About the car,' he said, and his voice pulled me back into the present. 'We haven't found it. We looked through all the CCTV footage and it isn't there. We don't know where it came from and we don't know where it went after it hit Klaver.'

'So we're stuck?'

He nodded. 'It seems that way.'

There was one easy answer. One simple short cut. Maybe I owed it to Barry to take it.

Chapter 17

All weekend I weighed up the reasons for and against being interviewed for the *Right to Justice* podcast. In my study, I made a list of pros and cons. The cons list was much longer. There was only one pro item, but it was of crucial importance. Hours later, I still hadn't decided, so I called Mark and asked him if I could pick his brains about something. He said he'd be right over.

Even though I wanted to rush up and kiss him as soon as I heard his footsteps on the stairs, I forced myself to stay in my chair for the sheer pleasure of watching him let himself in with his key. It seemed more intimate even than sleeping together. It was nice to have him here. We had been spending a lot of time at his place.

'I'm thinking about going on the *Right to Justice* podcast,' I said.

Mark hung up his coat and took a seat next to me on the sofa. He put his arm around my shoulder and pulled me close. I snuggled up and curled my legs under me. Pippi was eyeing him up as if to decide whether to jump on his lap. He wasn't that keen on cats, but she loved him. Not as much as she loved me, I told myself, but he was a close second. Go figure.

'Are you sure that's a good idea?' he said.

I wanted to talk to him because he was always the voice of reason. I needed him to say that I was doing the right thing. I was also fully aware that I couldn't ask for his opinion without telling him why I didn't want to go on the podcast, because I had to balance that with the reasons for doing it.

He reached for my hand and wrapped his fingers around mine. 'Sandra Ngo isn't going to be sympathetic towards you. She'll grill you.'

'I know. The thing is, I really need her information and this is the only way to get it. She says she's got proof that Ruud Klaver was innocent.'

'Yes, I heard that on the podcast. But you didn't think he could have been.'

'I never found any evidence for it.'

'Are you starting to doubt that now?'

'Maybe the witness didn't see what she said she saw.' My voice was sharper than I intended it to be. I didn't want to seem defensive. In the back of my mind I thought that maybe this was a rehearsal for the real thing.

'But you had forensic evidence too.'

I nodded slowly. He had been listening to the podcasts closely, as well as to my muttering afterwards.

'Are you worried there was something you missed?' he asked.

I pulled my hands through my hair. The problem about checking your own work was that it was so hard to judge

131

whether you'd done a good job. Maybe I should never have agreed to work on this case. It had seemed like a bad idea from the start. 'If I missed something, then I should definitely go on *Right to Justice* and admit to it, don't you think?'

'So that's a yes?'

I took a deep breath to tell him, but the words didn't come out. 'I need a drink,' I said. 'Do you want one?' Without waiting for his reply, I got up and walked to the kitchen. 'I'm just a normal human being,' I said loudly. 'It was an early case for me; I wasn't as experienced. So it's possible that I made a mistake.' I grabbed two glasses and put them on the table. 'And if I did, I should try to make it right.'

'Do you want to tell me what was going on with this case?'

I opened the fridge and got out a bottle of Chablis. I rummaged in the drawer for the corkscrew.

'I've seen how you react to the podcast,' Mark said. 'I can tell it's making you upset. I'm . . . worried.'

I sat back down. 'Worried about what?' I looked away and concentrated on cutting the foil on the top of the bottle.

'About you, of course. Did something happen during that case? Something that shouldn't come out?'

Shouldn't? I guess you could say that. 'Yes, I suppose there's something that shouldn't come out.' Even thinking about it hurt. I pulled the foil from the neck and exposed the delicate cork underneath.

'Is it something you did?'

Something I didn't do. Something I could have stopped, maybe. Something a child did and that was therefore classified. I stabbed the point of the corkscrew into the cork. 'My boss got injured during the arrest. A life-changing injury, we'd call it now.' I drove the point down and for a second wondered if a cork had feelings, and if being stabbed like this hurt as much as this conversation was hurting me. 'I think Sandra Ngo knows something the family aren't willing to share with the police.'

'Why wouldn't they tell you? Wouldn't they want to prove his innocence?'

'Now that he's dead, they're angry and probably feel there's no reason to cooperate with us. But I need to know.' I turned the corkscrew and watched the cork being penetrated further and further, until I could ease it out of the neck of the bottle.

'For most people,' he said, 'having to admit they were wrong would be enough to make them not want to be interviewed. But you seem to be okay with that.'

If I couldn't talk about this tonight, I couldn't do the podcast on Monday. It gave me an indication of how hard the interview was going to be. I put pressure on the corkscrew to lever the cork out of the neck. When it finally gave up its grip on the bottle, it came out with a satisfying pop.

I used to wonder when the right time was in a relationship to talk about the most painful things in your life. Now I knew the answer was: when you could bear it, when you were strong enough to talk about it.

'I was pregnant at the time,' I said. 'Four months pregnant.' I filled both glasses. I handed Mark his and then took a large gulp from mine. The flinty coldness filled my mouth.

Mark looked at me but stayed silent. He looked surprised. This wasn't what he'd expected to hear at all. In the back of my mind, I wondered what he'd thought I was going to confess to. That I'd tampered with evidence maybe? Framed the suspect? That Ruud's confession had been coerced after all?

He must have seen how much the memory was affecting me, because he reached out for the hand that wasn't clutching the wineglass. He didn't say anything. I appreciated that he let me finish the story. It would have been so easy for him to interrupt, to say that he didn't know I'd had a child, to ask where it was now.

To ask why I hadn't told him this before.

Instead, he gave me time.

'I lost the baby.' Part of me was proud of myself because I didn't cry. I gulped down the entirety of my glass of wine, then freed my hand to fill it up again. 'Two weeks after the arrest. And even though the doctor said there was nothing I could have done about it, I was sure that it was because of what happened that night. And every time I hear about this case, every time I think about it,' I took another big gulp from my glass, 'I keep thinking that it was my fault, that I shouldn't have gone into the house, that I shouldn't have run the risk.' Because my choice had put everybody else in danger. It had hurt Barry. I put my glass down and pressed the palms of my hands against my eyes. 'And the worst thing was that the main witness, Nancy, was pregnant too. I went to Carlo Sondervelt's parents' house and saw all these photos of their granddaughter, and I knew that this was how old my daughter would have been.'

Mark wrapped his arm around my shoulder and pulled my face to his chest. 'I'm so sorry,' he said. 'I'm so sorry.' He slowly rocked me from side to side.

I fitted into his embrace and tucked my face in the corner between his shoulder and his neck. I held him tight, as if he was my life buoy. As if only the touch of his body was going to keep me from drowning. I slid my right hand under his jumper to feel the warmth of his skin under my cold hand. He didn't flinch.

Even though I wasn't going to mention any of this to Sandra, it was possible that being interviewed was going to hurt. This was the price I was going to have to pay to get the information she had. But didn't I owe it to the dead man to do at least this much? If he'd been innocent, shouldn't I try to obtain the information that would make all the difference to the case? And most of all, didn't I owe it to Barry?

I made up my mind. I wasn't going to back out.

I took my phone from my bag. I called Sandra Ngo and set up a time for the interview. We agreed that I would see her tomorrow.

After I'd disconnected the call, I poured myself a final glass of wine.

Mark stayed, and it wasn't just having someone else in my bed that made me lie awake for most of the night. I was going through the case again in my head, running through the events of Ruud Klaver's arrest. I remembered that arrest so clearly.

After the incident, I stayed upstairs. Someone else went with Barry to the hospital. Dennis was taken away. I volunteered to watch Angela and Remco. I stayed behind and looked at the blood on the floor, and for the first time understood how terrible it felt to put your own safety before that of a colleague. Guilt washed over me, even as I still thought that Barry would probably be fine. I would never do this again, I promised myself.

As I'd told Mark, two weeks later, I had a miscarriage.

What I hadn't told him was that it was the day after I'd found out that Barry would never walk again. He'd been unlucky: the knife had severed one of the main nerves in his spine. A couple of centimetres either side, and he would have been fine.

If I'd done something, grabbed the kid's arm, he would have been fine.

I never told anybody how I felt. My husband thought I was depressed because I'd lost the baby and was extra nice to me. That only made me feel worse. Because I definitely didn't deserve it.

All those memories tumbled through my mind as I lay awake that night.

The fact that Sandra had sounded triumphantly pleased when I'd spoken to her was the least of my worries.

Chapter 18

'Don't do it,' Chief Inspector Moerdijk said when I went to see him first thing Monday morning.

Up to that point I'd felt rather good about doing the right thing and asking the boss for permission to be interviewed by Sandra Ngo. You'd have thought that by now I'd know that bowing to authority was a mistake. 'Boss, I don't know if we've got a choice.'

'Of course you do. Don't do it. Don't get involved with that *Right to Justice* lot.' He grabbed some papers from his desk.

'Has something happened?'

'They asked for comments on the first case they covered.'

I remembered that. At that stage, the police had worked with Sandra Ngo. We'd very quickly learned the error of our ways. 'I know, but this is a bit different.'

'I don't see how. She asked for a comment, and the police's official stance is that we do not cooperate with Sandra Ngo and her programmes any more.'

'She says she's got something that proves Ruud Klaver was innocent of Carlo Sondervelt's murder.'

'And?'

'Well, it could be crucial for finding out who killed Klaver.'

The boss frowned. 'And?' he said again.

'Don't you see?' I said. 'If Ruud Klaver didn't kill Carlo Sondervelt, then someone else did.'

'And you think this person could have killed Ruud?'

'I really don't know. I'm still pretty sure Klaver was guilty, but I need to see what Sandra Ngo has dug up.'

'Lotte, I trust you. Whatever Sandra has found, you'll find too.'

I shook my head. 'Not this time. The family refuse to speak to me and Sandra seems to be treated like a beloved daughter. If it's based on something they've told her, they're not going to share it with me.'

'Lotte, I want to be very clear: don't do it. We know she can't be trusted. We know that she likes stitching people up. She'll pretend to be nice and then knife you in the back.'

The expression made me feel sick. 'I don't think she's going to do that with me.'

The boss gave me a dubious look, as if to say that I was overestimating myself.

I remembered the acrimonious conversation that Sandra and I had had a couple of days ago. 'At least I know what I'm getting myself into.'

Moerdijk shook his head. 'I don't understand why you'd even think of doing it.'

'I've got nothing much to lose,' I said.

'Sandra thinks she's found some evidence that proves we were wrong. She says that you locked up an innocent man, and you think you've got nothing to lose?'

'She's going to broadcast that anyway. I can't stop her from putting her podcast and her opinion out there.'

'So just wait. Wait for the podcast and then you'll have the information.'

'You're asking me to wait for a week, or two weeks, in the middle of a murder inquiry?'

'The murder of a convicted murderer.'

'Does that matter?'

'It makes it all a little less urgent.'

I shook my head. 'If he was actually innocent, we wouldn't be talking like this.'

'Seriously, Lotte, do what you do best. Get digging. Look through the old case notes again. Forget it was you who originally investigated this. Imagine it was Bauer's case, for example, and try to stitch him up for taking one of our team.'

I left, as strongly decided as I had been before, regardless of what the boss had said. Still, his suggestion was an interesting one. How would I view this case if it had been someone else's? When I got back to our office, I opened my files again. I had been too busy thinking about myself when I thought about Carlo Sondervelt's murder.

It was great that Thomas was back from his holiday. Ingrid and I hadn't really talked since our falling-out on Friday, and having our third team member return defused the atmosphere. I wasn't going to rate it any higher than that.

'How was your break?' I said to Thomas.

'I'm glad to be back. My kids are more stressful than work.'

He had two. Eight and ten years old.

'Love your tan,' Ingrid teased. 'It even looks real this time.'

'Very funny,' he said.

He did like to have a tan all year round. He'd once told me that he thought it made him look younger. I wasn't sure about that, but it did make him look healthy.

'I saw that your guy died. I didn't think we were going to be working on that. Any leads?'

'Nothing so far,' Ingrid said. 'We haven't found the car. We haven't found a motive for the murder. Carlo Sondervelt's parents have got a very solid alibi, so it doesn't seem to be revenge for that murder either. Klaver's family are extremely uncooperative.' She didn't look in my direction.

'That shouldn't be a surprise. Ex-cons' families normally are.'

'Sandra Ngo says she's got evidence of his innocence,' I said.

'Ruud Klaver was innocent?' Thomas asked.

'That's what she says.'

'Didn't he confess?'

Yes, he'd confessed and we had been relieved. Of course there had been weak points in his conviction. There always were. We never found the gun. There had been no gun-powder residue on Klaver's hands.

I looked at our whiteboard and chewed the end of my pen. The boss had suggested that I try to think of the case as Bauer's work. Or maybe, even better, I could think of it as the work of an unnamed inexperienced CID detective desperate for a result. Someone willing to cut corners in order to get the results she wanted. Was that what I had done?

It was so hard to think of this as someone else's case. My memories of that time kept getting in the way.

I remembered being exhausted during the long interrogation of Ruud Klaver. I'd been about to give up when I'd shifted in my chair and the tight waistband of my trousers had made me suddenly aware of my baby I'd protected at such a high cost.

And even though I knew it was all in my head, I remembered that it felt as if my baby was saying: you're doing well, Mummy, let's get him to admit what he's done and I'll be here to listen to him say the words. I'll be your witness as you make amends.

I remembered that it gave me new energy so that it seemed as if both of us together got Ruud Klaver to confess. I was strengthened by the knowledge that there was a second being with me who noticed my every move, thought and emotion. At that moment, she was being fed by the feelings of deep relief that I wasn't showing externally.

And now I had to consider that it had all been wrong. How was I going to accept that this moment had been . . . what? An error? Force? Coercion?

I closed the file that I had been reading and pushed it across to Thomas's desk. It was pointless for me to look at it any longer.

Thomas was the expert in finding my mistakes.

Chapter 19

I zipped up my thick coat against the gale that whipped cold air along the canals. Where the wind hit the skin around my neck, it felt as if it was wicking away any trace of body heat. Mark had told me to wear a scarf this morning, but I had laughingly scolded him for mothering me. Now I was regretting it. He'd been right. He often was.

The house was on the corner of a road overlooking a little park. In spring and summer it would be a pleasant place to be; it would be green and there would be flowers. Today there was none of that. The trees were stripped bare of their leaves. The wind had free range and blew the empty branches this way and that. What might go back to being a lawn was now a brown expanse of mud edged with puddles. A play area off to the right was empty. The metal bars of the climbing frame were covered with beads of water. The shock-absorbing tiles underneath it were made slippery by the rain. All the kids who normally came here to play were sensibly indoors.

This morning, Thomas and Ingrid had spent an hour trying to talk me out of doing this. She'd even played me clips of the previous *Right to Justice* series, where the cop on the case had been completely crucified. This was my last chance to follow her advice. I could just not turn up. That way I would keep my identity hidden. But I would also not get the information I needed.

I had to do this.

I had expected a proper recording studio, like the TV channels had. I'd been on *Opsporing Verzocht* in the past, when we were looking for information from the public on a case where a single witness would make all the difference. Instead this seemed to be Sandra's house. Or maybe her parents'. I triple-checked the address. I knew I was at the right place and only procrastinating. There was no point in delaying any longer.

I rang the doorbell. I wasn't surprised when it opened only seconds later. Sandra must have been waiting for me. Maybe she'd even watched me as I dilly-dallied on her doorstep.

As soon as I stepped through the front door, she gestured towards a door off to the right.

'There's a light on your left.' She closed the front door behind me before I'd even found the switch.

When I flipped it, a bare light bulb illuminated the tiny corridor. There were wooden steps down. The walls were painted a deep red. The sound of every footstep on the stairs told me that this was a bad idea, but I kept going down.

'It's straight in front of you.'

I opened a thick metal door and saw a basement room with padded walls. As if I needed a reminder of my total insanity in being here.

'We've soundproofed it so you can't hear the traffic on the recording,' Sandra said.

Two people were already crammed into the room, and there was paper everywhere and yellow Post-its plastered over every surface. It reminded me of Dennis's newspapered walls. There were no windows. I looked at the Post-its. Sandra didn't stop me, so I knew there wasn't any information about Ruud Klaver's case on any of them. What I could see were recording schedules and notes about the software. A timeline for the podcasts: whom to interview when.

My name was on a Post-it right in the centre. *Lotte Meerman: 16 October @ 11.45*. It was written in red ink.

In the privacy of her own home, Sandra seemed to have made an effort to look as slovenly as possible. One advantage of doing a podcast was that your appearance didn't matter. Her light-grey jumper had a large red food stain down the front that might have once had something to do with tomatoes. Her hair was released from its customary topknot and fell down to skim the edge of her jaw. As she walked ahead of me through the basement, her moccasin slippers made a swishy sound on the concrete floor.

The other two people in the room were a young girl with lanky hair, who stared at me as though she needed glasses but was too vain to get them; and a man a little older than me with a bald head and pale skin. Both of them looked as if they never went outside but were stuck in this basement forever, forced to research crimes. It wasn't so different from my own life, but at least I was allowed out every now and then.

'Please sit here,' the bald man said. He pointed at an office chair by a black table. This must be the guy who'd visited

Carlo's parents with Sandra. The guy with the same first name as Ruud Klaver's son.

'Thanks, Dennis,' I said, to mess with him, because he hadn't told me his name.

I was successful, because he stared at me open-mouthed like he was a goldfish. Then he almost fell onto a chair behind a desk and put on a large set of headphones, as if that would guard him against my special mind-reading powers. To avoid looking me in the eye, he focused on the screen of the laptop in front of him.

All this time, while I was playing mind games with her staff, Sandra had been watching me with a courteous smile that didn't fool me in the slightest. She might be holding papers in her hands but she might as well be brandishing a knife. Now that I was here, I was reminded of the boss's advice that I shouldn't be doing this. That nothing good was going to come from it. But if I wanted the information on Ruud Klaver that I so desperately needed, I had no choice.

'I'm not your enemy,' Sandra said.

Well, it sure felt as if I'd infiltrated behind enemy lines.

The girl picked up a pile of books from the floor, put them on the table and placed a small silver recording device on top so that it was close to our mouths. Even though I couldn't see the spines of the books, I knew they had been chosen for their thickness rather than the quality of the writing within.

'Can you say something?' the bald man said.

'Can I have some water, please?' I asked.

'Perfect. I can hear you clearly.'

I looked at the girl. 'Could you get me some water?' My mouth was dry, as if all the moisture in my body had gone to my sweating hands.

'Oh, sorry. Of course.' She darted off.

'Sorry, Lotte, I should have offered,' Sandra said. 'Do you mind if I call you Lotte for this?'

'Detective Meerman will be fine.' The temperature in the room seemed to drop by a degree. I smiled to take the sting from the words. 'I think your listeners will find it easier to follow our conversation if you do that.'

'Sure. If that's what you prefer.' She smiled back as sincerely as I had done. 'I want you to be comfortable.'

'And just to be clear, after we've done this interview, you will give me the information you've got on Ruud Klaver. You will tell me why you think he didn't kill Carlo Sondervelt.'

'Why I *know* he didn't,' Sandra corrected me. 'And yes, I will tell you that. That was the deal, after all.'

I put my phone on the table and pressed record. 'I'm sure you won't mind if I have a record of this conversation as well.'

'Are you concerned about how we're going to edit it? Worried we'll take your words out of context?'

'I'm sure you wouldn't do a thing like that.'

'Go ahead. I don't mind at all.'

'When are you going to broadcast it?'

'It's scheduled for Wednesday.'

I was glad when the girl returned with a glass of water. I took a small sip, just enough to moisten my tongue. 'Can we start?' The sooner we began, the sooner it would be over.

146

Sandra looked at her sound man, who nodded. 'I'll record the introduction later; no need to go over that now.'

'Sure.'

She got an elastic band out of her trouser pocket and tied her hair back. That must be part of her *Right to Justice* persona. 'I'm here with Detective Lotte Meerman to talk about Ruud Klaver.' The timbre of her voice had changed, dropping maybe half an octave and taking on a mellow honey characteristic. In contrast, her face didn't change at all. She looked at me with a mixture of politeness and mischief that I found disconcerting. There was a half-smile around her lips that threatened to change into a smirk. 'Welcome, Detective Meerman, to our *Right to Justice* podcast.'

'Thank you, Sandra, it's interesting to be here.'

She bit her lip both at my use of her first name and at my choice of words. I should have just said: nice to be here. Who cared that it would have been a lie.

'I'm sure the listeners will be very interested in what you have to say about Carlo Sondervelt's murder. You were the investigating detective on that case, is that right?'

'I was one of the team, to be precise, but yes, I worked on that case.'

'For those people who tuned in to the previous episode, Ruud Klaver told us he'd felt coerced into a confession. You were the detective questioning him, weren't you?'

'I was. What Klaver didn't tell you, or at least I didn't hear it on the podcast, was that his lawyer was with us in the room the whole time. I'm sure she would have stopped the interview if she'd felt I was putting undue pressure on the suspect. Actually,' I took a sip of water, 'before we get into the details, I do want to say how sorry I am that Ruud Klaver died. My sympathies are with his family at what must be a tough time for them.' I didn't think Sandra would leave that in, but it was worth a try.

'Are you saying that because you no longer believe he was guilty?'

'Whether he was guilty or not is irrelevant in this.' Sandra's eyebrows shot up, but I kept talking. 'A man has died and that's hard on his family.'

'But if he was a murderer—'

'That doesn't matter,' I interrupted her. 'He was convicted of a crime, he was sentenced to time in jail and he served that time. We treat his murder as we would anybody else's.'

'Right.' The scepticism was clear in her voice. 'Let's go back to Carlo Sondervelt. I hear what you're saying, but in my eyes, someone was imprisoned wrongly for ten years. You might think his innocence or guilt is irrelevant, but I think Ruud's death has made it even more heartbreaking that he was locked up for a crime he didn't commit.'

Her challenging look made it hard, but I managed to stay silent. I knew that I didn't have to win every argument. In an interview like this, it was easy to get dragged off course, and I should only say what I was willing to.

'You were convinced that Klaver was guilty because you had a witness,' she said.

'Correct.'

'A witness who saw Ruud shoot Carlo.'

'That is correct.' All of this was in the court records anyway.

'And you believed her.'

148

'There was no reason not to. She was a reliable witness.'

'But you only had her testimony.'

'Well, her witness statement backed up a large amount of circumstantial evidence, such as the blood we found on Klaver's clothes.'

'For the listeners, let me just point out that Klaver always maintained that this blood came from the fist fight he'd had earlier in the evening with Carlo Sondervelt.'

'Our forensics team argued that this was highly unlikely, based on the pattern that the blood had formed on his clothes.'

'But highly unlikely doesn't mean impossible.'

'Correct. Highly unlikely just means highly unlikely.' I thought I managed to keep the sarcasm out of my voice. However much I wanted to aggravate Sandra, I knew it wouldn't sound good. 'So when that was backed up by the witness, we felt there was a very strong case to arrest Ruud Klaver for Carlo Sondervelt's murder.'

'I find this very interesting,' Sandra said.

I was wondering what the girl with the lanky hair was doing at this point. She was busy behind me somewhere. If I looked for her, I would probably miss Sandra's next question. I hated having someone at my back that I couldn't see.

The bald man with the headphones was still staring intently at the screen of his laptop. Our voices must be coming through loud and clear because he didn't give us any signals to the contrary.

'The reason why I'm bringing this up,' Sandra said, 'is because it interests me to see why you believe one person and not another. I know that this is the job of the police, but you are still human beings and you can be swayed.'

'Of course we're still human, and that is why we like to have our opinions backed up by forensic evidence.'

'But there was no CCTV footage of Carlo's murder.' She took the elastic band from her hair, shook it loose and tied it back again. All without making a sound.

'Correct.' Instead of looking at Sandra playing with her hair, I tried to read one of the Post-its on the wall behind her. The writing was tiny.

'Do you think you believed the witness, Carlo's girlfriend, because she was pregnant?'

'If her pregnancy had anything to do with it, it was only because it meant she wasn't drinking and therefore was a very reliable witness.'

'Did you breathalyse her?'

I stopped looking at the yellow Post-its. 'I can't remember, to be honest. I would have to check in the files.'

'I know you mentioned this same point in court, and I went through the case files, but I couldn't find anything that mentioned a breathalyser test. You just made the assumption that she was sober, but maybe she wasn't. Not everybody is responsible during their pregnancy.'

'She told us—'

'Well she would have done, wouldn't she? She was the only witness who was going to get the suspect locked up. What was she going to say otherwise?'

I was in two minds now. Would staying silent be the wise choice, or would it look as if I was giving in and agreeing with Sandra? I took another sip of water and put the glass down carefully so that it wouldn't make a sound on the recording. 'What she saw lined up with our forensic evidence.' It seemed a safe factual statement to go with.

'But there was someone else who saw the incident, wasn't there?'

'Yes.'

'And this person didn't identify Ruud Klaver.'

Ruud's defence lawyer hadn't done nearly as thorough a job. 'To clarify: the other witness said he didn't get a good view of the perpetrator and therefore couldn't identify him. It's not as if he said that he'd seen the murderer and it wasn't Klaver.'

'But you had two witnesses, one the pregnant girlfriend, the other a neutral bystander, and one of them identified Ruud, the other didn't. You don't think that's strange?'

'No, it's not strange at all. One of them got a clear view, the other didn't. That happens a lot. And don't forget that Ruud Klaver pleaded guilty.'

'What if I told you that the barman in the pub said that your pregnant witness had been drinking?'

I sat back on my chair. That was her big reveal? That ten years later the barman said Nancy might have had a drink after all? That was what I was doing this interview for? 'Would that have made a difference?' Sandra asked.

'I don't think it would have. Not with the forensic evidence to back the statement up.' I was careful not to let my voice broadcast my relief.

'The *circumstantial* forensic evidence.'

'Anybody would have said that our witness was credible

and reliable. The judge in the case ruled that she was.' I took another sip of water.

'Only she wasn't. We have proof that shows that Ruud Klaver was innocent.'

'Discrediting our witness doesn't make him an innocent man.'

'I know that. What I'm saying is that you believed the witness so implicitly that you never checked other facts that you should have checked. You never followed up on other lines of enquiry that would have ended with Ruud Klaver declared innocent. You believed this pregnant woman and got an innocent man convicted. A man who is now dead. You lost him ten years of his life because you felt sympathy with the victim's girlfriend.'

My throat suddenly felt as if I had swallowed shards of glass. I had to stay focused. I had to ignore that this was going to be broadcast all over the country. I pressed the nails of my middle fingers into the pads of my thumbs. I needed to create pain in another part of my body to keep my mind sharp. 'I think everybody would have had sympathy with a twenty-year-old pregnant girl whose boyfriend had been murdered in front of her eyes.' The physical pain felt good. It gave me control back. Now that I was hurting myself, Sandra wasn't hurting me with her questions. I pressed harder. 'I understand what you are doing in these podcasts: trying to show that certain convicted criminals weren't actually guilty, but you also need to understand that there were victims in this case. That there were people for whom this was really hard. And as I said, I don't think I would be the only one to feel for a young girl in that situation.'

'It's interesting, isn't it, that you're here, doing this interview, to find out the truth about this case. You didn't find it out for yourself because you were so fixated on your witness. Even now, even after I've told you I have evidence, you haven't figured out what it is. That's really poor policing. And the fact that you're here shows me that you know it.'

I would have got angry if I hadn't known she was right. I hadn't discovered what evidence Sandra had. It wasn't just that I had to accept that she might be a better investigator than I was. It was that I had to accept that I had failed. Oddly enough, that knowledge made me calm. I had nothing left to give and it was about time I saw what I was getting in return. I released my fingers experimentally to see if I could stay in control of my voice without the physical pain. 'What is your proof that Ruud Klaver was innocent?' The control held; my voice was still steady even if the painful shards were still there.

'I'm sure,' Sandra continued as though I hadn't spoken, 'the family are pleased that someone as competent as you is working on Ruud's murder case.' The sarcasm cut through the honey of her voice like vinegar. I knew it was just to rile me. I knew that this would never make it into the broadcast version of the podcast. 'You never found the gun, did you?'

'No, we didn't. Are you going to share your so-called evidence with the listeners?'

'Of course. I hope this episode has shown that there is serious doubt about the police's case. Their forensic evidence was circumstantial and their witness was not as reliable as they presented her. Now we've found that the weapon used in Carlo's murder had been used in another murder three weeks earlier, a murder for which Ruud Klaver had a rock-solid alibi.' She looked at me in triumph. 'You locked away an innocent man and you can no longer do anything to right that wrong.'

The same gun had been used before? Oh, that was a basic error. We should have checked the database to see if the weapon had been used in any prior unsolved incidents.

She pressed a button on the recording device and stopped it. 'It's good, isn't it? My evidence.'

The evidence of another murder with the same weapon could only be a bullet with a matching striation pattern. How had Sandra found out about it? And, more importantly, how had Forensics missed it? 'Which murder? Is someone else in jail for it?'

She pushed a file towards me. 'I've printed everything out for you. Have it.'

I grabbed the file and stuffed it in my bag. I wasn't going to give her the satisfaction of looking through it here. I could tell by her face that she was disappointed. I was hoping that she was disappointed by the entire interview. I thought I'd done well. I'd held it together and answered all her questions.

'You were right,' she said. 'There were things the family didn't want me to ask you about.'

'I know.'

'I'm really curious.'

'I'm sure you are.'

'But I respect their wishes.' She grinned. 'And they'll tell me at some point. Or maybe you will.'

The podcast was going to be released on Wednesday. That gave me a day before the whole country would know that I'd worked on this case. It was something I would have preferred to keep hidden.

As I stepped out into the rain, I felt the weight of the file in my bag. Had I ever bought anything at a higher price? I had the murderer of Ruud Klaver to find. And I had to look at this second murder. Surely doing the interview had been worth it.

I grasped the file tight with the hand that wasn't fighting to hold onto my umbrella. I didn't want to examine its contents at my desk. If the information turned out to be garbage, I wasn't sure what I'd do, but smashing up Sandra's recording studio was one option. Bursting into tears was another. Both of these were best avoided.

I rushed back through the storm to my flat and opened the file with trembling fingers. As I skimmed through the pages, I saw that Sandra's evidence was solid. Klaver's alibi was backed up with photographs.

Everything tumbled around me.

I had made a mistake. It now seemed likely that Ruud Klaver had indeed been innocent.

Chapter 20

'The next time I see Sandra Ngo, I don't know if I should hug her or kill her,' Chief Inspector Moerdijk said.

His running gear was drying over the radiator in his office. He must have gone for a run at lunchtime and got caught in the rain. The bottoms of my trousers were still a little damp from where my umbrella hadn't kept all the rain off. It was harder to stay dry when there was also a force 8 wind trying to pull the umbrella from your hand and you were attempting to keep a file with important papers from getting soaked.

'Kill her,' I said. 'Or just give her a kicking. I won't tell anybody you did it.'

I had gone to the boss's office after I'd examined the file and had a chance to absorb what I'd found in there. Barry had said that I'd focused on Ruud Klaver exclusively from the start. That after Nancy's evidence I'd only ever looked at him. I knew I had needed it to be him because otherwise we wouldn't have gone into the Klavers' house in the first place. But that didn't make it the truth, and now it turned out that the gun that had killed Carlo Sondervelt had been used in another murder and Ruud Klaver had a solid alibi for that time.

'I'm not sure she deserves that. But you do. I told you explicitly not to give an interview to *Right to Justice* and you went directly against my instructions.'

I shrugged. What was done was done. Nothing the boss could do would make me feel worse than I already did. I'd had some time to calm down after the interview, and it no longer felt as if old wounds had been ripped open. Instead they throbbed with the familiar ache of a previously broken bone during rainy weather.

'You do know that I'm your boss, don't you? You haven't forgotten that? And you also remember what that means, right? It means that if you ask me if you can do something, and I tell you you can't, then you don't. You don't do it sneakily behind my back.'

There was a joking edge to his voice, so I wasn't worried by his words. I knew him well enough to be aware that the fact that he was kidding meant that he was secretly pleased. In a way, I did deserve to be told off. Not for going against his wishes, but because Sandra's evidence had nothing to do with information that the family had given her. I'd thought it would be impossible for me to unearth the thing that she had found, but I could have done. In fact, I should have done. Ten years ago.

'What do you want us to do now?' I said.

'You never looked into this at the time?'

'No, we had no idea the gun had been used before. That murder was at the other end of the country. We never compared the bullets.'

'But Sandra Ngo did. How many people are shot each year?'

'Fewer than twenty countrywide last year, if you include non-lethal shootings,' I said. 'But it's on a downward trend, so maybe there were around thirty the year Carlo Sondervelt died.'

'Ha. It probably wouldn't have taken her long to narrow it down and find the right one.'

I could have done it in a day: looked at the striation marks on the bullet and gone through the database to find one that matched. I couldn't shake the thought that someone within the police station must have given Sandra access to our database, or even run the query for her.

'So, yes, this does prove that the same gun was used in two murders, three weeks apart,' I said. 'The first was committed in a forest just outside Arnhem, between two and four o'clock in the afternoon, on the seventh of January. No witnesses.' I took a sheet of paper out of the folder. 'Here is a statement by Dennis Klaver, saying that the seventh of January is his birthday, and his father was at his party that afternoon.' There was a pile of photos of a children's party, with Dennis and both his parents very clearly present. I had looked through these photos quickly; I didn't need any more reminding of what Dennis had looked like as a kid. 'It takes about an hour and a half to drive from Amsterdam to the woods outside Arnhem where the body was found. Or an hour by train to Arnhem's centre, plus at least half an hour to get to the exact location. And the same to come back, of course. So we'd be looking at three hours' travel time, and according to Dennis, his father was at his party the whole time.' I took out a second page, signed by Angela Klaver. 'This is from the wife, stating the same thing.'

'It's pretty solid as alibis go.'

'There's even an invoice from the place where the party was held, and a party invitation with the exact date and time.'

'Sandra Ngo is very diligent. Maybe we should ask her if she wants to come and work for us.'

'Not funny,' I said.

'I would say she's out-Lotted Lotte. This is the kind of thing you'd do.'

I ignored his joke. Or jibe. Or whatever it was. Instead I pushed a photo of a man in a red T-shirt across the table. 'This is the other victim: Maarten Hageman, forty-five years old. From the database, I can see that the Arnhem police thought this might have been organised-crime-related or a revenge killing. Hageman was well known to them. Completely different to Carlo Sondervelt. I couldn't find an immediate connection between the two.' But I had only been looking at the information for about an hour before going to the boss. 'I also don't know what impact this information has on the ongoing investigation into Ruud Klaver's murder.'

'It's certain that it's the same gun?'

'Yes, from the photos, the striation marks look identical. But I have asked Forensics to double-check everything. Ngo seems to have hired an expert to write a report. In both cases, the bullet was recovered from the body with minimal damage.' I collected all the bits of paper up and put them safely back in the file. 'If this had come up during Ruud Klaver's trial, he probably wouldn't have been convicted.

Even though it doesn't prove his innocence, of course. Two different people could have used the same gun.' I placed the file on the floor underneath my chair. 'But it certainly would have put reasonable doubt in the mind of the judge.'

The boss stood up and stared at the storm outside. 'This isn't good.' He directed his words to the window.

'What do you want us to do now?' I spoke to his back. 'Are we still concentrating on Ruud Klaver? Or do you want us to work on Maarten Hageman and Carlo Sondervelt's murders again?'

The boss turned around abruptly. 'You've made this the death of a man who had been wrongfully convicted.'

I was only too well aware of that. 'Nobody else knows about the second murder. The podcast hasn't talked about it yet.' I had promised not to expose the information outside the police station until after the podcast was aired. I had to give Sandra her scoop. I didn't see the point in telling the boss that that was only two days away. It would just annoy him more.

'True. Anybody listening to those damned *Right to Justice* podcasts would still assume Ruud Klaver was guilty.'

'Not quite. When Ruud was hit by that car, the podcast had just reached the stage where Ngo said there was going to be evidence that proved his innocence.' I knew that because it was what I'd been listening to when I saw the family come out of the hospital.

'But they hadn't said what the proof was. What if the real murderer of Carlo Sondervelt wanted to make sure that none of this came out?'

'Then he'd kill Sandra Ngo, not Ruud Klaver,' I said.

160

'Or he'd have a chat with her first to find out what she'd got,' the boss said.

My phone bleeped. As if she knew we were talking about her, Sandra Ngo had sent me a text. She was going to change the broadcasting schedule; my interview was going to be aired tonight. I looked at my watch. I had six hours of normality left.

'Once that podcast airs,' Moerdijk said, 'everybody will know that Klaver had been locked up for ten years for a crime he didn't commit. There will be a huge amount of pressure on us.'

I showed him my phone. 'It will go out tonight.'

He swore softly. 'Okay, I'll get some more resources as soon as possible. You should probably stay away from Ruud Klaver's family for a bit. Thomas and Ingrid can communicate with the Klavers. You concentrate on the old murders – Carlo Sondervelt, Maarten Hageman – see if there's any link between them and Ruud Klaver's death.'

'If you're getting us more resources from other teams,' I said, 'there's this traffic cop . . .' I didn't necessarily want to help Charlie Schippers, but I also didn't want to have my debts stack up any higher than they already were.

Chapter 21

'None of this makes any sense to me,' Ingrid said. 'You seem so convinced that his death and this podcast are linked. You could be completely wrong.'

'Here's the timeline as I see it.' I grabbed a blue marker pen. 'Twelve months ago, Ruud Klaver was released from prison.' I wrote the date on the whiteboard. 'There were no incidents. He didn't get beaten up, threatened, nothing.'

'As far as we know.'

'True. Then Sandra Ngo starts to look into his case. She meets with Carlo's parents and with Nancy Kluft two months ago.' I wrote their names down. 'That was at the start of her research, when they were still cooperating with her. Before they knew what angle she was going to take.'

'I see where you're going with this. Still nothing happened to Klaver or to Sandra Ngo.'

Nothing had happened to her then, but something had happened later. Ingrid's words triggered a memory. Of course. I remembered the afternoon I'd come down the stairs of the police station and heard Sandra Ngo shouting that she'd been burgled but nothing had been taken.

That had been after the first airing of the podcast in

which she'd said that Ruud Klaver had been innocent, but before he had been killed. A burglary that nobody had taken seriously. I doubted anybody had even bothered to dust for fingerprints at Ngo's house. She had been angry because nobody had visited her. I sighed. This was just brilliant. She would claim that the police had messed up again.

'On the afternoon of the tenth of October, Sandra Ngo declared in her podcast that Klaver was innocent,' I said. 'There was a break-in at her house later the same day, and at eight p.m., Klaver was hit by a car.'

'This could all be a coincidence. Just to play devil's advocate, of course,' Ingrid said.

'I didn't know this was a game where we were allowed to just spout baseless theories. Can I go next?' Thomas said. 'Someone close to Carlo, say Nancy, is clearly pissed off when she hears that Klaver now claims he was innocent. After all, she saw him with her own eyes. So when she happens to spot him on the pedestrian crossing, she gets a case of the red mist and drives into him.'

'Oh, I've got one,' Ingrid said. 'The family must have had the information about his innocence beforehand. They contact the investigating detective to tell her she's been wrong all along, and she is so pissed off that when she sees him, she decides to hit him with her car just to make matters worse.' She grinned at me and then high-fived Thomas.

'Very funny.' I wiped the timeline off the whiteboard.

Thomas stared thoughtfully at the file he had in front of him. 'I can see why you want to link those things. I'm guessing we'll reopen the investigation into Maarten Hageman's murder.'

163

'Yes, apparently the Arnhem police are sending their paperwork over. They wanted to lead the investigation, but the boss refused. That will come to us too. Or rather, to me. The boss wants you guys to concentrate on Ruud Klaver's murder and will get you more resources.'

'I hear you're going to have that traffic cop working with you?'

'Yeah, I owed him one.'

'Great.' Thomas grimaced. 'You know that his colleague, Arnaud, said he's as thick as two planks of wood.'

No wonder he was still a traffic cop after ten years. It didn't really matter. I could work around him. He just had to not get in my way.

Thomas opened the file that Sandra had given me and turned over the pages I'd looked at earlier. 'This guy Maarten ran a couple of restaurants and bars in Arnhem and Amsterdam?'

'Yes. The police suspected they were a front for a money-laundering operation,' I said. 'He was shot twice. Once in the stomach and once in the head.'

'There was nothing dodgy about Carlo Sondervelt, was there?'

'No, nothing. I know we always say good things about the dead, but Carlo genuinely seemed to be just a hard-working student. Never been in trouble with the police. His fellow students, his professors, they only had good things to say about him.'

'Apart from getting his girlfriend pregnant. Did the parents know?'

'No, they didn't. It was a total surprise to them.'

'There was nothing iffy about the girlfriend either?'

'No, no reason to suspect anything like that. So if there's nothing that links Carlo and Maarten,' I said as I made notes of things to check, 'maybe the murders were committed with the same weapon but by two different people.'

Thomas laughed. 'You still don't want to admit that maybe you were wrong?'

'It's not that.'

'You know that people don't trust evidence that goes contrary to their beliefs? Confirmation bias, it's called.'

'I know. I went on the same internal course.'

From the corner of my eye I could see that Ingrid was flipping through the photos of Dennis's birthday party. I tried to look away – I didn't want to see Dennis as a kid – but I still caught glimpses of him with his parents, his friends, a cake and a pile of presents. When I'd been that age, I would always do the same thing on my birthday: we'd go bowling, I'd have some classmates round and my mother would make pancakes. Every year the same friends, every year the same thing. My mother didn't have any imagination. Dennis's brother was obviously absent from the photos, because what self-respecting eighteen-year-old would want to be at his baby brother's birthday party?

Ingrid looked up and caught my eye. 'Are you still convinced that Ruud Klaver killed Carlo Sondervelt?' she asked.

I wasn't convinced of anything any more. 'It's not that. It's just that the murders took place under different circumstances, at very different locations and times of day. We can't find a link between the victims.'

'We've been looking for about five minutes! We'll find

something. And sometimes there just is no obvious link, you know that. It could have been a friend of Ruud Klaver's who had also been involved in the earlier fight.' Ingrid paused. 'That's actually possible, isn't it? Was Ruud alone earlier in the evening?'

'I'm not sure.' That was an interesting idea. Maybe someone else had known that we'd find Ruud's DNA on Carlo and Carlo's blood on Ruud, and had taken advantage of it. Someone could have seen the fight. The fact that I had been looking at these files ad nauseam for the past few days was now coming in handy. I knew exactly what was in them and where everything was located. 'But Carlo Sondervelt was with one of his friends. Tristan.'

'Did he come from Arnhem?'

'I'll check on that.'

I also wanted to talk to Nancy Kluft again. I needed to verify exactly what she'd seen. I had postponed this meeting for as long as I could, but now I could no longer avoid it.

I looked up her address and cycled to her house. I should have taken someone with me, but I was worried: not about the questions I was going to ask, or about the answers she was going to give, but about the questions she might ask me.

That was why I was here by myself.

I locked my bike and walked to her front door. As I paused with my finger centimetres away from the bell, I knew that this was my last chance to turn back. But I also knew I wouldn't. I had to figure out where I'd gone wrong.

I'd first spoken to Nancy at the scene of the crime, when I'd decided that I shouldn't wait for Barry, but should talk to the crying girl myself.

As I got closer, she turned towards me. Her eyes were swollen and red, and snot was coming down her nose. She had high cheek-bones, and long dark hair streamed from underneath her bright-pink hat.

I opened my handbag to get a pack of tissues out and handed them to her. 'Can you answer a few questions?'

She nodded and wiped her face with the back of her hand.

I sat down next to her on the damp pavement. The waistband of my jeans dug into my stomach. It was only just starting to feel tight. 'What's your name?'

'Nancy. Nancy Kluft. I'm Carlo's girlfriend.'

She used the present tense. The reality of what had happened obviously hadn't sunk in yet. In the distance, three men sang an old André Hazes song about a lover who would never return. This girl's lover would never come back either.

'I'm so sorry for your loss,' I said. The words were inadequate. I wondered how many years I would have to do this job before they became routine. 'What did you see?'

'The guy came from around that corner,' she pointed down a dark alley paved with cobblestones, 'and then he shot Carlo.' She started to sob.

I put my hand on her back and felt her ragged breaths. I stared down the darkness of the alley and waited as she slowly calmed down. I rubbed her back until she could talk again.

'Sorry,' she said.

'It's okay. Take your time. Where did you come from?'

'We were in this bar.' She nodded backwards to the place she was sitting in front of. She breathed deeply as if to pull herself together. White fog streamed from her mouth. 'He was waiting for us.' She put her hands in front of her face.

'And then what happened?'

'He disappeared down the alley again.'

'What gave you the idea he was waiting for you?'

'Because I'd seen him before.' Her voice was as steady as it could be between gulps of tears.

I felt excitement building up in my body. 'You got a good look at him?'

'Yes, yes I did. They'd been fighting earlier.'

The door opened. Nancy was as beautiful as she had been ten years ago. Maybe she no longer had the perfect skin and glow of a twenty-year-old, but she would still turn heads in the street. It had been those looks that had started the fight in the first place. Sometimes it really didn't pay to be too pretty. She looked at me, puzzled at first, with the expression on her face that people get when they're expecting someone else – a delivery man or a friend – and find a stranger standing on their doorstep instead. Only I wasn't a stranger.

It took her a few seconds before she realised. Then her face broke out in a wide smile and she opened her arms as if to give me a hug, before quickly dropping them when she realised it would probably be inappropriate to hug a police detective.

'Detective Meerman,' she said.

I smiled. 'Call me Lotte. You used to, remember?'

Her smile grew wider, displaying perfectly white teeth. She reached out and put a hand on my arm. 'Come in, come in.'

I followed her down a corridor plastered with photos that I tried my best not to look at. My eyes were firmly on Nancy's back. I was doing well, I thought.

168

'Can I get you anything? Tea? Coffee?'

'No, I'm fine.' But I smiled, because the warm welcome I was receiving was a wonderful antidote to the attitude of the Klaver family. This was the difference in reaction between the family of the victim and the family of the perpetrator. The only odd thing about this case was that the family of the perpetrator had *become* the family of the victim. And I was about to ask this lovely girl if it was possible that she'd been wrong all these years. Maybe turning my friends into enemies would turn my enemies into friends. I unzipped my coat. Experience had taught me that it was far more likely that I was going to turn my friends into enemies and then only have enemies left.

Nancy sat down at a table that had a pile of laundry on top of it. I sat opposite her, trying not to look at any of the photos dotted around the room.

She pointed at the pile of washing in front of her. 'Do you mind if I continue with this?'

'No, go ahead.'

She grabbed a dark-blue T-shirt from the pile and gave it a shake to bounce out any creases. 'I thought you might come to see me. Jelte called me after you'd visited them.'

'Yeah, we talked to them a couple of days ago.'

She smoothed the fabric of the T-shirt, folded the sleeves to the centre and then the other side over. She brought the bottom seam up to the neck and folded it double again. All in a few seconds, a few practised hand movements.

I knew I was only watching her because I didn't want to ask the questions I was going to have to. I was here now;

there was no point in stalling any longer. 'So you know that Ruud Klaver died?'

'Yes, Jelte called me straight away. I might not have known otherwise. I don't really follow the news, but he reads the entire paper. Even scans the obituaries religiously to see if any of his friends have died.' She picked up a second T-shirt, a red one. 'And this was a big story, after Klaver had been on that podcast and lied about being innocent.' Her hand paused with the flat of it resting on the red fabric. 'Jelte said you asked him questions about the night of Ruud Klaver's accident, but you can't think we have anything to do with it?'

'It was your birthday, wasn't it? You had dinner with Carlo's parents and your daughter, Wietske. I managed not to grimace at saying the girl's name.

'Yeah, and we were all at our favourite Chinese restaurant.'

'That's why I don't think you've got anything to do with it. But there is something I want to check with you.' I leaned forward in my chair and gave Nancy a deep look.

She stopped folding.

'Be honest with me. It doesn't matter any more because Ruud is dead and it's all a long time ago.' I swallowed, not too happy with what I was going to ask her. 'But if you didn't see Ruud shoot Carlo that night, you should tell me now.'

She picked up another T-shirt and folded it with abrupt movements. As if to punish me for my questions, she had chosen a pink one printed with golden stars and emblazoned with the word 'PRINCESS' on the front. It was a T-shirt that a ten-year-old girl would wear.

'I won't think badly of you.' I continued to look into

Nancy's eyes, if only not to have to see that T-shirt. 'If you just caught a brief glimpse of him . . .'

'You think I lied?'

'No.' The word came out of my mouth automatically, but I realised it was the truth. 'But it's easy to make a mistake under those circumstances.'

'You think I lied.' The words were harsher this time.

She'd been so secure when she'd told me what had happened. I hadn't doubted her words. Especially as her evidence was so crucial. How often did you get a witness who saw everything as clearly as she had?

'They'd been fighting earlier,' she said.

'They were in a physical fight?'

'Yes. Carlo punched the guy a couple of times. But the other guy started it.'

'He punched him? Hold on just a second.' I rushed over to the forensic scientist and told him. If Carlo had hit the guy, there might be some of the gunman's blood on his hands and clothing. There was always a high chance with gun crime that there was some previous form, and that this person would be on our DNA database.

'Let me take you to the police station. We'll look at some photos and see if you can pick him out.'

'He had blond hair and he was a little taller than Carlo. Maybe one-ninety?' Some life returned to her eyes. She took her hands out of her pockets as if she could drive me on towards finding the murderer if only she was more animated.

'Age?'

'Thirty-ish.'

'This is all really useful,' I said.

'I recognised him straight away,' she said. 'I'll call Carlo's friend *too. Tristan broke up the fight. He can help me identify him.'* She got her phone out.

'Had you been drinking?' I said before she could make the call.

'Carlo had. I hadn't.' She looked at me with large brown eyes. 'I'm four months pregnant.'

I covered her hand with mine. I wanted to say: so am I, but I had to keep quiet in case any of my colleagues overheard me.

I'd had a miscarriage before. I'd told everybody about the pregnancy, exactly at the three-month point, and when I'd lost the baby afterwards, I had to tell them all about that too. The sympathy in my colleagues' eyes made the loss harder to bear, and I'd started to realise that it was better not to tell anybody. This time I was going to keep it a secret until I showed.

Nancy folded up another 'PRINCESS' T-shirt. This one was lilac. I'd never liked those T-shirts that confirmed girls' roles. I would have . . . No. I stopped myself. Don't think about that. Get on with this interview. Get it over with.

'I honestly don't think you lied,' I said, but I knew only too well that people misremembered things. They thought they'd seen something but they hadn't. They thought something had happened at three o'clock but it had actually happened at four.

'My boyfriend was shot dead and you think I lied about that?' Nancy pulled two matching socks out of the pile, lined them up, toe to toe, and folded them in half. She rolled the top of the ankle over the toe. It became a perfect little parcel.

'I'm concerned,' I said it compassionately, 'because there might be proof that Ruud was innocent. I know that night must have been really confusing. Everything happened so fast.' Witness statements were notoriously unreliable. People looked at the weapon, not the face of the attacker.

'I saw him. Yes, I only saw him briefly, but I recognised him because he and Carlo had been in that fight earlier. He'd been pestering me in the bar, so I'd got a good look at him then.' There were tears in her eyes. Tears of anger, I thought. 'So yes, it all happened in a flash, as you said, but it was long enough to recognise him.' She still sounded so certain.

'Did you drink that night?'

'No, of course I didn't. I was pregnant.'

'The barman said that maybe you did.'

She frowned as if she was trying to remember everything about the night. 'I bought drinks, sure. For Carlo and Tristan. And there are only so many soft drinks you can have in an evening, so later on I probably only bought drinks for them. Maybe that's what he meant.'

'Maybe.' That was definitely possible. 'If you hadn't seen Klaver earlier in the evening, would you have been able to pick him out?'

Her hands stopped moving and she looked at me. 'How can I answer that now? These what-if questions are really hard. I had seen him before and I can't erase that from my brain.' She was such a thoughtful witness. She considered the options and then was honest. It was why I'd believed her. 'Maybe I wouldn't have been as sure, but it's like when you see a friend, you look at them for a second and you recognise them.'

'Were you worried that he'd follow you after the fight? Ruud Klaver, I mean.'

'Yes, I was. That's why I was annoyed with Carlo for wanting another drink. He said he needed to calm down, but I wanted to go home. I was really worried Klaver was going to come after us. He seemed the type.'

'So when someone shot Carlo . . .'

'I automatically assumed that it was him? Is that what you're suggesting?'

'It was a cold night. Everybody was wearing hats and scarves.'

'Lotte, it was him. Yes, he was wearing a hat and a scarf, but I recognised him from before.'

'There was a second witness . . .'

'Who wasn't as sure.' She finished my sentence. 'I know. I was at the trial, remember? That guy just didn't get a good look at his face. I was right behind Carlo.'

I wished I'd accepted her offer of a cup of tea, as that would have given me the chance to break the intensity of her stare. I only hoped my sudden worry wasn't visible on my face.

'Ruud was facing us when he shot Carlo,' she continued. 'I saw him. It was him.' She swallowed. 'I dream about it most nights, me behind Carlo, Ruud coming at us, shooting him. The other guy, the one who called the ambulance, off to the left.'

'You've always dreamed about it, haven't you?' I rummaged through my handbag.

'Yes, right from the start.'

I got my notebook out, and a pen. 'Draw it for me,' I said. 'Draw where you were, where Carlo was, and the other witness.'

'I was here, right behind Carlo. Ruud came from here. The other guy was here.' She drew the street with the pub quickly, stabbed crosses where she had been, where the others had been. That the pen was so certain in her hand only increased my doubt.

Because the picture was all wrong.

She hadn't been behind Carlo. She'd been to the side. Ruud had come between the two of them. The other witness had come out of a side street, but to the right rather than the left. Even where she'd said the scene had taken place in relation to the pub was wrong. It was the opposite side of the road.

This was how it looked in her dreams, not how it had been in reality. As I studied the drawing, my hair fell down in front of my face and I pushed it back behind my ear. Had I asked her to do this when I interviewed her initially? Her certainty hadn't worried me a day after the murder. Not like it worried me today, when she was still so adamant ten years later. When there had been no doubt, no pause, no *I can't remember it as clearly; what was it I said?*

It didn't mean that she'd been wrong, of course. It could just be that over time, how she dreamed it had replaced the actual memory. I was more grateful than ever that we'd had forensic evidence to back her story up.

I put the notepad back in my bag. I only hoped that I'd asked her for this same drawing ten years ago. That then she'd drawn it correctly. That then it had been right.

'You believe me now, don't you?' she said. 'Now that you see that I still remember it all as clearly as if it had happened yesterday.'

175

'This has been a great help.' I put my coat back on.

She sat back on her chair. 'I'm sorry, I didn't even ask you—'

'Thanks for your time,' I said quickly before she could voice what she'd been going to say. I walked back to the front door without looking right or left, as if I had blinkers on.

Charlie Schippers came bouncing into the office like his enthusiastic canine namesake. 'I didn't think you'd do it,' he said. He was wearing a pair of bright-orange trainers. Maybe they gave him the extra spring in his step.

'It's only temporary.' I pointed at the desk opposite me.

'What can I do?' he asked before he'd even put his stuff down.

'We're looking at Maarten Hageman's death.'

'The Arnhem guy.'

I narrowed my eyes. 'You're well informed.'

'I did my homework.' He blushed. 'This is my big chance, you know. He was involved with money laundering, wasn't he?'

That was better than I'd expected, mainly as I'd expected nothing whatsoever after Thomas's comments. 'Yes, that's what the original investigation focused on.'

'We should look into that.'

I pointed at the whiteboard behind him. 'That's what we're doing.'

He turned round on his chair like an obedient schoolboy.

'We're also looking at the possibility that someone framed

Ruud Klaver. So we're going to have a chat with everybody who knew about the fight earlier that night.'

'Nancy and Tristan,' he said over his shoulder.

'Yes. And anybody else who saw it.'

But if they'd framed Ruud, they must have had a reason to kill Carlo. Which meant it wasn't a spur-of-the-moment thing as we had been assuming so far, but something much more calculated. And as Maarten Hageman had been laundering money, we should find out if there was more to Carlo Sondervelt than we'd originally thought too. Tristan had been there when Ruud and Carlo had had that fight. He would have known that Ruud probably had Carlo's blood on his clothes. We should pay him a visit.

Chapter 22

Tristan de Kraan worked as a software developer in one of the office buildings on the Zuidas. When we'd called him, he'd been very willing to talk to us, and Charlie and I had taken the tram to meet him. He was no longer a dark-haired teenager. He was now an overweight young man with glasses who wore a Foo Fighters T-shirt and jeans.

'I've been expecting you.' Tristan smiled. 'No, actually I've been expecting Sandra Ngo, but she hasn't been here.' The smile turned into a fake sulk.

We were in a tiny room on the eighth floor, and from the window I had a perfect view of the train station way down below. One wall was lined with cardboard boxes that had once held computer equipment. They made the office look like a padded cell.

'What do you want to know?' Tristan said.

'How well do you remember that punch-up between Carlo and Ruud Klaver?'

'It's been a while now. Ten years, right?' He twirled a pen between his fingers and paid more attention to that than to my question.

'Yes, that's right. Do you still remember what it was about?'

'I'm really not sure. I was still inside the bar when it all went off. I was talking to another one of my friends.'

The cardboard boxes were giving me a mild feeling of claustrophobia. At any point, the closest pile could topple over and fall on my head. I shuffled my chair slightly forward.

'When we spoke that evening, you had no doubts that it was Ruud Klaver.'

Tristan shook his head. 'I still don't. It was definitely him. I saw the fight through the window and rushed outside to break it up.' He stopped twirling for a second. 'I grabbed Ruud's arms and pulled him away. Nancy kept Carlo back.' He finally made eye contact. 'So yeah, I saw him really up close. It was easy to pick him out.'

'You didn't hear what the fight was about?'

'Afterwards Carlo said that the guy had been obnoxious. He'd been touching up Nancy or something like that.'

I nodded. That was what Nancy had told me as well. 'Was Carlo ever involved in anything?'

'Like what?'

'Anything criminal? Did he have a lot of money?'

'No, I don't think so. I remember he had a car before the rest of us did – he had to drive us around all the time – but I think his parents bought that for him. We rented a flat together near the university.'

'Is there anybody else who was close to him at the time?' Charlie asked. He had his notepad in front of him and his pen to the ready, keen to write down anything that Tristan said. I let him take over asking questions for a bit.

Tristan must be at the bottom of the pile in this firm if

his office had been turned into the cardboard recycling area. Maybe they wanted to get rid of him but couldn't because he had a permanent contract, so they kept putting more boxes in his office in the hope that he'd leave. He could flatten them all and then he would have twice the space he had now.

'I think I was probably one of their closest friends. They were really tight, Carlo and Nancy, always together. Preparing lunch together the evening before to take to university the next day, things like that. They were like Siamese twins. Still, it was a bit of a shock when it turned out she was pregnant.'

'Did his parents know?'

'No, he hadn't told them yet. I don't know how they would have reacted. Then of course Carlo was murdered and everything changed. Nancy became the beloved daughter, with the grandchild.' His voice was bitter.

'Did you like her?' Charlie said. He and Tristan were probably the same age.

'You know, it's tricky when you've got a good friend and then he starts going out with a girl and you never see him without her,' Tristan said.

But Nancy had phoned him straight away.

I'd driven Nancy to the police station to take her statement and create a montage of what the suspect looked like. She'd called Tristan from the car.

Barry Hoog arrived just a few minutes after we got there. His blond hair was damp and combed back, his eyes thick with interrupted sleep, and he wore a pink T-shirt that was probably just on top of his pile of clothes when he was hurriedly getting dressed.

His presence immediately relaxed me. I was now no longer walk-
ing this high-wire without a safety net. The very first thing he did
was to tell me off for not giving Nancy a cup of tea. He asked her
if she'd be okay for a minute, and at her nod, we walked away
together to the coffee machine. It was his tried-and-tested excuse to
discuss a case. We did some good thinking by this coffee machine.
Even after just a year of working for Barry, I'd started to associate
coffee with thinking time and drank more of the stuff than I ever
had before.

'I'm sorry I got you out of bed,' I said, but my guilt was over-
ridden by an enormous sense of relief that he was here. I loved
working with him and hoped I'd be in his team for a long time.

'Don't worry about it. What have you got?'

'The girlfriend saw him,' I said as soon as I'd checked that she
couldn't hear me any more. 'She said Carlo was in a fight with a
guy earlier in the evening. Around midnight. I told Forensics. Their
friend helped break it up. He's on his way. Then the guy came back
for Carlo an hour later with a gun, and shot him.'

'The same guy?'

'Yes, the girl recognised him. They might be able to get his DNA
from the victim's hands.'

'Good. That's good. It seems you've got it all under control.'

My phone rang: Carlo's friend, the second witness, was here.
Tristan was a dark-haired boy who would probably call himself a
man, with a diamond earring, most likely fake, in his left ear. I took
him to our office. As soon as he saw Nancy, he wrapped his arms
around her and gave her a hug. She leaned against his shoulder
and cried.

'I'm so sorry,' Tristan said softly, 'I'm so sorry. They'll get who

did this.' He stroked her hair as if he was petting a beautiful and cherished dog. 'I would never have left you if I'd thought . . .'

'You couldn't have known,' she said. 'Don't feel guilty.' She pulled back from the hug.

He wiped the tears from her face with a careful thumb.

I could picture it: two close friends, mates for a decade, share a flat and go to university together. And then one of them gets a girlfriend. Tristan must have felt left out. Jealous maybe. I couldn't decide if he'd been jealous of Carlo or of Nancy. Or maybe both. I now saw the stack of cardboard boxes in a new light: they could be a barrier to keep people away. It would be very effective: I wouldn't voluntarily step into his office and risk getting buried by them.

'You'd known him for a long time?' I asked.

'We'd gone to primary school together. Best friends.'

'Did he ever do anything illegal?' Charlie asked.

'He never even smoked a joint. Seriously.'

There was a double-height row of thick books on his desk, manuals for programming languages. If Tristan ducked his head down, nobody would even be able to see him. It all spoke of a man who wanted to be left alone.

'Were you surprised that Carlo got into a fight?' I asked.

The twirling pen stopped again. 'You know, I was actually. I can't remember that he ever did that before. The other guy must have started it.'

'And you got in between them to break it up?'

'Yes.'

I couldn't picture the overweight man I saw in front of me breaking up a fight. At the time, ten years ago, I hadn't doubted him at all. Today I doubted everything. I should have done so at the time. Either this wasn't what had happened, or he must have cared about his friend a great deal. His friend who had moved his girlfriend into their flat, who had been doing everything together with her.

'We'd been drinking,' Tristan continued. 'It was all a bit of a blur, you know. One minute I was inside having a beer, the next I was trying not to get hit.'

'Okay. So the fight stopped, what happened then? Did Ruud say anything? Was he shouting at Carlo? Swearing?' I asked.

'Not that I can remember. I went home.'

'Straight away?'

'Yeah, I'd sobered up by then. A fight is a bit of a buzz-kill, you know.'

'Carlo and Nancy stayed?'

'Yes. I think they were going to get some food.'

'They had another drink.'

'Okay, well, it's been a while, I can't really remember.'

'And then she called you to come to the police station.'

'Yes. I was still watching TV. I'd been home for an hour or so. I must have been waiting for them. I was so shocked that Carlo had been murdered. Especially when she said it was the guy who'd beaten him up earlier on.'

'She said that?'

'That's why I came to the police station. To identify that guy he'd been in a fight with.'

I thought about how they were when he'd seen her in the station.

'You came in and gave her a hug.' I was probably mistaken about the animosity I'd imagined between them.

'I knew how she felt about him. He was everything to her.'

I nodded. That moment had seemed real. 'And you said: "I shouldn't have left you alone", or something like that.'

'I don't remember that.'

'But you remember picking out Ruud Klaver? Picking out his photo?'

'Are you ready to look at some photos?' I asked when I thought I'd given them enough time.

'I remember what the guy looked like,' Tristan said. 'I had to break up the fight.'

I got the books of mugshots out and put them in front of the two of them. 'Take your time,' I said.

'Remember that it is very possible we haven't got a photo for him,' Barry added. 'And don't say it's him unless you're sure.'

Both Tristan and Nancy nodded like the serious students they clearly were. For the next few minutes, the silence was only interrupted by the slap of plastic on plastic as pages of the album were turned over.

'What was the fight about?' I asked.

Tristan and Nancy exchanged glances.

'It was about me,' Nancy finally said.

'You?'

'Yeah, the guy was obnoxious in the bar. Touching me and looking down my top. Carlo told him to stop and then the guy started laying into him.' Tears were streaming down her face. 'They went outside. He punched Carlo a couple of times and Carlo punched him back. And then Tristan got in between them and broke it up.'

Tristan wrapped an arm around her shoulders. Such a pointless death; such a waste of a life. Nancy went back to turning the pages of the book. I left them to it and called Forensics from the room next door.

They told me they had recovered the bullet from the body. It had been wedged in one of the internal organs so it had hardly been damaged. That was good news. It hadn't been misshapen by bone or a wall. If we ever found the weapon, it would be straightforward getting a match. The guy was still telling me about the marks he'd found on Carlo's hands, and that he was going to see if he could get any DNA from them, when I heard Nancy call my name. I disconnected the call and went over to her as quickly as I could.

'This is him.' Her voice was high and excited. Her face was lit up, as if she expected that identifying the killer would bring Carlo back to life. 'This is the man who shot Carlo.'

'If you lived in the same place, how come you didn't go home together?' Charlie said.

'I probably wanted to give them some time alone.'

Instead of being the interloper who had broken the two friends apart, maybe Nancy had fitted in well with their lives. They could have been three friends instead of two friends and a girlfriend. 'Are you still in touch with her?'

'She lived in the flat for a few months and then moved in with Carlo's parents. We lost touch after she had the baby.'

I thanked him for his time and got up, careful not to disturb the boxes.

I thought about the two students sharing a flat. I'd studied as well, the education my mother kept telling me I'd thrown away by joining the police force. I had lived with my mother all the way through. I couldn't afford to move out. 'Did your parents pay for your flat?' I managed to keep the jealousy out of my voice.

Tristan grinned. 'No, we worked. Earned our own money.'

'What did you do?'

'This and that. All part-time jobs.'

'Did you ever work in a restaurant?'

'I did some kitchen work.'

'Did Carlo?'

'Yes, we worked at the same place, on different days.'

'Do you remember where?'

'I have no idea. It was such a long time ago.' Tristan ducked back behind his computer-manual wall.

I couldn't help but wonder if it was in one of the restaurants that Maarten Hageman had owned.

Chapter 23

Charlie and I went back to the office. He seemed pleased that he had a temporary desk on our floor, because he sat down with a huge smile. 'Van Persie,' he said. 'He's my favourite. I have a picture of that goal against Spain as my wallpaper.'

There was no arguing with taste. At least someone liked our new artwork.

'Do you mind if we look at these?' He held up a CD-ROM that he'd got from one of the boxes with my investigation notes. 'It would really help if you could talk me through what happened during Ruud Klaver's interrogation.'

I didn't like watching myself on the screen. It was excruciating, like hearing a recording of your own voice. I would have liked Thomas to go through my old interviews, but his time was now taken up with re-interviewing the elderly woman who had witnessed Ruud Klaver's fatal accident. Maybe he thought his good looks would persuade her to remember some vital bit of information. I wasn't holding out much hope.

'We can have a look,' I said. The CD-ROM had the time

and date written on the front in blue marker pen. It was an early one, before we'd had any evidence, and it had been hard going. I had sat opposite the suspect and his lawyer, a stern-faced woman with dark hair tied back in a ponytail.

'What should I look out for?' Charlie asked as he slotted the CD-ROM into the slot.

'He was still denying everything at this point,' I said, 'probably because his wife had given him an alibi.'

'I'm pretty sure he came home around midnight,' Angela said.

He must have told her to give him an alibi for the fight too. Nancy had told me that the punch-up was after midnight, so as long as she and Tristan had identified the right person, Angela was lying. If I'd been Ruud, I would have confessed to the fight and only denied the shooting. We already had two witnesses to the fight.

Or maybe he hadn't had a chance to brief his wife. Maybe he had still been wearing his jeans because he'd only just come home, not because he'd been planning to go out again. And now Angela was guessing as to what lie she had to tell. This could work out well for us.

'Were you still up?'

'No, I'd already gone to bed.'

'But you're sure it was midnight, not later?'

Two of my colleagues came out of the bedroom with clothes in a bag. The coat rack at the top of the stairs had been emptied already. If we had the jacket that Ruud had been wearing this evening, it could make things a lot easier. I would expect gunpowder residue on the sleeve, and maybe some of Carlo's blood.

'No, it was midnight.' Her voice was firmer now, as if she had talked herself into believing it, or as if she had decided that she might as well stick with the lie.

I made a show of getting my notebook out and writing down the time. Remco had stopped studying the ground and was back to staring at me.

The guy who'd been at my side when we'd burst through the door now came up to me and pulled me into the kitchen. 'No gun,' he said.

'Shit.'

'But we've got his clothes, plus what he was wearing when we arrived. Let's call it a day.'

I nodded. I could finally go to the hospital and check on Barry. But this was also when the clock started ticking: once his lawyer turned up, we had twenty-four hours to question Ruud Klaver.

'Look at his body language and the interaction between him and his lawyer,' I said. 'Within fifteen hours of this footage, he will confess to having shot Carlo.'

'Okay.' Charlie pressed play on the video footage.

On the screen, the image of the interview appeared. The camera had been at the side, so you could see both me and Ruud and his lawyer at the same time. I remembered that I'd been tired. I'd been home for a few hours but I hadn't slept. I could only hope that Ruud's night had been as bad as mine. If his clothes were anything to go by, it hadn't been great. His white polo shirt was definitely grubby after a night in the cells.

'Why did you get into a fight with Carlo?' I asked. I noticed that I was turning my wedding ring round and round. I'd had no idea that I'd had a nervous tic like that. I had been really worried about Barry, I remember that. No wonder I was fidgeting as I was talking.

'You've got the wrong guy,' Ruud said. 'I was home by midnight last night. Didn't my wife tell you?'

'We've got two witnesses who said you were in a fight with Carlo Sondervelt,' I said.

'You've got the wrong guy,' he repeated. 'It wasn't me.'

It was strange to see myself on the screen, this ten-year-younger version. I still had long hair, tied back into a ponytail, and I'd tried to look businesslike and mature by wearing a trouser suit. I remembered I always used to wear clothes like that. These days, I didn't need that; there's nothing like having wrinkles to make you look mature whatever you're wearing.

I could see the time at the bottom of the screen and I could tell we'd been at it for two hours at this point. On the one hand we'd had two witnesses, but on the other hand we'd had a man with an alibi. Nancy and Tristan had been adamant that Ruud had been the one, but I remembered that she'd described a thirty-something man with blond hair and then picked out a forty-something man with brown hair from the photos. On the screen, Ruud's brown curls looked closer to blond because they were shot through with grey. There was a deep line between his eyebrows, but otherwise he had a youthful face that was soft around the jaw and cheeks with a little bit of extra weight.

'What did you do with the gun?'

Ruud shook his head. 'I didn't have a gun. I haven't got a gun.' He threw a glance at his lawyer. 'Look at the stuff I've done. When have I ever shot anybody?'

'Okay,' I said, 'let's look at the stuff you've done, as you

190

call it.' I sounded really sarcastic and made a show of going through a pile of papers.

When Nancy first identified the man who had shot Carlo, I was surprised. I knew Ruud Klaver. He had been arrested a few times for GBH and a couple of muggings. I could totally see him for the fight. I had once arrested him before I joined CID. The next morning he'd told me that he got the red mist whenever he was drunk. He was drunk far too often. So yes, that fight was sadly in character.

The only thing that surprised me was that he'd had a gun. If Carlo had died as the result of a beating, I would have had no doubts at all. Now I had to ask once more.

'This guy? Are you sure?' I looked at Tristan. 'Do you agree?'

He nodded. 'Yes. Yes, it was him.'

'Okay. Thanks.'

I left the room to talk to Barry.

'Klaver?' he said. 'Seriously?'

'It's what they said.'

'Okay, well let's go pick him up.'

So, regardless of my initial doubts, there had been plenty of previous. 'A long list of assaults,' I said. 'I think you've paid us a visit, what? Twice a year or so?'

'I really didn't do this.' Ruud pulled at his lower lip.

I didn't say anything, but allowed a silence to develop.

'I had a couple of drinks earlier on,' Ruud volunteered. 'Maybe they saw me then and got confused.'

'If you don't have any evidence,' the lawyer said, 'I suggest you let my client go.'

She was right: at that point we hadn't had any evidence.

Charlie paused the footage. 'He doesn't sound convincing, does he?'

'No,' I said. 'He doesn't. And I never understood why he denied having been in the fight. If I'd been him, I would have admitted to that early on, and only denied the shooting.'

'Even today, Tristan sounded certain that he'd identified the right guy.'

I pointed at the screen. 'This part was never in question. Ruud Klaver is definitely lying here. We know for a fact that he was in that fight.' I sat back in my chair and looked at myself on the screen, paused in the middle of staring at Ruud, my hands folded. 'Study that footage closely. This is what Klaver looks like when he's lying. It might be helpful.'

I got up and went back to my own desk. I didn't want to watch the rest, and put my headphones in to block out the sound of my own voice.

My music was interrupted half an hour later by Charlie laughing loudly. I switched it off. 'What's so funny?'

'Oh, I just didn't think anybody actually would say that. But you did. You said: "It's all over, Ruud." So funny, just like on TV.'

'When was that?'

'After you got the forensic evidence.'

Ah yes. I'd rushed back from the hospital after the call from Forensics and waited with ever-increasing impatience for the official report to come through so that I could confront Ruud with it.

I walked over to Charlie again to watch this bit on the screen over his shoulder. He pressed play.

'We got into a fight. He punched me.' Ruud's voice was sullen, like a child surprised to have been hit by his classmate in the playground. He felt his jaw and wiggled it as if he could still feel the impact of Carlo's fist.

'Did you hit him back?' I asked.

'I did.'

'But we didn't find any of his DNA on your hands.' Charlie paused the footage. 'Why was that?'

I shrugged. 'His hands were clean. No blood, no gunshot residue, nothing. I remember thinking that he must have washed them very carefully.'

Charlie nodded. 'He must have thought he was going to get away with it.'

'We didn't find anything on any of the coats at his house either. But there was blood splatter on his jeans, so we knew he must have discarded the jacket he was wearing at some point, because there was no way there could have been blood on his jeans but not on his coat. He'd clearly tried to clean up, so the scrubbed hands were in line with getting rid of the jacket.'

I knew exactly what to say, because Barry had questioned the same thing.

I went to the hospital often to give Barry updates. It helped me to pretend that he was going to be fine. That as long as he was lying here resting, he would heal and would be back at work in no time.

'*He could be innocent, you know,*' Barry said. '*It wouldn't be the first time a witness picked out the wrong person.*'

'I know.' I was sitting at his bedside. There had been an uncomfortable silence for the first ten minutes of my visit. Egbert had been in tears. It was discussing the case that had brought normality back.

I'd come here after three hours of needless interrogation, because there were only so many times that you could ask the same questions before you went slightly insane. My colleague had taken over. He'd known how desperate I was to check on Barry. I sat with my hand on my stomach. 'But Nancy and Tristan both identified him. Do you think he didn't do it?' My scheduled pre-natal check-up was in a couple of weeks. Maybe I should ask them to move it forward.

'What about his alibi?' Barry sounded like a patient schoolteacher faced with an overexcited student. He often acted as if his main job was to keep my enthusiasm in check.

'His wife is lying. There's no way he was home that night by midnight.'

'There was no gunshot residue on his hands.'

'He washed them.'

'You didn't find marks on any of the jackets.' He tapped his hands on the bedding.

'He probably stuffed the coat he was wearing in a bin on his way home.' I had to stay upbeat. I had to argue my case energetically, because otherwise I would dissolve into tears at seeing Barry here like this, and that wouldn't do anybody any good. Arguing helped me dissolve the lump in the back of my throat.

'Did you find the gun?'

'No. He must have dumped that somewhere too.'

'At least you're keeping an open mind,' but there was a hint of a smile on Barry's face. 'You haven't forgotten that we have to prove he's guilty, have you?

'*I know, I know.*'

And now Charlie had picked up on the same point. He pressed play again.

'He hit you because you were chatting up his girlfriend,' I said on the screen. I looked at my watch. I must have been bored with asking the same questions over and over. Or maybe I'd been checking how close it was to hospital visiting hours.

'Yes. He followed me out of the bar and punched me in the face.'

'And then you punched him back. And after the fight, you waited for him outside the bar and shot him.'

'No. I walked around for a bit, to clear my head, and then I went home. My wife saw me arrive back.'

Unfortunately for him, his wife had said he'd come home around midnight, but the fight with Carlo had taken place after midnight, so that had either been wrong or was a definite lie.

'But you weren't surprised when we arrested you for murder.'

'I thought the guy had died after I'd punched him.'

'So that's why you lied about getting into a fight in the first place.'

'Yes. No.' Ruud threw a look at his lawyer.

'My client admits that he was in a fight with Carlo Sondervelt,' the lawyer said. 'But unless you have evidence that he shot him, you should let him go.'

'Stop,' I said. 'Can you rewind that?'

Charlie did, and I watched it again. 'That's interesting,'

I said. 'Did you see? He wasn't sure what he was supposed to confess to.'

He played the same bit again. 'He looked confused, didn't he?'

I wasn't sure the look was confused per se, but he had definitely looked for confirmation and the lawyer had stepped in. 'He should have gone with that from the beginning,' I said. 'He should have admitted to the fight and denied the shooting.'

'But if he really was innocent, maybe he didn't know there had been a shooting in the first place,' Charlie said. 'That's what he said, wasn't it? That he thought you'd arrested him because Carlo had died after the punch-up.'

That was true. And that was why it had been such a relief when we pressed him for another hour and he'd confessed to the shooting too. I'd been far too triumphant to realise that this had been really suspicious. Had I just been too inexperienced? Or too preoccupied with everything else going on? On the other hand, I'd had forensic evidence and I had a confession. How could I have known it was all wrong?

That evening, I listened to the podcast. I had to admit that Sandra had edited it fairly. Her closing words stayed with me. I hadn't really taken them in when we were actually recording, but now I heard them. Really heard them, because they so closely mirrored what I was thinking.

'You locked away an innocent man and you can no longer do anything to right that wrong,' her voice said.

Even though her words mirrored what I'd been thinking, I knew that there *was* something I could do. I could find Ruud Klaver's murderer. I could find out the truth about what had really happened.

I looked at the architect's table in my office, studying what I had so far. The fact that I had been wrong about Ruud Klaver's guilt, and that I hadn't been able to see it, sat heavily in my stomach. I wasn't saying that I'd never made mistakes before. As I'd said in Sandra's interview, we were all human and everybody could make mistakes. But the worst thing was that I'd never even considered that he could have been innocent. Ever since the *Right to Justice* podcast had resurrected the case, all I'd been able to think about was about being proved right. I only cared about what was going to happen to me, to my reputation. I had overlooked that here was a real person whom I'd locked away in prison for a crime he hadn't committed. Someone who'd been killed.

All I could do now was accept the mistake I'd made and live with it. Maybe try my hardest to make sure that nothing like this happened again. That would be a good way to make amends.

And I could find out who had really killed Carlo Sondervelt. This must be terrible for his parents, too. And for Nancy, whose witness statement had wrongly locked Ruud Klaver up.

All those people suffering because of my mistake.

Sandra Ngo might be a nuisance, but that didn't mean she was wrong. In fact, I admired the persistence that had got her to the truth. Her dogged pursuit of this case and of the facts. I was impressed that she had found the second murder committed with the same weapon. And even more impressed because I had missed it. I had been so convinced of Ruud's guilt that I hadn't checked everything I should have. I could have found that second murder.

Instead, I had been so convinced of my own infallibility that I'd made the assumption that Sandra's evidence must have been something the family weren't willing to tell me, because surely she couldn't have uncovered something that I hadn't. My exaggerated self-esteem had caused all kinds of problems in this case. That the judge had convicted Ruud Klaver, that the forensic evidence had backed me up, none of that mattered. This had been my mistake. This had been my doing. I had been wrong and I had messed up.

Now what was I going to do?

I got my blue marker pen out and started to scribble on a new piece of paper. I wrote Ruud Klaver's name in large letters in the centre of the page. I no longer had to force myself to see him as a victim. He was now not only a victim; he was someone I owed something to.

The next morning, the files from Arnhem arrived. Charlie and I divided up the boxes.

'Look for anything that links to Carlo or Ruud Klaver,' I said.

I started looking at the photos. Maarten had been in his forties when he'd been killed, a corpulent man with a suntan and combed-back blond hair. An entrepreneur, according to his obituary, but the Arnhem police had done a great job of showing that none of his restaurants made any money, and that if they'd been run as proper businesses, they would have been closed down years before. They'd all made a loss, whereas Maarten had had plenty of money to spare.

I stuck his photo on the whiteboard, next to one of Carlo Sondervelt. What could the money launderer and the student possibly have in common? Who would have wanted to shoot these two people? Had it been random? Had they targeted the wrong man?

Sandra Ngo had found proof that the same gun had been used in both murders, and then she'd been burgled. I had to take her word for it that nothing had gone missing. If the murderer was the burglar, then all the files that he could have seen were now in my possession. Was it linked to that second murder? The murder of Carlo Sondervelt? I didn't know the answer to that yet, but I was going to find out.

Chapter 24

The wind pushed me in the back and propelled me forward faster than my feet could keep up with. Being buffeted like this, it was difficult to keep my balance. The water almost had waves, with white-edged foam, as it rushed through the canal. The boats that were normally as steady as houses now rolled lightly. A cat on the roof of one houseboat looked perturbed, as if the rolling had brought on a feline type of seasickness. In the little park on the corner, the last few leaves were ripped from the branches by the sudden gusts. They raced across the road and overtook me, as if they were looking forward to their inevitable end in a canal. I locked up my bike and rang Sandra's doorbell.

'Hi, did you forget something?' she asked. 'I have to admit, I hadn't expected you back here so quickly. What can I do for you? If you have any questions about that file, if there's anything you don't understand, let me know.'

I ignored the dig. 'I've come to ask about the burglary.'

She frowned. 'Which one?'

'The one at your house, last week.'

'Ah, that one.'

'Can you show me where they got in? Not through the basement, I assume.'

'You're interested in that now?'

'Well, as we had such a nice chat together earlier on, I thought I'd do you a favour and look into it for you. You know, help you out.'

She narrowed his eyes. 'Seriously, why are you interested?'

I shrugged. 'It's a crime. I'm a police officer. Doesn't seem that unusual.' I couldn't believe she hadn't put two and two together herself yet. 'Can you show me the point of entry?'

Sandra showed me round. The intruder had come in through the window at the back. Had lifted the door handle and pulled the garden door open. They hadn't even had to break the window. 'And nothing is missing?' I said. 'No papers, nothing?'

'No, but I'm pretty sure someone looked round the office. My papers were in a different order from how they had been before. But they were all there.'

I nodded. 'The papers on your investigation into Ruud Klaver.' It wasn't even a question. 'That's what they must have come for. Someone looked through them a few hours before he was killed.'

Sandra lifted an eyebrow, as if she was surprised I was willing to share that with her.

'Thanks, Sandra, I'll be in touch.'

It was as I was leaving her house that I saw Remco Klaver. I found it hard to read the look on his face.

'Are you okay?' he asked. I was even more confused when he added, 'Sandra Ngo can be such a cow.' He no longer looked as if he'd just come back from holiday, because his tan had faded. 'How are you coping?' He seemed friendly and quite willing to chat with me.

I was a little surprised by his attitude, even though I'd noticed the animosity between the two of them when I'd first seen them together at the hospital. 'Can I buy you a coffee?' I asked.

He looked at his watch.

'Or were you going to talk to Sandra?'

'She can wait.' He smiled. 'It won't do her any harm.'

'You're making it sound as if you've had run-ins with her yourself.' I'd noticed a bar a few doors down from where Sandra lived, and I set off towards it, Remco walking beside me. The place was more a snack bar than a proper café, but it would do for our chat. I wasn't surprised when the only coffee they did was filter.

'Do you mind if I have something to eat?' Remco wore a very thick V-neck sweater over what looked like a turtle-neck jumper.

'Be my guest.'

He ordered a veal croquette. I took my coat off and hung it over the back of the red plastic chair. The square table was covered in white Formica that had seen better days. Our coffee came in white mugs, and Remco's croquette was crammed in a white plastic tray with lashings of mustard to the side.

He looked at it as though it was the most exquisite food he'd seen in his life, or as if he hadn't eaten in days. He dipped the croquette in the mustard. 'They don't have these in Dubai,' he said. 'It's one of the things I really miss.' He took a large bite and breathed with his mouth open. 'Hot, hot,' he said with a wide grin on his face.

Nope, I didn't really understand his attitude. It wasn't what I'd come to expect from his family. Here he was bad-mouthing Sandra and seemingly happy enough to sit and have coffee with me. It wasn't how he'd been the first couple of times I'd met him. It was, after all, the way he'd talked about me that had got Sandra interested in me and in this case.

I waited for him to get his phone out again, like he had done last time, but he didn't. 'Don't you want to record us?'

'Don't worry. I'm not on Sandra's side. My mother is, but I know what Sandra can be like. I've never seen her so puffed up as she is now. She's a very happy woman.'

'So why were you going to see her?'

'She wanted to speak to me.' He took another bite from his croquette. 'She wants to know why we didn't want her to talk about the arrest itself.'

'Ah, yes.'

He looked at me. 'I'm really surprised you've kept it quiet.'

'Why? Did you think we would have leaked it?'

'No, but Dennis has been making all this trouble for you, by talking to *Right to Justice*. It must have been tempting.'

'He was only twelve at the time.'

'I know. Then I will say thank you on his behalf, because he won't. How is the guy? Are you still in touch?'

'Barry?' I sat back on my chair. 'Do you know, you're the only one of your family ever to have asked after him. He's in a wheelchair.'

'I know that. We might not have asked after him, but we all know what happened to him.'

I nodded. 'Okay. Fair point.'

'You know, that's why Dennis has been so obsessed with our father's innocence. Because if Dad wasn't guilty, then you should never have arrested him, and therefore it wasn't Dennis's fault but yours. It's messed up.'

I got it. I probably shouldn't have, but I totally did, because I'd been thinking about it the other way round. For me, he had to have been guilty, even though I had been surprised when Nancy and Tristan had first picked him out. Maybe my initial doubt had been right.

'Is that why he got in touch with Sandra?' I asked.

'Yeah,' Remco said. 'And he had so much stuff already – he's spent years looking into every detail – so that worked well for her. I don't know what he's going to do now. Find a proper job, I guess. Sandra was in her element. She likes digging for secrets and she doesn't care if anybody gets hurt.'

'How is he now? Happy?' This had to have been good for somebody at least.

'I worry about him. I think he's at a bit of a loose end. His dream has come true and now he has to look for a new dream, you know.'

'He's young. He can study or something. You went to university, right? Wasn't that where you met Sandra?'

'Yes, I met her just as I was trying to keep my head down. I was running away. That's what I'm good at.' He put his croquette down. 'My father was on trial for murdering a student. Sandra found out and started to play her little mind games. She said that if I told her something about myself, something I didn't want her to know, then she wouldn't tell anybody about my father.'

'Sounds familiar. She still does that.'

'She does? That figures. It's probably worked well for her.'

'Did you do it? Did you tell her something?'

He nodded. 'Yeah, I did. It seemed a price worth paying for not having my father's identity outed.'

'What did you say? What secret did you tell her?'

He leaned forward on the table and locked eyes with me. 'That I wished my father was dead.'

Chapter 25

I stayed behind and watched him leave the snack bar, more confused than I'd been before. The first thing I did after the door closed behind him was to check his alibi. I cursed myself for not having done that before. But twenty minutes of foreign phone calls later, I had confirmed it: on the day his father had been hit by that car, he had definitely been in Dubai. However much he might have wanted his father dead ten years ago, he hadn't killed him.

Now I started to wonder if the murder of Carlo Sondervelt and the conviction of Ruud Klaver had caused a split in the family. On the one hand there was Dennis, who believed his father was innocent and who'd dedicated his life to clearing his name; and on the other hand there was Remco, who'd hated his father, wanted him dead, and who'd left the country. Suddenly the almost-fight in the hospital made total sense. On which side did the mother sit?

Before I could think about it more, my phone rang. It was Nancy. She was in tears.

'I heard the podcast,' she said. 'I don't understand. I saw him. I saw him! It was him. And now . . .' There was a muffled sob at the other end of the line. Maybe she was wiping her nose. 'Now you're saying that maybe he didn't do it? I hadn't been drinking. Was that why you asked me about it? Because that podcast woman suggested it?'

It was the call I'd been dreading, and I had to take a gulp of coffee before I could talk. I didn't want to say that it was irrelevant whether she'd been drinking or not, because she was right, I had asked her about it. 'I'm sorry, Nancy. I've looked through the evidence and it seems probable that Ruud Klaver was innocent.'

I hadn't wanted to accept that, not after what had happened at the arrest. But Barry had warned me at the time. There were a lot of things I hadn't wanted to accept.

'That doesn't make any sense.' The initial anger was gone from Nancy's voice and had been replaced with an immense sadness. 'I saw him. It *was* him.'

'It's easy to misremember things.' I said it gently. 'Don't blame yourself.'

'But I can't have done.'

As I listened to the sound of her tears, I had to fight to keep mine back. 'Can I ask you something? Do you remember where Carlo worked?' I felt bad about asking her to remember stuff after we'd pretty much discredited her other memories.

'It was a pizza place.' She sniffed. 'I definitely remember that because we used to joke about it.' I thought I could hear a smile in her voice. 'Because he was called Carlo and baked pizzas. Not that he was Italian in the slightest.'

'Do you know what it was called?'

'Something corny like Pizza Italy. I'm not sure of the

name. It's probably closed by now. It was always so quiet, Carlo would complain that there was never anything to do.'

Had there been a pizza place on the list of restaurants that Maarten Hageman had owned? I thought there might have been.

'But Detective Meerman – Lotte – Ruud Klaver did it. I saw him,' she said again, and I wondered if at this point she was trying to convince herself as much as me.

I needed to talk through what I'd found so far, but when I got to our office, Thomas and Ingrid had gone. Even Charlie wasn't there. He'd probably gone upstairs to talk to his traffic-cop colleagues. It was lunchtime; I should have eaten something when Remco had. Carlo had worked at a restaurant without any business. What if he'd seen something? It was very possible that he had. He was a smart kid. Tristan had said he'd never done anything illegal. It seemed very possible that he'd discovered the restaurant was just a front and had threatened to tell the police about it. I hadn't looked in that direction at all. I'd been too focused on Ruud Klaver from the start, as Barry had said.

Barry.

I knew he'd been following the *Right to Justice* series. I'd also kept him informed of every detail when the case was happening and we were all still pretending he was going to be fine. I grabbed my bike and cycled to his house.

When he opened the door, he didn't look surprised. He glanced at his watch. 'It's time for lunch. Do you want to grab something to eat?'

'Sure. Where do you want to go?'

He pointed at a café across the road. 'That place is pretty good. It's wheelchair-friendly too.'

As soon as I stepped inside, I noticed the group of young women wearing headscarves in all the colours of the rainbow, chattering like a group of brightly coloured birds. In fact, I was the only woman, apart from the one behind the counter, who wasn't wearing a headscarf. There was no way they would serve a cheese sandwich with a glass of milk in here.

I removed a chair and Barry wheeled himself into the gap. I sat down opposite him. To avoid watching him carefully manoeuvre himself into place at the table, I looked at the menu. I didn't recognise any of the dishes apart from Soup of the Day with bread. Above the door, a line of TV screens pumped Turkish music videos into the room. If I were a short, bald man, I probably wouldn't make a video of myself crawling all over a sports car surrounded by tall women. Now he was getting a wad of cash out of his pocket and throwing it in the air. Hmm, maybe that was the point: even if you were fat and short and bald, as long as you had a sports car and money, you could get attractive women. It was so nice to see that certain values were truly universal.

'What are you having?' I said.

'Cacik and bread, I think. Maybe some baba ganoush as well. You?'

'Soup,' I said. It felt like a failure.

'Okay.'

The bald man was replaced by a Turkish version of Gary Barlow playing a small stringed instrument. A lute maybe?

Who knows. I looked around me. We were the only Dutch people here. The only Dutch people who weren't of Turkish descent, I corrected myself in my head.

'This was timely,' Barry said. 'I was going to give you a call anyway.'

'What about?'

'You go first.'

The door opened again and a blonde girl came in. We were now in a minority of three. She bought a bag full of loaves of bread to take away, and left again. But not without having thrown me a quick glance.

'Should we have looked more closely at the place where Carlo worked?' I asked.

'Where he worked? What's brought this up?'

'The other guy who was shot with the same gun, Maarten Hageman, he ran a string of restaurants that were fronts for money laundering. Carlo Sondervelt worked in a pizza place that never had any customers.'

'Did you investigate it at the time?'

'No, we had Ruud. He confessed. We were done, remember?'

The soup arrived. It was red, with bits in it. I took a bite of the bread. It melted in my mouth, soft and fluffy, and tasted of something other than just flour. I picked up another piece. 'What are these?' I pointed to the bits on top.

'Sesame seeds. Do you like it?'

'It's great.' I was relieved that I could be honest. 'How's yours?'

'Very nice.' What he'd called cacik looked like a thick

yoghurt with things in it. He scooped some up with his bread. 'Why did you want to talk to me?'

'You were my mentor. You know about this case. Who else should I talk to?'

He smiled. 'Happy to help.'

'Did you think there was anything wrong at the time? We had forensic evidence.' I had been with him when the call came.

I picked up the phone with one hand and held Barry's with the other. 'What have you got?' My mouth was dry and my question was more like a croak.

'We found blood on Carlo. Someone else's blood. We paid extra attention to his hands after you told us he'd been in a fight with the potential killer.'

'And?

'We've got a match. It's Ruud Klaver's.'

'Thank you!' I squeezed Barry's hand and disconnected the call with a huge grin. 'We've got him,' I said. 'It's him.'

'Let's not get ahead of ourselves,' Barry said. 'This is only evidence of the fight. It doesn't mean we've proved Klaver shot him.'

'I know. But at least it's evidence that he's lying and that his alibi is fake too. He wasn't home at midnight.' He squeezed my hand back as I was talking. That had to be a good sign? Right? 'If nothing else, the judge will give us an extension to keep him for another twenty-four hours.'

I left the hospital in a better mood than when I'd arrived.

Forensics emailed me through their report. They'd found Ruud's blood on Carlo's hands and on his jacket. They were still testing the clothes that we'd got from Ruud's house. The ones he'd been wearing when we arrested him had been clean. I'd pinned my hopes on a dirty pair of jeans that we'd found stuffed in the bottom of the washing basket.

'Surely with that it was watertight? Why didn't you say anything at the time?' I asked.

'I had a lot of things going on.' He tapped on the wheel-chair. I managed not to flinch. 'So I didn't follow your daily updates as closely as I should have, but I remember being surprised by Ruud's confession. I didn't like it.'

My stomach sank. 'No? I believed him.'

'I know you did. Sure, we had him for the fight, but the evidence for the murder relied purely on your witness. I was sure we'd have to let him go, and then he confessed.'

I didn't remember it like that at all. In my memory, I had felt triumphant that we had finally broken him down. Maybe I wouldn't have noticed if there'd been anything wrong at the time.

'And now I'm thinking, if he was innocent, as it seems he was, why did he confess?'

'People do.'

'Sure. But his lawyer didn't stop him. That lawyer bothered me.'

I remembered the footage that Charlie and I had been looking at yesterday, where it had seemed Ruud had checked with her to see what exactly he'd been admitting to.

Barry ate some more of his food. 'Do you want to try a bit?' he said. 'It's really good.'

'What's in it?'

'Yoghurt, cucumber and dill, mainly.'

'No thanks.'

'Try. Try it.'

I was uncomfortably aware that I was attracting a lot of attention from the table next to us by refusing. I tried a bit on my bread. It had quite a sting to it. Not from chilli, but from something else. 'What's in it? Apart from what you listed.'

'Salt and pepper. Oh and a lot of garlic.'

'Thomas and Ingrid are going to hate me when I get back.'

'It's not that bad.'

'It's easy for you to say; you're working on your second career. I have to sit in a small space with two colleagues.' I took a spoonful of soup, hoping that it would wash the garlic from my tongue.

'Anyway,' Barry continued, 'I wondered if someone made it worth his while to confess.'

'You think he was paid to take the fall?'

'Exactly. Ruud Klaver pleads guilty to shooting someone after a random fight over a girl, and we never find out about the money-laundering link, and never connect the two murders. Because we didn't, did we?'

I took some more bread and dipped it in my soup. On the screen, Turkish Gary Barlow was replaced by a man dancing with a large crowd behind him in a style that I would have thought was Indian because it reminded me of Bollywood movies. Even though I now doubted Nancy's witness statement, there had been forensic evidence. There had been blood on Ruud's clothes. Carlo's blood.

'You think he made a deal with whoever killed Carlo Sondervelt and Maarten Hageman,' I said.

'He only had to take the fall for killing Sondervelt, because we didn't know Hageman was killed with the same gun, remember?'

I shook my head. 'No, he got ten years, Barry. Nobody goes to prison for ten years in return for some money.'

'Who knows how much they offered. Maybe he thought it wasn't going to be that long. Maybe he'd thought he'd get away with just a few years.' Barry shrugged. 'Perhaps he thought that as we'd found Carlo's blood on his clothes, he was going to get done for it anyway so he might as well take the cash.'

'Ruud falsely confesses, keeps his mouth shut all these years and then starts spouting off on *Right to Justice* about how he didn't actually do it?'

'And then he gets killed.'

I nodded. 'And then he gets killed.'

'He was an idiot to go on *Right to Justice*.'

I thought about Dennis's fight to prove his father's innocence all these years. Maybe Ruud had done it for his son. 'Remco Klaver told me that his brother has been fixated on his father's innocence because of . . . well, because of you.'

Barry put down the bit of bread that he was using as a scoop for his garlic yoghurt. 'If he ever wants to talk to me,' he looked down at his plate, 'tell him to call me. I'll talk to him.'

That afternoon, there was a special edition of *Right to Justice*. Sandra Ngo talked about the new direction the investigation was taking. She said that we were now looking at money laundering and organised crime. I listened in shock. How could she know that? Of course she could have figured out for herself what the link between the two cases was, but she wouldn't have known for certain that this was what we were looking at. Had it just been an educated guess? No, that wouldn't have been worth a special podcast. Someone had told her.

Chapter 26

The last time I'd been in the Commissaris's office, two months ago, it had been to receive a special commendation. To be congratulated on closing a particularly difficult case, rescuing a child from a canal and helping to bring a murderer to justice. Then it had been all smiles. There had even been a photographer to make sure that pictures of all this happiness and success were broadcast and shared with the national papers. There was nothing the powers that be enjoyed more than basking in reflected glory.

Today I knew better than to expect a smile, a medal or a photographer. Being called in for an immediate meeting with your boss's boss was never a good sign. I had fully expected this telling-off for going on the *Right to Justice* podcast and admitting that maybe I had made a mistake. It seemed increasingly likely that we'd sent an innocent man to prison. The Commissaris was probably peeved because he hadn't been the chief of police in Amsterdam when Ruud Klaver was sentenced. So he hadn't had the glory but now he had to tidy up the mess. Like having to deal with a hangover even though you hadn't been the one drinking.

Like the last time I'd seen him, he was in full uniform.

There were no laughs today and no smiles on the Commissaris's face. The one on my face started to feel forced as I did my best to appear unconcerned. I was sure I wasn't fooling anybody. I was worried that my breath smelled of garlic. I should have got some chewing gum on the way here, but I'd rushed.

He didn't offer me a seat. I held my hands behind my back and stood with my feet slightly apart, as if I was a soldier about to get a kicking from her commanding officer.

'I'm sure you know why I called you here,' the Commissaris said.

I was going to say: yup, I shouldn't have gone on the podcast; yes, you're right, I was wrong, I'm sorry about that. Instead I thought I was better off being silent for a bit and hearing the Commissaris out, so I just gave a single nod of acknowledgement.

Behind him, a row of framed photos lined the wall. It was a cabinet of high-profile criminals that our police force had apprehended. In many of the photos they were posing in front of their house, their car or with a powerful person. I knew why the Commissaris had chosen those particular photos. They said that no matter how wealthy or well connected you were, you could not get away with breaking the law.

'I'm left with no option other than to give you an official reprimand,' he said.

I had to swallow the saliva that suddenly seemed to have pooled in my mouth before I could say 'I understand.'

That he was right didn't make me feel any better. I knew I should have checked the national database to see if the gun had been used before. I could have found that there was another bullet with the same striation pattern. That our forensics department had made the same mistake was in no way an excuse. It was an oversight of such a simple thing.

I didn't say any of those things, of course. I had learned that sometimes it was just better to say nothing.

'What you did has interfered with an ongoing investigation,' he said.

That caught me up. I had been trying to help with the investigation. I didn't think I had hindered it in any way. I knew that I could have sat back and waited for the next *Right to Justice* podcast to air, but I had felt it was important to get the information that Sandra Ngo had as soon as possible. And didn't the result bear that out? Now that another murder was linked to Ruud Klaver's death, didn't that prove that I had been right to work with Sandra?

'I know that you feel you were doing the right thing, and that is commendable, but the outcome is so severe this time that maybe you need to reconsider your position.'

'I'm not sure I understand what you mean.'

'Are you denying that you worked with *Right to Justice*?'

'Well, obviously I did the interview.'

'That's not what I mean. We've known for a while that someone is feeding them information. I've got to admit that I'm surprised it's you. You don't seem the type.'

'Me? I haven't been feeding anyone information.'

'You went to see Sandra Ngo. Someone saw you.'

'When?'

'Today.'

218

'Oh yes, that's right. I went to see her to discuss the burglary.'

'But you were by yourself. I know you talked about the direction the inquiry is taking.'

'No, I didn't.' I couldn't help but sound indignant.

'You must have said something.'

'I only talked about the burglary. I have no interest in helping *Right to Justice*.'

'Maybe something slipped out accidentally.'

'It didn't. No way.'

I wondered who, apart from Remco, had seen me. I somehow couldn't imagine him calling the Commissaris. It had to have been another police officer. Someone from my team? I should have taken Charlie with me. Had I told him I was going to see her? Had he ... I shook my head. I was getting paranoid.

'Well, just make sure it doesn't. I'm keeping an eye on you.'

Before I could respond, there was a knock on the door. 'Your visitor is here,' a woman said.

'Thank you. Perfect timing.' The Commissaris smiled at me, but the smile never reached his eyes. 'Take a seat. You should stay for this.'

The door opened wide and the visitor came in. It was Dennis Klaver.

He looked at me. Behind the round glasses, his eyes looked small and swollen, as if he hadn't had much sleep. 'She's here. That's perfect.'

She. There was no politeness here.

I rubbed the skin between my eyebrows. I wasn't sure I was

up for the second confrontation in fifteen minutes. If there was going to be another fight, surely I should be allowed to have a five-minute break? Before I could even suggest that I needed to use the bathroom, or whatever other excuse I was going to use to get a few minutes to gather my thoughts, the Commissaris gestured towards a chair. Now he wanted me to sit down? Dennis and I had seats side by side as if we were a couple in marriage counselling. I could feel anger radiating from him.

'I listened to the podcast last night,' he said.

I was surprised that Sandra hadn't given him a preview of it, but maybe she'd put it out as soon as it was ready.

'And I want this woman,' he pointed to me with his thumb, 'removed from my father's case.'

'Why?'

'I feel it's hugely insulting towards our family to have her investigate my father's death. She's the one who put him in jail. An innocent man.' He swallowed after the last words. 'Can't you see how thoughtless that is? Especially after she admitted to her mistakes on the podcast. I don't think we can work with her.'

I drew a circle on my notepad and crossed it through with lightning bolts. It wasn't as if they had been working with me before. If they had cooperated, I wouldn't have done the interview. Still, I thought about what Remco had told me. It was good that I'd talked to him earlier today. It had made me see Dennis in a different light. To me, he now was no longer just the kid with the knife. If I felt guilty about Barry, because I'd had a chance to stop Dennis and missed it, then I should feel guilty about this young man too.

He'd only been twelve years old at the time. If I'd stopped him, his life would have been different. Hadn't he been damaged by the incident just as much as Barry had?

'Detective Meerman, do you have anything to say?'

I looked at the Commissaris. I knew he was going to throw me under the bus. I folded my hands in my lap. My arms felt as if they weighed a ton. 'If I made a mistake, I want to atone for it.' I turned sideways to look at Dennis. 'The only way I can do that is to make sure that I get whoever killed your father. Can't you see that? I'll do whatever it takes to find his murderer.'

'You see, I can't trust that.' His voice was a sneer. 'I don't trust you. You want to make sure that your mistakes never come to light.'

I wanted to laugh at that. If I'd wanted to keep my mistakes hidden, I would never have done the interview with Sandra. I threw a quick look at the Commissaris's face. 'No,' I said. 'It isn't like that. It honestly isn't. Plus, we've divided up the investigation in such a way that I won't be dealing with you or your family.'

'I'll lodge an official complaint against the police if she isn't removed.' His hands gripped a piece of paper. 'I read about the police reorganisation. You're supposed to put victims and their families at the heart of what you do. I'm the victim's son. I don't want to see this woman on our doorstep ever again. I won't talk to her, I won't meet with her.'

Could I blame him? My own father had been locked up overnight once, on a false accusation. I'd done whatever I could to make sure he'd been released. If he had been killed, would I have been happy if the detective who had locked him up investigated his murder? No, I wouldn't have. The answer came quickly.

'Does your entire family feel the same way?' I turned my head to look at him again. 'I spoke to your brother Remco earlier today and—'

'Don't speak to any of us,' Dennis shouted. He turned towards the Commissaris. 'I'm serious. I'll file a complaint. I'll go to the press. Surely there must be other crimes in Amsterdam that she can investigate?' His voice was deeply sarcastic. 'I'll start an online petition on the *Right to Justice* website. You should see the comments on there already. If Amsterdam's police force wants to keep any shred of credibility, if you don't want people to just laugh out loud when you talk about your victim-centric policing, then you need to remove her from this case.'

He waved the piece of paper that he'd been clutching. 'This is the official statement about the response of the police to complaints. It says that "the main purpose of this is to restore the faith of the public in the police force".' He put the paper back on his lap. 'Do you think the public will have any faith if you keep her on this case? Everybody knows what's gone wrong in my father's case. Everybody can download Sandra's podcast and hear her admit to it. And now she's investigating my father's murder? This is clearly insane.' He looked at me again. 'You said you spoke to my brother. It's why I'm here. I don't want my brother talking to you. I don't want you talking to him.' He almost screamed the words. 'Don't you know how much it hurts to see you? For all of us? To have the police's mistakes rubbed into our faces?'

That I understood his feelings only made matters worse. If he was going to file an official complaint, I would be invited to an open discussion with the police mediator. There was no point. I knew that there was nothing I could say or do that would make Dennis dislike me less. There was no way of explaining my actions that would make this right.

I pushed my chair back. I knew what the Commissaris was going to say. 'I'll leave the two of you to discuss this further,' I said. 'I'll accept whatever you decide.'

The Commissaris nodded. 'I'll inform your boss. He'll talk to you later.'

I went back to the office and decided to watch the footage I'd wanted to see ever since Barry had told me over lunch that he didn't like the confession. I knew I had very limited time left before I'd officially be taken off this case, and I had to brief Charlie quickly.

Luckily he was sitting at his temporary desk.

'Let's look at that confession again,' I said to him before I'd even hung up my coat. 'We need to check if anything looks odd. Especially if there is any eye contact between Ruud and his lawyer.'

'Okay,' Charlie said. 'It's right here.'

I knew the time of the confession to the minute. The footage was lined up to exactly the right point. He must have been looking at it when I was out. I didn't blame him; it was probably the part that I would have watched first too. He pressed start.

'We've got his blood on your trousers,' I said on the screen. 'We've got a witness.'

Ruud sighed. He looked exhausted at this point, the bags under his eyes deep. 'I did it,' he said. 'I shot him.'

He didn't look at his lawyer. She didn't look at him. She wasn't surprised at what he was saying. She must have known from the start of this session that he was going to confess. She didn't try to stop him. She let him talk.

'Why?' I said. 'Why did you kill him?' A smile broke out on my face. My hand went to my belly. Even now, watching it on the screen made me feel infinitely sad. That happiness that I'd been feeling, I could still remember it.

'I was angry,' Ruud said. 'I was drunk. We'd had a fight. I had a gun.' He never looked at the woman beside him. 'I was unlucky that I hit him.' His voice was resigned. He sat back on his chair. The die was cast, the deed was done.

'Let's look at it again,' I said to Charlie, and he rewound the footage.

'He looked certain, didn't he?' he said after we'd watched it twice more.

'He really did. He never looked away, he retained eye contact throughout.' That had been a very convincing lie. Very different from the stuttering we'd seen the day before.

Even now, with the years of experience that I'd gained since, I would have gone with that confession. I wouldn't have doubted it. Sure, Barry didn't like it, but that was mainly because it had been unnecessary. Contrary to what Ruud had said on the *Right to Justice* podcast, it was not a forced confession. I hadn't said anything like: just confess, Ruud, then this will all be over. He would have known only too well that it was only the beginning. If anything, I would probably have put more pressure on him if I questioned him today.

On the screen, I sat back in my chair, looking content. I must have felt as if the balance had been restored. I watched it again. If I had to find anything suspicious about it, it was the calm with which he confessed. No anger, just acceptance. I leaned forward to watch his face more closely. He looked tired but together, as though he'd thought it all through and this was his best option.

'What are you looking for?' Charlie asked.

'Anything odd.'

'It looks really normal,' he said. 'Is that strange?'

'This confession is only strange,' I said, 'for an innocent man.'

Chapter 27

The chief inspector was still away from his office an hour later, probably in an extremely important internal meeting. As I waited to see what my punishment would be, I got a call to say that there were two people waiting to see me. Maybe I was being punished right now, because Carlo Sondervelt's mother Anke was here with Nancy.

I was in two minds as to where to speak with them. I could take them to the canteen to create a less formal setting for our conversation, but if they were angry and upset, this might be uncomfortable. I should provide them with some privacy. In the end, I asked the desk sergeant to show them to one of the interview rooms.

As soon as I entered the room, I realised that that had been a mistake. The cold setting made their grief even more obvious. Even though I'd known that Nancy was upset when I'd spoken to her earlier today, I hadn't appreciated how bad it was. Her face was pale, as if her tears had washed any colour away. Anke's hair was uncombed, and the stoop of her shoulders made it seem like she'd aged at least a decade overnight.

They huddled at one end of the room as if that would

keep them safe from questions and accusations, their arms wrapped around each other's waists for warmth or comfort.

'Please take a seat,' I said. 'I'm sorry we can't talk somewhere more comfortable.' I'd thought that I'd had to pay a high personal price for Sandra Ngo's information, but I hadn't taken Carlo's family's upset into consideration. I hadn't realised that the podcast would make their agony raw again. I could feel the pain coming from them, as if someone had taken a sharp knife to the stitches of a not-quite-healed wound.

'Why did you say those things?' Anke said before she had even pulled out her chair. 'Those horrible things. You said that maybe Ruud Klaver was innocent.'

'The evidence that Sandra Ngo has—'

'It's all a pack of lies,' Anke said. 'Klaver did it.'

'There's a second man who was shot by the same gun. Klaver has an alibi for that day.' To avoid her eyes, I looked at these walls that over the years had listened to hundreds of suspects' confessions and angry denials.

'What do you mean?' Nancy said.

'Unless two different people used the same gun, Klaver didn't kill Carlo. I'm sorry.'

'Who was the other victim? Another student?' Tears were streaming from Anke's eyes. I couldn't tell if it was because of her son, or because another man had been killed.

'No.' I said. 'He was a man in his forties who was known to the police.'

'That doesn't make sense. Carlo was a good kid. He never had any dealings with the police,' Anke said.

'I know. There's nothing to suggest that he knew the other victim.'

'The other man was killed before Carlo?'

'Yes. Three weeks before.'

'But I saw him,' Nancy said. 'I know what you said, that I could have misremembered things, but I didn't. I saw him.'

I took the piece of paper with her drawing from the file that I had brought down with me. I didn't want to show it to her, but I knew it might be the only way she would accept that what had happened wasn't as she recalled it. 'You drew this for me a couple of days ago, remember?'

'Yes.'

'And you said that this was where you were,' I pointed with the point of my pen to the leftmost cross, 'this was Carlo, this the other witness and this,' I indicated the circle, 'Ruud Klaver.'

She nodded vigorously. 'Yes, exactly. Because I was behind Carlo, I could see Ruud's face.'

'Nancy, this wasn't how it was.' From the impact of the bullet, we had been able to trace exactly where the gunman had been. There was no need to go into those details. 'The gunman was much further to the left. He was actually really close to the second witness. You weren't here, but much more here.' I drew for her what the forensic evidence had shown.

'You're saying I lied?'

'You didn't lie. You misremembered. That's a very different thing. It's hard to remember exactly what happened, especially during such a traumatic event as the murder of your boyfriend.' I could have added that many witnesses were so glued to the sight of a weapon that they never even looked at the attacker's face. That could have happened to Nancy and she could have filled in the gap in her knowledge with the face of the man she'd seen earlier in the evening.

Nancy looked at Carlo's mother and pointed with a trembling finger at the drawing. 'That was how it happened,' she said. 'I swear that's how it was.'

Anke avoided Nancy's eyes and instead looked at me. 'You didn't question it at the time.'

I bowed my head. I'd checked in the files and I hadn't found a drawing. 'I know. That's my fault. I should have asked Nancy to draw it back then and I never did. I was as certain as she was.'

Anke put her arm around Nancy's shoulder. 'And what's going to happen now?'

'Now that we know that two murders were committed with the same weapon, we're going to reopen both cases.'

Anke threw me a sharp look. 'But Nancy is no longer a credible witness. Is that what you're saying? Is that what Sandra has achieved?'

'I'm sorry,' I said.

She got up from the chair quickly, took Nancy's hand and dragged her out of the room behind her.

I stayed where I was. I'd been worried about what kind of punishment the boss was going to give me, but it couldn't be any worse than this guilt I was feeling.

When he called me into his office ten minutes later, I knew I'd been right. Because even whilst I was being told that I had to stay away from Ruud Klaver's family, all I could think about was the grief and pain I'd caused Carlo's family by going on that podcast.

When Moerdijk had finished with me, Remco called. He wanted to talk to me; could I come to the house tomorrow morning? I suggested we meet at the same place where we'd talked last time, but he said he didn't have enough time to go there. When I explained that I'd been told to stay away from the family, he said that he'd make sure his mother was out. I tried to get him to meet me anywhere other than at their house, but he insisted. It would be quick, he said. He had to tell me something before he headed home to Dubai.

I left the office early and went over to Mark's place. It said something about the whirl that my mind was in that the sparse decoration of his house was perfect for me. It soothed my head. As soon as I stepped over the threshold, he enveloped me in a hug. I felt bad that I hadn't wanted to see him last night. That I hadn't been able to listen to the podcast in his company. There was a certain pain that was more bearable when you were by yourself. He held me until the clock in the kitchen started to beep and demanded his attention instead.

No longer being wrapped in his arms, I felt cold and vulnerable suddenly. I started to develop a real dislike for that oven clock. I followed Mark to the kitchen, where he had been summoned to take the lasagne out of the oven.

'Sorry,' he said, 'it's a little basic. But there's garlic bread and a salad too.'

'That's great. Thanks for cooking.'

'Can you open this?' He handed me a bottle of Chianti and a corkscrew. He knew that was my favourite job. As he divided the lasagne in half, I pulled the foil from around the neck of the bottle and eased the cork out, then poured the wine.

We sat down to eat.

'Are you in a lot of trouble?'

At least he had waited until I'd drunk half my glass of wine before he asked me about the podcast. He probably thought I needed the alcohol to take the edge off.

'Yes. I shouldn't have done it. I should have worked it out for myself. I knew it was going to be bad for me, but I hadn't appreciated how awful it would be for Carlo Sondervelt's family. Especially Nancy.'

'Did you talk to her?'

I swirled the wine round in my glass. 'She came to see me. With Carlo's mother. She's still adamant that she saw Ruud Klaver.'

'How is she?'

'Very upset. I don't know if it's because deep inside she's starting to doubt herself, or because now people will think that Ruud Klaver was innocent.'

'How are his family?'

'Odd. I spoke to Remco. He seemed surprisingly fine. And then I got shouted at by Dennis. That was much more in line with expectations. But I don't know what to do.'

'What do you mean?'

'Well, now that his father has passed away, I don't know what's right any more.'

'Find his murderer, I guess.'

I shook my head. 'I'm off that case. At Dennis Klaver's request.'

'Then maybe you should just stay away from them.'

'I guess. I've promised to meet Remco tomorrow, and that will be it.' I wanted to tell Mark that this was actually the least of my worries. I sighed.

'Is that smart?'

'Probably not. I've had an official warning. I might get myself sacked this time. So I guess the answer is: no. I don't trust that family. Maybe I'm being set up.'

'That's okay. You can come and live here and cook for me.' He grinned to tell me it was only a joke.

'My cooking is terrible. You'd hate me within a week.'

'Okay, you can live here and I'll cook.'

'Maybe.' I finished my glass of wine and filled it up again. Mark had hardly touched his. 'If I get sacked, I'll consider it.'

It was after midnight when I cycled back to my own flat. I would have loved to stay the night, but I had a cat to feed.

In the darkness, I wondered what I was going to do. Mark and I might have joked about me getting sacked, but there were other ways of being punished that weren't quite that blatant. So why was I even considering meeting with Remco tomorrow?

My mother would say that I was secretly trying to sabotage myself. That I wanted to live with Mark and give up my job. It clearly wasn't that. Even in my imagination she managed to annoy me.

I had to push hard on the pedals to move my bike against

the storm. The wind blew any exhalation away within seconds.

I fed Mrs Puss, who meowed at me with a sound that managed to convey gratitude and annoyance at the same time. I cleared out her litter tray and fell into bed.

Even though I'd been drinking, sleep wouldn't come. Mrs Puss jumped onto the bed, curled up beside me and started to purr, but tonight it didn't comfort me. All I could think was that I'd put an innocent man in prison, an innocent man who was now dead. The only redeeming feature was that I hadn't known. I had been convinced that Ruud Klaver was guilty.

I turned onto my other side. I'd caused so much pain to the victim's family by going on that podcast. I was trying to make things right but I just kept adding to my guilt list. After my talk with Remco, I realised that my failure to stop Dennis hadn't simply put Barry in a wheelchair; it had damaged Dennis as well. It had had a bigger impact on him than I'd realised. There had to be a way to make amends.

Chapter 28

The next morning, it was windy but it was no longer rain-ing. I had a couple of hours before my meeting with Remco Klaver. It seemed prudent not to go into the office. I sat in my front room for ten minutes and looked out over the canal. My shoulders itched with a desire to do something. All night I had been wondering who was giving Sandra her information and had helped her compare the bullets. There was one straightforward way to find out, and that was to go to her house and ask her about it.

Clearly it wasn't a particularly clever solution, but when had I ever cared about that? Sandra would just play her little mind game and I'd pay the price. Even if I was supposed to stay away from Ruud Klaver's case and his family, nobody had told me to stay away from *Right to Justice*. Apart from the Commissaris saying he was keeping an eye on me, of course. I had made this mess and I should go clear it up.

I quickly fed Pippi, then rushed down the stairs and grabbed my bike. I would record our conversation on my phone and that would help me with the boss.

The weather agreed with my approach, because it still wasn't raining by the time I got to Sandra's house. I should have used the cycling time to think of smart ways to ask my questions, but my thoughts were whirling so quickly in my head that I still hadn't thought of anything when I rang the doorbell. So when she opened the door, I simply said, 'Who is it?'

'Who's what?' She had an annoying smile on her face, as if she knew exactly why I was here.

'Who's talking to you? Who do you get your information from?'

'Surely you don't expect me to tell you?'

'You're interfering with an ongoing police investigation,' I said.

'If it hadn't been for me, you wouldn't even have known to look in this direction.'

'I know that. Trust me, I do. But we're trying to solve Ruud Klaver's murder.'

'I heard you were no longer on that case.'

Anger coursed through my veins. I had to control my voice. 'Please stop broadcasting this kind of information.'

As if the weather thought it ought to give me a hand cooling down, just then the heavens opened. The downpour was as heavy and sudden as a cold shower.

'Come in,' Sandra said. 'Don't stand out in the rain.'

'I've said what I wanted to say.'

'I'm not going to stop.'

It was pure stubbornness that kept me standing outside in the downpour. That Sandra Ngo was so young made this conversation even more annoying. 'You have someone inside the police force who feeds you information. I understand.

This is exciting. I understand that too. It gets you a lot of listeners. I get all of that. But please stop.'

'Inside the police force? Are you sure?'

Not inside? Then who? Who would know otherwise?

Barry. The name came to me immediately. What had he said he was doing? Some consulting work? Was he working for *Right to Justice*? I kept my face impassive and tried not to show how betrayed I felt. Rain started to drip down my nose. I wiped it away.

'Are you sure you don't want to come in?' She looked at her watch. 'If you're soaked, you won't have time to change. You're meeting Remco Klaver in half an hour, right?'

'You know that?'

'His mother told me.'

Angela wasn't supposed to know. And why had she told Sandra? Maybe I shouldn't go to the meeting. Maybe I really was being set up. 'What would it take for you to stop broadcasting?'

'Come in. That would be a good start.'

A thin trickle of rain ran between my neck and the collar of my coat. It was that that made me change my mind. Not that Sandra had me backed into a corner. I stepped over the threshold.

The last time, I'd gone down the stairs into the basement. Now I followed Sandra into a living room. 'Let me get you a towel,' she said.

'I'm fine.'

'Tell me,' she said. 'Tell me why I should stop making these podcasts.'

'I said the wrong thing. You don't need to stop them.

Just don't talk about information that's still crucial to our investigation.'

'You wouldn't have found the connection between the two murders without me.'

'I know that. I'm very aware of it. But you're putting people's lives at risk. Carlo Sondervelt and Maarten Hageman were probably both killed by the same people. Maybe they killed Ruud Klaver too. Three murders. These are dangerous criminals.'

'You're doing this for my own good?'

'Yours?' A drop of water ran from my hair down onto my forehead. I wiped it away. Who needs a towel when you've got a perfectly good coat sleeve? 'I hadn't even thought about you.'

'They could kill me for all you care.' Sandra laughed. 'At least you're honest.'

'I'm worried about the people who witnessed the original fight: Nancy and Tristan. I'm worried about Ruud's family. Plus, if they know the direction we're looking in, they'll know what we're going to do and it will help them.'

'So, what deal are you going to offer me?'

'Deal? I wasn't going to offer you a deal.'

'You did last time.'

'I'll find out who your informer is. In fact I've got a pretty good idea already.'

'I was right last time.'

'You were. Well done. Now stop putting things in the podcast that hinder our investigation.'

'I don't know what would hinder it. Maybe you should

keep me more informed. If you come here to brief me, I'll know what to leave out.'

'Send me your podcast a couple of hours before broadcast. If there's anything in there that shouldn't become public knowledge, I'll let you know.'

'That's not going to work.'

'Okay.' I moved towards the door. 'I'll get a total ban then. I didn't want to do that, but you leave me no choice.'

'I'm going to see Angela Klaver,' Sandra said. 'Do you want a lift?'

'No, I'm fine.'

She made a show of studying the outside. 'It's raining hard. You'll be soaked before you get there, and I'm going in that direction anyway. Put your bike in the boot.'

I rang the doorbell of Angela Klaver's house. Nobody came to the door. I looked at my watch. I was ten minutes early, but I'd thought Remco wouldn't mind. I rang the bell again. The house stayed silent. I rang Remco's mobile but he didn't pick up.

I took a couple of steps back so that I could look up to the first-floor window, but I didn't see anybody. There was a buzzing noise beside me. Sandra opened her car window. 'Are they not here?'

'I think Remco's decided not to talk to me.' More than ever I wondered if I was being set up. Maybe the best thing to do was to leave as quickly as I could, before anybody saw me.

'I can give you a lift back?'

And having Sandra Ngo give me a lift here had clearly been stupid. 'Weren't you meeting Angela?'

She shrugged. 'Maybe I made that up.'

'I'll wait.' I said. If this was some kind of trap, I'd already stepped into it. I might as well wait it out. I hoped that Remco was on his way. 'Just in case he's popped out for a few minutes.'

'Do you want to get back in the car?'

'No, I'm okay.' I looked for a dry place to stand. There was a small overhang by the garage door that would keep the worst of the rain off. I leaned with my back against the blue door and was vaguely sheltered.

Then, from behind the door, I thought I heard something. A soft sound. A one-tone hum. Was it the sound of a car engine running? Had Remco decided at the last minute that he was going to drive away without talking to me?

I would wait here until he came out. I could stop him as he was driving off. 'Remco,' I shouted. 'Just give me a few minutes. Let's talk.'

I stood looking at the garage door, expecting it to tilt up, but there was no movement.

I banged on the door. 'Open up. Don't be like this.' I put my ear against it. The engine was still running.

I banged more loudly. There were no exhaust fumes coming from under the door. I called Angela's mobile but wasn't surprised that she didn't answer my call.

Something was wrong here.

Behind me, a car door opened and slammed shut again. 'What's going on?' Sandra said.

I kneeled down on the ground in front of the garage.

I could just get my fingers underneath the door, but the concrete floor scraped the back of them. I felt something soft. The gap at the bottom of the door was blocked up from the inside. A blanket? I prodded it. It moved. The first step should be to make that gap bigger so that the fumes would leave the garage. That would buy me time to bash the door in.

The storm had torn plenty of branches from the trees in front of the house. By my left hand was a stick that seemed roughly the right size. I thrust it through the gap between the door and the floor and felt the cloth move. I pushed it sideways and fumes gushed out from underneath the door like water through a breach in a dyke. I pushed my fingers through the slit and pulled hard. The door didn't budge. 'Call an ambulance!' I shouted at Sandra. 'Carbon monoxide poisoning.'

'Ah, shit,' she said, but she started dialling.

For a second it crossed my mind that the family would not be happy if I destroyed their garage door. Was I over-reacting? Then I thought that with all the trouble I was in with them, a broken garage door was going to be the least of my problems.

I needed to get whoever was in the car out as soon as possible. My heart was pounding. What was easiest? Quickest?

I got my gun out and fired four quick rounds around the garage door lock.

'Jesus!' Sandra shouted.

I yanked the door. It didn't open. 'Help me pull!'

She dropped her phone and crouched beside me. Both of us put our full weight into trying to prise the door open.

I heard Sandra's heavy breathing and saw her shoes slip on the wet concrete. The sharp edge of the metal door cut into my fingers. The muscles in my upper arms felt as if they were straining to breaking point.

Then there was a sound like chalk on a board as the metal tore and sheared off around the lock. The door gave and swung upwards.

I ducked under it and rushed to the car. I could see Remco inside. His eyes were closed. I grabbed the door handle and pulled hard, nearly falling backwards when it opened easily.

Remco slumped sideways. I caught him. His lips were cherry red and his skin was pinker than it had been before. I grabbed him under the armpits and tried to pull him out of the dark Mercedes. Sandra quickly killed the engine, gripped Remco's belt and helped me drag him from the seat. She took hold of his legs and together we carried him into the open air.

Rain streamed down on all three of us as I felt for Remco's pulse. It was very faint. I tapped his face. 'Remco? Remco, wake up.'

He didn't move. I expected him to open his eyes, but he didn't. I held my hand under his nose, but the only air I could feel was the gusting storm. I wasn't going to take any chances: I closed his nostrils and blew oxygen into his lungs.

Sandra kept her fingers on his wrist and nodded re-assuringly every now and then. 'He's got a pulse,' she said. 'We're good. We're good.'

I had to admit that she was solid under pressure. The rain washed us clean of fumes until I finally heard the sound of an ambulance in the distance. I prayed that it was ours. It was getting blessedly louder and eventually came haring round the corner.

The paramedics bustled over, put an oxygen mask over Remco's face and lifted him onto a stretcher.

I rocked back on my heels and then sat down on the ground. Sandra collapsed beside me. Her hair streamed bedraggled around her face. She looked at me and grinned.

'Well done, partner,' I said.

'I can't believe you shot that lock out. I thought people only did that in the movies.'

'That door had it coming.'

She laughed, then joined Remco in the ambulance. I stayed behind on the pavement. Adrenaline was still coursing through every centimetre of my body, but I didn't move. Not even when the rain drenched my hair to saturation and I could feel it running down the back of my neck. My shoulders ached and my biceps throbbed as if I'd finished a two-hour workout. My throat felt like I'd smoked a packet of cigarettes.

It was strange to sit here. After the ambulance had left and taken its emergency siren with it, the street was silent and peaceful. Only the trees moved as they swayed in the wind. The clouds must be moving too, but the sky was so universally grey that there was no way of telling. The mangled garage door spoke of what had happened.

I lifted my face to the sky. 'I just saved your son's life, Ruud Klaver,' I whispered. 'Did you see that?'

Chapter 29

It was a few hours later that I went to see Remco in the hospital. I'd gone home first to dry off and get changed, and then headed to the police station to talk to Forensics about what they'd found at the Klavers' garage. This time I was sensible and had driven.

I knew I'd been told to stay away from the family, but as Angela already knew that I had planned to see Remco, she must understand that I would want to check on his condition. But as soon as I came up the stairs, I saw her standing guard outside his room, glowering like a Cerberus.

'Go away,' she said.

I paused.

'Seriously, go away.' Even though I'd saved her son's life, she didn't seem to hate me any less.

'Can I just talk to him for a couple of minutes?'

'He's sleeping right now and can't see any visitors. He needs his rest.'

I didn't believe her for a second, but a hospital corridor wasn't the ideal place for an argument that I wasn't going to win anyway, so I beat a tactical retreat and went back to the downstairs reception. I got myself a disgusting coffee in a plastic cup from a vending machine and sat down on the one blue plastic chair that had nobody sitting on either side. A hospital was a perfect place to catch a lurgy. I sent Remco a text, telling him that I was downstairs and would wait for him if he wanted to talk to me. Then I sent him a second text to give him the out that if he wanted me to get lost, he could tell me that as well.

There was an almost instant response. *Give me ten minutes.* I wasn't sure what he was going to say to get rid of his mother. I couldn't imagine she was just going to let him escape to talk to me like that.

Forensics hadn't found anything untoward in the garage. Maybe the strangest thing had been that Angela hadn't objected to the police going through her house. Concern about her son might have mellowed her somewhat towards us. Not enough to let me see Remco, of course, but then that was entirely personal. There had been three obvious sets of fingerprints in the house and garage: Remco, Angela and Dennis. Then they'd found my fingerprints, and Sandra's, on the door and the car. Nothing that was out of sync with this being a suicide attempt, including the blankets that had been stuffed against the garage door from the inside. I just didn't think Remco seemed the type, and I would have liked a note. If he couldn't cope any more, I would have expected him to fly home to Dubai without giving any notice, but not to try and kill himself. Unfortunately, it was not that easy to tell who was going to commit suicide. I wished I hadn't seen so many parents who'd insisted that their son or daughter would never have done a thing like that. That their children had been happy. People can be very good at faking happiness.

The thought had crossed my mind that Remco, of course, had timed it perfectly to be rescued by me. Maybe this had been a cry for help more than anything else.

Ten minutes crawled by, and I watched patients and visitors come and go. A doctor walked past. Her headscarf had a bold pink pattern that brightened up the hospital. A young woman rushed through the door, her wheelie bag rattling loudly behind her. The sound of the wheels on the floor echoed in the corridor. She stopped, threw me an embarrassed look, pushed the handle down and lifted the bag instead. That was how Remco must have arrived a week ago when he first went to see his father, straight from the plane.

Sitting here reinforced my dislike of hospitals. It brought back far too many memories. I would forever equate the smell of antiseptic with pain. Being here reminded me of that overriding feeling of powerlessness as nurses and doctors did things to you that made you feel like a puppet, no longer an individual but an object to be handled and dealt with, no matter how kind and careful they were. You were no longer a person but a patient. I'd been here too often.

But then more than once was probably too often.

In the end, it was almost twenty minutes later when Remco came out of the elevator in his pyjamas and dressing gown. It jolted me back in time. He looked no older than he'd done when I'd arrested his father.

'How are you?' I asked.

'I've got a terrible headache. Otherwise I'm fine.'

'You did this to yourself?'

He nodded. 'Yes. I blocked off the garage door with blankets, set the engine running and took the pills. I wanted it to be peaceful.'

'And you wanted me to find you.'

'I'm sorry. I couldn't do that to my mother. Not so soon after my father had died.'

'And she would have coped with your death just fine? Just not with finding your body?'

'I know. I wasn't thinking straight.'

'Right.'

'I'm just curious about one thing,' he said. 'Did you get to the house early?'

Of course. I'd forgotten about that. 'Yes, about ten minutes early.'

'Interesting.' He nodded again slowly. 'Well, thanks to that, I'm alive.'

If I hadn't waited right in front of the garage door, I wouldn't have heard the engine running. I wouldn't have been able to save him. I wouldn't even have known he was there.

'How long are they going to keep you in?'

'Just overnight. Under observation.'

'And then what?'

'Then I'm going to take the first flight home to Dubai.' He shrugged. 'I need the sunshine. Not working, constant rain, it's depressing me. I guess that's why I did it.' With his grey face and in his pyjamas, he did seem a different person from the confident tanned guy he'd been last week.

'Do you want a coffee?' I asked. 'Or something else?'

'I'll have some tea.'

It came out of the machine looking like brown water with white scum on top, but he drank it. 'If I ask you a question,' he said, 'will you give me an honest answer?'

'I'll do my best.'

'Do you still think my father murdered Carlo Sondervelt?'

I swallowed. 'I'm no longer sure,' I admitted.

'That's interesting.' He leaned forward and studied my face. 'Are you hedging your bets?'

I didn't break the eye contact. 'No, I'm being totally honest with you. Until about a week ago, I was one hundred per cent sure that he'd killed him. Now we know that the gun was used for a second murder, and there are problems with Nancy's witness statement. I'm no longer as sure as I used to be.'

'But you don't think he's definitely innocent either.'

'You're right, I don't. All I can say for sure is that if the case had come to trial, with the information we have today about the second murder, your father wouldn't have been convicted.' I paused. 'Your family would still have been together.'

Remco took another sip of his tea. It must be his way of buying time, because it couldn't taste very nice. 'You saved me,' he said.

'You were just lucky that I was there.'

'No, I mean you saved me ten years ago. I knew it at the time. You saved all of us. You locked my father away.'

I wanted to ask him to explain himself, the words on the tip of my tongue, but if experience had taught me anything, it was when to keep quiet and just let people talk.

He stared at the wall as if he could see the past projected

there. 'Dennis is probably too young to remember what it was like, but I don't understand why my mother refuses to accept it.'

She'd even given him a false alibi at the time.

He fell silent as a man in a wheelchair was pushed past by a nurse. Push faster, I wanted to urge her. My heart beat hard as I waited for Remco to continue. His mother or his brother could arrive at any minute and stop him.

'Remember when Dennis said that I hated my father? He was absolutely right. I did. I told you, didn't I, that I wished he was dead?'

I nodded.

He rested his elbows on his knees. 'If I think back to my childhood, my overriding memory is of always being scared. Of hearing his footsteps coming up the stairs and trying to hide. Of smelling alcohol on his breath and knowing I should stay as far away as I could. You might not know whether my father was innocent,' he turned his head, no longer staring at the wall but looking me straight in the eye, 'but I know. He was guilty as hell. I remember the night of Carlo Sondervelt's death. I saw him when he got home. My father shot that guy, that student who was only a year older than I was. He did it.'

Chapter 30

I was shocked at Remco's words. Having finally accepted that I could have been wrong and arrested an innocent man, it took me a few seconds to process what he was telling me.

'He did it? You saw him?' I asked. That wasn't what he had said at the time.

I'd had to stay behind after Ruud had been arrested. Dennis had been taken away, and I was careful not to look at the blood on the floor. I'd wanted to go with the ambulance, but I had to continue doing my job. I had to watch the family as my colleagues searched the house. It wouldn't be the first time a criminal had hidden a gun in his child's bedroom.

Angela had still been wearing her pyjamas. She'd put a thick jumper on over the top. She was sitting on the sofa. Remco sat apart from his mother, slouched in a chair. His cheekbones and nose were too big for his face, as if they had grown up first and the rest of his features had to play catch-up. He observed me in total silence. I couldn't read his expression, but unlike his brother, he didn't seem angry. I didn't think he was a threat.

'How long is this going to take?' Angela asked.

It also wouldn't be the first time that a wife had covered for her husband.

'If you have somewhere else you can stay, with family, friends, I would call them.' If they left, I could leave as well, go to the hospital, check on how Barry was doing.

'We're not leaving the house,' Angela said.

You're also not leaving this room, I thought, but I didn't say it.

'Do you know what time your husband came home last night?' I asked.

'Around midnight, I think,' Angela said.

'Are you sure?'

Out of the corner of my eye, I could see that Remco was shifting in his chair. He was looking down at the floor, no longer watching me. *'Did you hear your father come home?'* I asked him.

He didn't say anything; just slowly shook his head.

Now his testimony was the complete opposite. 'He came home for a few minutes. I heard him. I was still awake; I used to stay up all night playing *GTA*. I looked at him around the door, as I always did, to check what state he was in, and I saw his clothes. His jacket was covered in blood. He had a gun. I was petrified. I knew it was different from normal. This wasn't just a fight. I switched off the lights, switched off my PlayStation, made sure I didn't make any noise and pretended to be asleep. Then I heard the front door open and close again. Fifteen, twenty minutes later I heard him come back, but I didn't leave my room. Not until you showed up.'

'And you're sure he had a gun?'

'Yes.'

'Are you willing to testify to that?'

Remco shook his head. 'No. I wanted to tell you so that you didn't think you locked up an innocent man. It's the least I can do for you for saving my life. Don't feel guilty. He did it.' He paused to drink some of his tea, holding the plastic cup between both hands. 'I told you, didn't I, that I wanted my father dead? But now that he is, I don't know any more. My mother keeps telling me that he'd changed. That I should have come home and seen for myself. I feel terrible. As if I'd got the thing I'd always wished for and then found out it sucked. And like Dennis said, I was the one who killed him.'

I waited, but he didn't say anything else. 'Your father's death wasn't your fault.'

'I was the one who stopped the doctors. I keep wondering what would have happened if I'd let them resuscitate him.'

'He was in a vegetative state. He'd broken his neck. This wasn't your doing.'

'Maybe. Anyway,' he made an effort to change his tone of voice, 'I heard Sandra was there. That she helped you.'

'Yeah, it was lucky she was. I might not have got that garage door open by myself.'

He leaned forward and put a hand on my arm. 'Can you stop her? Stop this? My father killed Carlo, but he'd done time in prison for that anyway. Sure, he claimed that he was innocent, but now that he's dead, what difference does it make? He had an alibi for the other murder. He was hit by a car, but that was probably just an accident.' He shivered and wrapped his dressing gown tighter around himself. 'I'm going home as soon as I'm allowed to leave. I'm hoping you won't stop me. This place is getting me down.'

'Are you sure you won't testify?' I had to ask him again.

'There's no point. Why not let the rest of my family believe what they want to? I was happy when he got convicted and I didn't have to tell anybody what I'd seen. Anyway, I would like this to stay between us.'

'You never told them?'

He shook his head. 'No. At first I couldn't, because Dennis was locked up.'

Of course. I knew that he'd spent a year in a juvenile detention centre.

'And when he came back, he wanted to believe in his father so much. It would have been like telling a six-year-old that Santa didn't exist. Even though he was a teenager by then, but you know what I mean. Later, I tried to persuade him that maybe our father was guilty, but it was too late by then. Maybe that's why I left Amsterdam, left the country, because I couldn't look at them. Whenever Dennis and my mother were talking about how wonderful our father was and how unfair the police were, I couldn't join in. But I was also too cowardly to go against them. I didn't like being a coward. It was easier to just leave. And now it's all got too much.' He shrugged. 'It'll be fine when I'm back in Dubai. I'll be busy and won't have so much time to think.' His face was pale as death. As pale as it had been when he'd been lying on the pavement. 'I think I'll go back to bed now. I'm exhausted.'

I nodded. 'You do that. Thanks for telling me this.'

As I watched his pyjama-clad figure go back up the stairs, I felt immensely sorry for him. It must have been hard to be the only person in his family who knew the truth. I remembered his watchful stares as I'd arrested his father. I remembered the way he'd looked at me during the court case. I wondered how he would have reacted if the judge had decided that we hadn't done enough to prove his father's guilt. Would he have spoken out then? Probably not. He would have been too scared to go against his father. It was lucky that the judge had ruled in our favour.

This confession had been his present to me, but it had also come with a request: that we drop the investigation into his father's death. It was different from how Sandra operated. Unlike her, Remco had made a trade without forcing me to accept or refuse it.

I left the hospital and thought about what to do next. As I drove back to the police station, rain streaked the window and the wipers had to work hard to give me any kind of view. I understood why Remco found the weather depressing.

Could we do what he'd asked and leave things the way they were? Ruud Klaver was dead and we might never find the driver who caused the hit-and-run accident. We'd had the right man for the murder of Carlo Sondervelt all along. Maarten Hageman's murder was still unsolved, but at least we knew that he was shot with a weapon that later ended up in Ruud Klaver's hands. The Arnhem police could take that information and run with it. If it helped them in any way, then great. If not, nothing had changed.

I was still pondering on it as I drove up to the station entrance. I looked at the statues that represented the duties the police force was supposed to uphold: to protect the people and provide justice. I parked, swiped my card at the entry gate and went through the turnstile. I walked up the stairs and paused at the door of the boss's office. It was open.

'Can I talk to you for a second?' I said. 'I want your advice.'

Moerdijk clicked his mouse to close down whatever he

had been looking at. 'Of course. Come in. Take a seat. What's up?'

'Remco Klaver just told me that his father killed Carlo Sondervelt. He saw him come home covered in blood. He saw the gun. Then his father went out, probably to discard his clothes and his weapon at the bottom of a canal.'

The boss frowned. 'He never said this at the time.'

'I think he was afraid. He was scared of his father and didn't dare go against his mother and brother. He was only eighteen.'

'Do you believe him?'

'Yes, I do.'

'Why did he tell you this now?'

'Because I saved his life. I think he didn't want me to feel guilty about having locked up an innocent man. He said he won't testify in court. He'd like the case closed. Ruud's death treated as an accident.'

'What about Maarten Hageman?'

I shook my head. 'He didn't know anything about that.'

Moerdijk scratched his head. 'He won't testify?'

'No. I asked him twice. He refused.'

'If we leave it, it will look like we locked up an innocent man.' He looked at me. 'It will look like you were wrong.'

I hadn't even thought about that. 'I guess so, but I don't really care about that, to be honest.'

'You don't have a burning desire to show Sandra Ngo that she was wrong and you were right all along?'

Maybe yesterday I would have, but since we saved Remco's life together, I felt far less acrimonious towards her. If she hadn't insisted on giving me a lift, Remco would have died. If she hadn't helped me pull open the garage door, he might have died. 'She can have this one,' I said.

'That's surprisingly magnanimous of you,' Moerdijk said. 'If you're sure, I'm tempted to go with what Remco wants.'

It certainly made a difference that I knew I had been right all along, but I didn't need the whole country to know as well. This was enough. I was grateful to Remco for having told me and I fully appreciated how hard his position with his family was going to be if I revealed the truth. That might have been the reason why he'd wanted to kill himself in the first place.

If Remco had committed suicide, I would never have known that Ruud had been guilty. This was the universe's way of rewarding me for having saved a life.

'Okay,' the boss finally said. 'We'll dismantle the team, but the family will have to agree. I don't want to get into any more trouble with Angela Klaver. Tell Remco to have his mother confirm his request, and we won't call it an accident but we'll scale the investigation down. If we ever find the car, then great, we'll look at it again, but I'm not holding out hope after all this time.'

I called Remco and he said he'd talk to his mother. I didn't know what he said, but an hour later, Angela emailed the boss, and in addition, Dennis withdrew his official complaint against me.

There was only one problem.

I didn't know what to say to Carlo's family. I had no idea what I was going to tell Nancy.

Chapter 31

I had to talk to Nancy at some point, but I had no idea how I was going to approach it. I couldn't let her believe that she'd been wrong about the events of that night, but I felt caught between a rock and a hard place, responsible towards both Nancy and Remco. How was I going to balance both their needs? It was easy for us to say that we were just going to drop the case or reduce the scale of the investigation, but the last time I'd talked to Nancy I'd tried to get her to understand that she'd misremembered the events of that night. Now I knew that she had been right all along. I wanted to tell her that she *had* seen Ruud, but I also had to explain that we wouldn't take this any further. I knew full well that she wouldn't be happy, and so I delayed it.

Neither Ingrid nor Thomas was surprised by the boss's decision. If this had been a normal suspicious car accident, without the extra tension of the victim being a murderer-who-might-have-been-innocent, this would have been roughly the amount of time we'd afford it anyway. As we hadn't found the car or any new witnesses, scaling the investigation down was the usual chain of events.

There was only one person who was upset, and that was Charlie.

'Can't we look at this for a bit longer?' he said.

'No, we're calling it a day,' I said. I slowly packed up the files that I would send back to the Arnhem police force. They'd done a good job investigating Maarten Hageman's background.

'But I went through all this paperwork.'

Maybe he'd realise that traffic policing wasn't so bad after all, if he was already complaining after having checked only one box full of files.

'And I found this link,' he continued. 'I checked all the restaurants against the employment records. It took me forever.'

I took pity on him. 'Show me,' I said. I could do the Arnhem police a favour by looking at what Charlie had found in their documents before sending them back, though I knew I was just procrastinating.

'There were four restaurants that Maarten owned that the police paid particular attention to. These were the ones that they were certain were only fronts for money laundering.'

'Okay.'

'Then there were a few more that they thought were legitimate businesses. Those were right at the back.' He sounded indignant about having to read to the end of a fifty-two-page document. 'You said it was something like Pizza Italy, but that wasn't it. It was Casa Italy, and I pulled up their employment records from that time. Carlo's name was on the list, as well as Tristan's.'

'So?' I asked. 'We were pretty sure about that already, weren't we? Pizza Italy, Casa Italy, same difference.'

'But it's proof.'

'You're right. But it's not new. It's proof of information that we were already pretty sure of. So it won't change things at all. We're still going to ship all these boxes back to Arnhem.'

'Okay.' He looked so disappointed that I felt sorry for him.

'It's great for the Arnhem team that you've uncovered this. It will really help them.'

'Can't we see Tristan? Interview him once more? Can I ask him some questions?'

And as had happened so often with my ex-boyfriend's parents' dog, I couldn't help myself. I threw the stick one more time.

The stack of cardboard boxes seemed to have grown since we'd last been here. There was now a double wall of them on the left-hand side. Tristan was twirling his pen, flicking it up and turning it around his thumb without even looking at it as he asked me how he could help us this time.

'Casa Italy,' I said.

The pen clattered onto the desk.

I looked around, but the wall of boxes held steady, unaffected by the shock I'd clearly given Tristan.

'What about it?' he said.

'You worked there,' Charlie said.

I'd forgotten that I'd promised him he could do the questioning. I now stayed silent.

'Yes,' Tristan said.

'You and Carlo.'

'That's right.'

'What was the place like?'

'It was just a pizza takeaway joint. We mainly did deliveries.' He picked up his pen and started twirling it again.

I couldn't help but watch the spinning pen. I wondered how he rotated it around his thumb. I wished I could do that.

'Was it busy?' Charlie asked.

'No, it was probably the easiest job I'd ever done. We didn't have many orders so there was a lot of time to study. It was perfect really.'

'Did you ever meet the owner?'

'You mean Maarten Hageman?'

Charlie nodded.

'He didn't come often,' Tristan said. 'He wasn't Italian enough, he used to say, so he stayed away. He would be there one evening every other week, mainly Fridays. Carlo told me he'd sit at a table in the corner, mostly on the phone.'

'Had you ever seen Ruud Klaver before the fight with Carlo?'

'No, I hadn't.'

'Not with Maarten?'

Tristan shook his head.

'Did you listen to Maarten's conversations?'

'No, I only saw him a couple of times. I did Wednesday and Thursday nights, Carlo did Friday and Saturday. That paid more.'

So Carlo would have been there on the nights that Maarten came in. Suddenly a whole lot of things became much clearer to me. I gave Charlie a sign to wind it up.

After we left, I bought Charlie a coffee in the café on the ground floor of the office building. It would be unfair to leave it at this. I was reminded of the many times that Barry Hoog and I had talked about our cases. It was appropriate to do this over coffee. He and I had always talked in the office by the coffee machine.

'What did you learn from that?' I asked as soon as we were sitting down. Just for today, I could treat Charlie as if he was my star pupil.

'That they worked at the same place?'

I took a sip of my latte. It gave me enough of a pause that I could calmly say, 'Okay, but you knew that already. It was in the employment records.'

'Oh yes. True.' He added sugar to his cappuccino and stirred thoroughly. 'Oh!' He pointed at me with the spoon. 'That they worked on different days.'

I waited for him to continue and make the connection, but if he did, he didn't say it out loud. 'And that's important why?' I prompted him.

'Because . . .' He took a gulp of coffee. Then he put the cup down on the saucer and sat back on his chair. 'Because one of them was there on the nights that the main guy came.'

I nodded.

'And that was the one who was shot.' He prodded the spoon into the air rapidly. 'With the same gun!'

I couldn't help it, his enthusiasm made me smile. 'Well done,' I said, and then wished I hadn't because it sounded more condescending than I'd meant it to. 'I think he must have overheard something, or seen Maarten with someone he shouldn't have.'

'But I thought he'd been killed because Ruud Klaver got into an argument with him over the girlfriend?'

I drank some more of my coffee and let Charlie figure it out for himself.

He finally did. 'She lied,' he said. 'It was never about her.'

'Shall we go and see her?' I said.

He jumped up straight away.

'After you've finished your coffee,' I added. Maybe I hadn't annoyed Barry as much as I'd always thought.

At least Nancy wasn't folding her laundry this time.

'I'm really sorry about barging in like that before,' she said. 'With Carlo's mother. I hadn't listened to the podcast properly. We were just angry.' Her eyes flicked from me to Charlie.

We were sitting on the sofa. Thick drops of rain were hanging from the windows. Sheltered from the wind by the gutters, they were clinging on and fighting gravity. A bare rosebush at the end of the garden swung angrily in the wind, pushed down by every gust and then straightening itself after the air had passed to next door's garden.

'You were right,' I said. 'You saw him. You saw Ruud Klaver.'

Nancy put her hands to her mouth. 'He did it?'

I nodded. 'He did it.'

'Didn't he have an alibi?'

'Only for the other murder. Not for Carlo's. I'm sorry I doubted you.'

Nancy buried her face in her hands for a second. She took

a couple of deep breaths. Then she had herself under control again. 'What's going to happen now?'

'Nothing. I'm sorry.'

'But *Right to Justice* has to tell everybody they were wrong. That we were right.'

'Nancy, Ruud Klaver served his time in prison for the murder.'

'So they can just say that I'm a liar?'

'They didn't say that. They said that I never checked certain things. It's definitely grey, but there is no problem legally. As long as they don't defame you – and she didn't – they can speculate, they can make any statement they like. At the end of the day, the Klaver family is going to stop pursuing this.'

Nancy slowly nodded. 'It's strange, isn't it? We're back to where we were months ago, but somehow it doesn't feel like that any more. It feels as if everything was raked over again for no reason. Anybody who listened to those podcasts will think Klaver was innocent. It feels unfair.'

'I know. But with his death, this is the best outcome.' Especially given that Remco was unwilling to testify. It was that thought of Remco and his reluctance to speak out and point the finger at his father that made me say, 'You were brave, Nancy. You were really brave to identify Ruud Klaver and to be a witness.'

Nancy broke down in tears. She covered her face with her hands.

'Without you,' I continued, 'Klaver would never have been convicted. Without your testimony, he would never have been put away.'

She wiped her face and blew her nose in a tissue. She

threw it in a bin and sat back down. I took one of her hands in mine.

'And you were smart, too,' I said. 'Smart to lie about the reason for the fight. Because that *was* a lie, wasn't it? The fight wasn't about you. It was about what Carlo had seen in Casa Italy. Had he overheard Maarten saying something? Did he know something about Maarten's murder?'

'He always said there was something odd about the restaurant,' Nancy said. 'There was never anything to do, so he couldn't understand why it was still going. He did some digging into their finances, checked what the rent was and things like that, and he said it should have gone out of business years ago. Then when the boss of the place was murdered, he got worried but he didn't actually tell me why.'

'What really happened that evening?'

'What really happened? You're not pursuing this any further, right?' She looked at Charlie, who was taking copious notes.

'We're only investigating Maarten Hageman's murder. You won't get into trouble for lying.' This was actually the best outcome, I thought. Now everybody had a reason to keep quiet.

'Okay.' Nancy sighed. 'Carlo, Tristan and I were in that bar. It was after midnight. Klaver must have been waiting until we were on our own, because as soon as Tristan went to the toilet, he accosted us. He said that Carlo had to keep his mouth shut if he knew what was good for him. Then he dragged him outside and started to beat him up.'

'Nobody in the bar stopped him?'

'Carlo got a couple of punches in, he was defending himself, and then Tristan came and managed to hold Klaver back. Klaver pulled free and ran away. Tristan went home, but Carlo was really shaken and had another drink. I asked him what was going on, but he told me it was a lot of bad stuff and that I shouldn't get involved. These were dangerous people, he said.'

'So you lied about the reason.'

'I thought it was safer. I didn't say anything about the money laundering, I didn't say anything about the boss's murder. But I couldn't keep quiet about who killed Carlo. I'd seen him. I'd seen him clearly.'

'Thanks, Nancy. I'll tell my colleagues in Arnhem. It might help them solve Maarten Hageman's murder.'

'Will I get into trouble?'

'For lying under oath?' At Nancy's nod, I said, 'I'll keep your name out of it.' At the back of my mind I thought that here was Nancy's reason to stop pushing *Right to Justice* into making a public apology. I could just tell the Arnhem police that Carlo had worked at Hageman's restaurant, and they would make the association themselves. It could be significant in that murder case, because whoever was running the money-laundering business had probably supplied Ruud Klaver with the gun.

Charlie and I went back to the office and finished packing up the files to be shipped back to Arnhem. He thanked me for having taken him to the two interviews. Again he said he'd learned a lot, but he was subdued as he went back upstairs to his old department.

Chapter 32

'What do you want for dinner?' Mark asked. He was over at my flat. 'Shall I order a takeaway?'

'No, I'm going to cook for you. I'm going to make pancakes.'

'Really? Do you know how to?'

'Doesn't everybody?' I measured out the flour. 'What do you want in them? I've got bacon or apple, or you can have plain ones.'

Mark grinned.

'What?' I said with a little lift of my chin.

'I don't know. When you invited me round for dinner, I wasn't expecting this.'

I had agonised for at least an hour as to what to make. I wanted to cook something that I wouldn't mess up, but I also didn't want to just heat something up. Nor did I want to make it too special, because then it would be obvious that I was just following a recipe from a book. In the end, I hadn't really had the time to think about cooking because of Remco's suicide attempt, his subsequent rescue and confession, and I had gone back to the default recipe that I knew how to make. 'What's wrong with pancakes? I like pancakes.'

'There's nothing wrong with pancakes,' he said with a smile in his voice.

'So, what kind do you want?'

'Bacon, please.' He got a bottle of red wine from a plastic bag. 'It's a good thing I brought something decent to drink with your pancakes.'

I handed him the corkscrew over my shoulder. 'You can open that. I need to concentrate.'

I heard him laugh behind me, but I ignored him, because this was the complicated stage where I had to add the milk slowly enough that there were no lumps. 'Oh, an egg. I need an egg as well.' I took one out of the fridge and added it. I beat the mixture with a fork. There were some lumps. It would be fine once I started cooking it. I got both my frying pans out. I always started by frying the bacon rashers so that they were nice and crispy.

'What's going on with your case?' Mark asked. 'I heard that *Right to Justice* cancelled the current series.'

'Did they? Oh good.' It was a relief. 'I guess they achieved what they wanted.'

'They showed that Ruud Klaver was innocent.'

'He wasn't.' The butter had melted and I carefully added a layer of bacon rashers to the pans, laying them out side by side so that there would be a nice bacon base to my pancakes. Four rashers per pancake was about right. 'His son saw him after he came home. He shot Carlo Sondervelt.'

'And now?'

'Now nothing.' The bacon spluttered in the pan. Small

spats of fat kept exploding and hitting my bare arms. 'We've scaled down the investigation into his death. We looked in the wrong direction from the beginning. I really thought that he might have been innocent and maybe blackmailing the real killer. It turned out that he'd actually done it.'

'What about the evidence, then? The stuff that *Right to Justice* uncovered, I mean.'

'She did a good job, Sandra Ngo. The gun *had* been used to shoot Maarten Hageman, but it was a different killer. Maybe the Arnhem police force can do something with that.'

The bacon was turning a nice colour. It pulled into small hills and valleys. I hooked the ends with my fork and turned them over. 'It will be ready soon,' I said. 'Do you want to lay the table?'

Mark laughed again.

I'd had no idea that cooking pancakes was so funny. Maybe it was amusing if you were the kind of person who actually knew how to cook properly.

'Sure,' he said, 'and I'll open the wine too.' He took knives and forks from the drawer and carried them through to the front room, together with wineglasses and the nice bottle of Chianti that he'd brought. 'Do we need candles? Pancakes by candlelight?'

'Are you making fun of my cooking? Are you looking down at pancakes?'

'No, not at all. I wouldn't dare.'

'Hey, this is the first meal I've cooked for you. No pasta with tomato sauce from a jar; proper food, made from ingredients.'

Mark gave me a kiss on the cheek. 'Thank you. I appreciate it.'

There was definitely mockery behind his words. I whisked the batter one final time with the fork. I mashed a few of the biggest lumps and hoped the others would be hidden by the bacon. It would taste the same anyway. I poured batter into both pans. It splattered for a second, then immediately solidified.

I watched the pans until the edges of the batter browned. Now for the tricky bit: I had to turn them.

'Are you going to flip them?' Mark was looking over my shoulder. He sounded anxious.

'You can't flip bacon pancakes. Everybody knows that.'

'Okay.'

I got the fish slice from the drawer and liberated the bottom of the pancake from the pan. Once I had it entirely underneath, I took a deep breath and counted to three, then turned the pancake over. It folded double and I had to straighten it out with the help of the fork and the fish slice. It was now a bit of a mess, but it would still taste fine. Mark could have the other one.

'Do you want me to help with that?' he said.

'No, I'm fine.' The other one came out of the pan more easily and I turned it without any mishaps. It was very satisfying to have done it right. 'See, told you I could do it.'

I left the pancakes for a minute to brown on the other side, then loosened them again with the fish slice and slid them onto the plates. I gave Mark the perfect one and kept the slightly misshapen one myself. Bacon pancakes and red wine was a match made in heaven.

'Is this the only thing you can cook?' Mark asked.

'I can do omelettes too, with a number of fillings. My mushroom omelette is particularly good. And pasta. With tomato sauce.'

'I feel honoured that you cooked for me.' He took a sip of his wine. 'What did the family say?'

'They dropped the complaint against me.'

'Not that family. I meant Carlo Sondervelt's. Didn't you say they were upset after the podcast?'

I put my cutlery down. 'I think I convinced Nancy,' I said. 'I haven't talked to Carlo's parents yet.'

'But at least you were right.'

'I know. I think the Sondervelts would want me to push it with *Right to Justice*, to make sure it got aired that Ruud Klaver killed their son. But for Klaver's family that would be really hard, and the boss agreed with me that maybe we shouldn't pursue this any further, especially as we have no evidence. Remco isn't willing to testify, so that leaves us with nothing.'

'That's hard,' Mark said. 'It doesn't seem fair somehow.'

'I know. That's what Nancy said too.' I wished that Sandra Ngo had never started this. The only thing she'd achieved was to make me look bad and annoy the victim's family.

'Did you tell her how you knew?'

'No, I just told her that she was right. Luckily she didn't ask. I couldn't really say anything without breaking Remco's confidence.'

'He's left you in a tough situation.'

'Not really. He wanted to make things right for me. I now

269

know that I didn't put an innocent man in jail. That's something. I don't care what the rest of the world thinks.'

'What I don't understand,' Mark said, 'is why Ruud Klaver would have gone on *Right to Justice* when he was actually guilty.'

Later, as it slowly became light again and I listened to the soothing sound of Mark's deep breathing on the pillow next to mine, I mulled that over.

Because it was a very interesting question.

Chapter 33

It was with that question in mind that I drove the next morning to see the person who might be able to tell me why Ruud Klaver had agreed to go on *Right to Justice*. It was Saturday morning, so I wasn't expected at work anyway. I'd told Mark where I was going and he'd joked that he was pleased with how much of an effort I was making to find answers to what had only been a throwaway comment.

I'd been a bit naïve to hope that Sandra Ngo would just tell me what I wanted to know. Even having saved someone's life together didn't stop her from playing her little games.

'You know what I want,' she said. 'It's the usual deal.'

'Just answer my questions,' I said. 'You stopped the podcast series, so there's no need for the massive secrecy any more.'

'Tell me something about yourself, something you don't want me to know, and I'll answer your questions.'

'All my questions?'

'Well, I'm not going to reveal my sources, of course, but everything else is fine.'

271

'And there will be no limits on how many questions I can ask?'

'Oh, I can tell you're going to take the deal.' She giggled. I hadn't thought it possible. It was so unexpectedly girlish.

If I'd known beforehand that she was going to ask for something like this, I would have given it some thought. I had a choice – there were a lot of things about me that I didn't want her to know – but I thought it was in the spirit of the deal to tell her something to do with this case. It had to be something that wouldn't hurt anybody else. It had to only involve me. That limited my options.

I took a deep breath and then pushed the words out. 'I was pregnant when we picked up Ruud Klaver. Two weeks later, I lost the baby. I felt I was being punished for what I did during that arrest.'

Sandra nodded thoughtfully. 'Ask any question you like,' she said.

I was relieved that she didn't ask what I'd felt I was being punished for. I wouldn't have told her. 'Who approached you for the podcast on Ruud Klaver?'

'Dennis did. I thought I'd told you this already.'

'Yes, I just wanted to get everything straight. So he called you out of the blue?'

'He did. I'd never talked to him before. He said he'd listened to the previous series and wanted me to prove his father's innocence.'

'He gave you all his information? All the files he had?'

'Yes. I think so. He'd been collecting things and investigating for years, so he had a lot of information.'

'There was still a lot of stuff at his flat,' I said. 'All the newspaper clippings on the wall.'

'I went to his place and did a first cut of what I thought was going to be useful. Those newspaper articles are all online anyway, so there was no reason to dismantle his wall.'

'Do you know if Dennis talked to his father before he got in touch with you?'

Sandra thought for a few seconds. 'You know, I actually have no idea. Maybe he didn't.'

'Interesting.'

'It's not that unusual. The previous series started when the guy's wife emailed me.'

'Was Ruud eager to cooperate?'

'Not in the beginning, but the longer it went on, the better it got. In the end, he liked the attention, I think.'

'Dennis's stuff made no difference. It was all about the bullets. The second murder.'

'The fact that the same gun was used. Yes.'

'And I'm guessing you're not going to tell me how you found out about that.'

She just smiled and drew her fingers across her mouth to indicate that her lips were zipped shut on this topic.

'Okay. That's fair. When was it?'

'When?'

'Yes, what was the exact date you realised it was the same gun?'

'Let me check.' She opened up her laptop but angled it in such a way that I couldn't see the screen. I could only guess that she'd received an email with that information and didn't want me to be able to read the sender's name. 'The third of October.'

'The third? A week before Ruud's accident?'

'Yes. Yes, that's right.'

'Did you tell him straight away?'

'No, I had a friend of mine double-check it first.'

'That must have taken some time.'

She looked at the screen again. 'My friend got back to me on the eighth.'

Two days before the accident. 'Did you call Ruud then?'

She stopped smiling. 'To be honest, that's when I got worried. I thought I might have been interviewing a double murderer. I realised that there's a difference between working with someone who's still in prison and someone who's been released.'

Her answer pulled me up. She was being extremely honest with me. I could imagine it was disconcerting to talk to someone and then think that maybe he'd killed two people.

'What did you do?' I asked. The sensible thing of course would have been to call the police, but I understood that Sandra would never have done that. Because that would be to accept that she needed us for something. And she would have lost her scoop.

'I talked to Dennis. I gave him a call and said that I might have found something that incriminated his father.'

'Dennis? Really?' Of course she didn't know anything about his background.

'Yes, because he was the one who contacted me in the first place. He was the one who was convinced that his father was innocent, and I wanted to know . . . well, how he'd react if maybe he wasn't.'

'Did you tell him what you had?'

'No. I didn't.'

'What did he say?'

'He was incredulous. He said that there was no way, and insisted that his father was innocent. He didn't believe it for a second.'

'But at some point you told him what you knew.'

'I realised that Maarten Hageman had been murdered on Dennis's birthday – his last birthday before his father went to jail. I was certain that he would remember that day.'

'This was when? When did you tell him?'

She didn't have to check her laptop for this one. 'I spoke to Dennis and Angela the day after Ruud's accident.'

'What was their reaction?'

'They were very relieved because they could give Ruud an alibi for that day, so they knew he hadn't done it.'

'So the day after you'd been burgled.'

'Was it?' She looked at her diary. 'Yes, I think you're right. Actually, I met with them a couple of hours after I'd come to the police station.'

I wondered if Angela and Dennis had been on their way to talk to Sandra when I'd seen them leave the hospital that first day. I took careful notes of this timeline. 'You told Dennis that there might be something that proved his father was guilty, then there was the burglary, and then you met with them the next day and told them what you'd found?'

She paused and looked at me. 'Yes,' she said. 'I was really

275

shaken up after the burglary. I went to the police station and you all just laughed at me.'

I remembered seeing her in the police station that day. She'd been screaming and the duty officer had told her to calm down. I had realised that she was having a complete meltdown, but instead of helping her, I'd been tempted to take a photo. 'I'm sorry,' I said.

'I thought it was possible that I was dealing with a real murderer,' she said. 'My house had been broken into, and I was worried that it had been him. I didn't know about his accident yet. Angela and Dennis told me about it when they came to see me.'

'Why didn't you say—'

'Say what? Come to my house, please, police officer? I'm pretty sure I did say that.'

'You're right.' Would she have told me everything if I'd talked to her then? She seemed young suddenly. No longer an adversary, but someone we should have protected. Someone I could have worked with. 'I'm really sorry,' I said again.

She sighed. 'It was such a relief to me when it turned out that he was innocent after all. That the family could give him that alibi.'

Back in the car, I thought about what Sandra had told me. If Dennis had started this, had Ruud Klaver felt powerless to go against him? What was he going to tell his son: I'm sorry, I did it? It had been a gamble on Ruud's part to go with what his son wanted, and most likely it had got him killed.

Maarten's murderer might have been worried that he was going to say something else, like where he'd got the gun, for example.

I leaned my elbows on the steering wheel and pulled my hair back from my face. Dennis had only been a kid at that point, a slight kid in green pyjamas, with shoulder-length hair. I thought that maybe I should feel bad for that twelve-year-old, who had been so convinced that his father had been innocent of Carlo Sondervelt's murder. I felt sorry for the two brothers, who'd never been able to talk about it. Should I feel worse for Dennis than for Remco? At least Remco had moved on, whereas Dennis had been stuck for years, trying to find evidence that would vindicate his father.

I drove to the police station and parked. Upstairs, I had another look at the photo of Dennis's birthday party. The happy family around the table, Remco conspicuously absent. Dennis's classmates laughing and eating cake. His father standing behind his son with his hand on his shoulder, smiling. It was bittersweet, this image of a boy at the last party before his father was locked up, the last time they were still one family. A boy with his hair shaved at the sides.

Shaved.

Wait.

I thought of what he'd looked like when we'd arrested Ruud Klaver; hadn't he had shoulder-length hair?

I pulled up the files from the Kinderpolitie, the section of the police force that dealt with crimes against children, but also with those perpetrated by children. I opened the file on Dennis Klaver. I hadn't wanted to look at this because it reminded me too much of what had happened. Now that

my anger against Dennis had abated, I could actually open
his file. I could examine the photo of what he'd looked like
immediately after he'd been taken into custody.

It was as I'd remembered it: he'd had shoulder–length hair.
It was greasy and matted – he probably hadn't combed it in
days – and he wore it with a centre parting.

I looked again at the photo of the birthday party. The
hair on the sides of Dennis's head had definitely been
shaved. I held the photo up against the screen so that I could
easily compare it with the photo after the arrest. Nobody's
hair grew that much in three weeks. But it wasn't just
the hair. Dennis's face in the police photo was wider, and his
features larger. Sure, it was definitely the same kid, but there
was no way there had only been three weeks between the
two photos.

That birthday party hadn't taken place three weeks before
the arrest. It was at least a year earlier. It was the wrong party.
The wrong year.

It was suddenly clear what had happened. Sandra had told
Dennis that she'd found something that made her think that
Ruud might have been guilty. Then there had been the
break-in to find out what this evidence was. A burglary that
had taken place because Dennis panicked. Did he tell his
mother? Did he confront his father at this point? Because
with the second murder, Sandra hadn't proved Ruud Klaver's
innocence; she had proved his guilt. His family must have
known that he hadn't been at that particular birthday party,
otherwise they wouldn't have given us the photos and
footage of the one the year before. Whose idea had it been

to fabricate the evidence so that it showed Ruud Klaver's innocence?

The two people who had supported Ruud all these years, his wife and his younger son, now knew that he had lied to them.

Angela had given him a false alibi the first time round too. She'd claimed he'd been home at midnight, whereas that clearly hadn't been the case. The thoughts continued to tumble in my mind as I rushed back downstairs to my car.

I was suddenly really worried about Remco.

Because while his family had probably been in panic mode, trying to control the damage, he had been in Dubai, ignorant of what was happening in Amsterdam. The finger-prints on the inside of the garage had been his mother's and his brother's. There was nothing strange about that – his mother lived there, his brother visited often enough – but had they known what Remco had seen on the night of Carlo Sondervelt's murder? They had known that he was going to meet me; maybe they'd been worried about what he was going to tell me.

And I remembered that if I hadn't arrived ten minutes early for our meeting, he would have died.

I called his mobile, but there was no reply. I called the hospital. The nurse told me that Remco had been discharged first thing this morning and had left with his mother.

That was no reassurance at all.

Chapter 34

I kept hitting redial on my phone to contact Remco. I pressed down on the accelerator to force my car to get me to Angela's house as quickly as possible. Rain was still coming down heavily and the windscreen wipers had to work hard to clear the deluge. I found myself leaning forward to see the road in front of me. The puddles were so big that I could feel the car aquaplaning as I went through one of them. After the tyres got their grip back, I hit redial again. This time, Remco picked up my call.

'Where are you?' I said.

'I'm at the airport.'

He was making his escape from the rain, as he'd told me yesterday. 'Stay there,' I said. 'I need to talk to you.'

'I'm sorry I couldn't pick up your calls earlier.' His voice was cheerful, in sharp contrast to my anxiety. 'I had to switch my phone off as I cleared security.'

'You've gone through security already? Do not board that plane. Wait for me.'

There was a silence. 'Okay,' he said finally.

I disconnected the call, swearing loudly as I doubled back on myself and drove through the same puddles. I would have already been at Schiphol if I'd gone straight from the police station and hadn't first tried to get to Angela Klaver's.

To my left, I caught movement out of the corner of my eye. Because of all the water on the side windows, I only saw a small dark shape as it came up to the crossroads. I braked hard and swerved. The car bucked and I was thrown forward, but I came to a full stop just in time to avoid the cyclist, who was crouched low over his handlebars against the rain and wind. His hand gestures as he cycled over the crossing told me only too clearly what he thought of my driving.

My heart pounded at the near miss. I looked up and noticed that I'd gone through a red light. I wouldn't have minded a brief stop by the side of the road until I'd calmed down, but instead I pushed down on the accelerator again because I knew I couldn't waste time like that. I also knew that I couldn't keep driving like a maniac, or I would end up killing someone.

Part of my haste came because I was suddenly worried that Remco hadn't tried to commit suicide after all. That someone had fed him those sleeping pills and then rigged up the car so that he would die of carbon monoxide poisoning. He must have known who that was. Someone from his family. They must have known that he knew. I had a hard time believing that Angela had tried to kill him. She would probably kill me without a second's thought, but she didn't look like someone who'd murder her own son. His brother was a far more likely suspect, especially as he'd tried to punch Remco in the hospital. Still, Dennis seemed like someone who'd act on impulse. Not someone who'd give his brother drugs and then try to kill him in such a way as to make it look like a suicide. More the kind of guy who would hit his father with a car.

I needed to stop speculating for a couple of minutes and concentrate on my driving. I needed to get to the airport and talk to Remco. If he'd gone through security, at least he was safe. Nobody without a boarding card would be able to reach him there.

I remembered that he'd been supporting his family financially all those years, and that he'd seemed comfortable in their company. I could imagine him making a deal with them: he would leave the country and keep his mouth shut, as long as they kept theirs shut as well. Was that why they'd backed off so quickly? Even Dennis had withdrawn his complaint.

I turned onto the ring road and could finally increase my speed. All I needed was for Remco to testify. I silenced the voice in the back of my mind that told me he might not be willing to do that.

I called his mobile again. 'Where are you?' I said.

'Waiting for you, as you told me to.'

'How long until your flight leaves?'

'Just over an hour. I got here early.'

I nodded to myself. That was good. It meant I had time to get through security myself, talk to him and persuade him to give me a proper witness statement. If need be, he could get on a later flight. There was a puddle the size of a small lake coming up that covered the majority of my lane. I slowed up a little bit but still felt the tyres lose grip. The car seemed to float for a second, until I reached the other tarmac shore. I slowed down some more. I had time, and I was definitely not going to achieve anything by killing myself here on the road.

A viaduct was coming up and a large plane was taxiing across it. I drove underneath the plane. The airport was clearly visible. I'd be there in five minutes or so. I followed the short-stay signs and parked in front of the entrance, then grabbed my phone and bag and jumped out of the car. I should have checked which terminal he was departing from. I didn't even know which airline he was on. I hit his number on my phone again.

'Where are you?' I said.

'I'm sorry.'

'Where are you?' I said it louder.

'I'm on the plane.'

'I told you to wait.'

'I can't,' he said. 'I can't do what you want.'

'Get off now! When's the flight leaving?'

'I'm sorry I lied to you,' he said. In the background I heard a female voice say, 'Sorry, sir, please put your phone away now. We're ready for take-off.' Then there was silence. He'd disconnected the call.

'Fuck!' I screamed.

Around me, people pulling suitcases sped up to rush away from me. Only one person stopped and stared.

He'd lied to me on purpose. An hour. He'd said his plane was leaving in an hour.

As I ran to the departures board, I called the boss.

'I need to stop Remco Klaver leaving the country,' I said before he'd even finished saying his name.

'Is he a murder suspect?'

'A witness. I need to get his statement.'

'I thought he'd refused?'

I scanned the board. The departure time of the flight to Dubai was in five minutes. 'You need to get that plane stopped.'

'Lotte—'

'Now! Before he leaves.'

'Lotte, there are no grounds. We can't.'

At that moment, the flight status changed to Departed. Because I'd been slow in understanding what had happened, I'd let my main witness leave the country. I took the escalator up to the observation deck and watched a plane taxi by. I had no idea if that was the one Remco was on. What was it he had said a few days ago? That he was good at running away. He had done it again. Instead of giving a witness statement, he had gone as far away as he could. Ten years ago that had been to Maastricht, this time to Dubai. He must think he'd be safe once he'd left the country.

I stuffed my hands deep in my pockets. He was probably right. I couldn't imagine his family following him to kill him now that they were certain he wasn't going to testify. If I'd been in his position, I might have done the same. For the time being he was safe, but who knew what would happen in the future?

I watched a few more planes take off and then headed back to the ground floor to return to the office. I had to find another way to prove what had happened. What did I actually know? I knew that Ruud Klaver's alibi had been fabricated. I knew that the photos that had been handed in as proof were from another birthday party, another year, because Dennis's hair had been shoulder-length when I'd arrested Ruud but was closely shaved in the photos.

I knew that Ruud had killed Carlo Sondervelt because Remco had told me so.

That was it. That was all I knew and I didn't have a shred of evidence for it. I could speculate all I wanted, but I couldn't prove a thing.

I left the airport through the large glass sliding doors and went to where I'd left my car. It was no longer there. There was only a parking warden. I told him the make and colour of the car and the licence plate number.

He told me it had just been towed away.

Chapter 35

Sometimes you reach a point where you think your day cannot get any worse. For example, when your main witness has left the country, your car has been towed and you get hit by a penalty fare for not buying a ticket for the train from Schiphol to Centraal. I told the ticket inspector that I had just forgotten to check in when I got on at Schiphol. I even told him I was a police detective. He still made me pay the penalty.

So yes, that was all pretty bad, but then I had a meeting with Chief Inspector Moerdijk and I realised that it *could* get worse. Because he didn't find my conclusions as convincing as I did.

My speculations, he called them.

My memory of a haircut from ten years ago didn't make any difference, he said. No judge would take it seriously. Even when I showed him the photos from when Dennis had been taken into custody, he said that children changed a lot at that age, especially boys, and you would expect a kid to look very different at his birthday party and after he'd been locked away.

He even went so far as to say that he was relieved that

Remco was no longer in the country because he wasn't sure what I would have done if I'd managed to stop him from getting on that plane.

Remembering how I'd doubted Nancy's statement about what had happened ten years ago, I felt as if my own prejudices were coming back to haunt me. That the boss was doing to me what I'd done to her didn't make it any better.

After that, I decided to give myself a break from the police station and walked home. I'd liberate my car later.

My cat meowed a happy greeting when I opened the front door. I didn't normally get home in the middle of the day. She must think she was going to be fed early. I gave her some Felix, really to delay having to open that particular drawer in the front room. She purred happily as she was eating, with a noise that sounded as if she really appreciated her lunch but was really just the sound of cat food being scoffed at breakneck speed. Normally she would lick the jelly off first. Had I forgotten to feed her this morning?

I opened the drawer. Right at the bottom, hidden under long-ago paid bills and old postcards, was an envelope. I fished it out and held it carefully between both hands. It looked so innocuous, as if it might contain a birthday card. I undid the flap. I knew there were six photos inside. They had been in my scrapbook for about a year, until I couldn't bear to look at them any more and had taken them out, leaving an empty page that was as telling as the photos had been.

I slipped them from the envelope and spread them out in front of me. The first picture showed me on the witness stand, hand in the air as I took the oath, with Barry in his wheelchair in the first row of the audience. The next one was of me and a heavily pregnant Nancy side by side, discussing the case and her testimony. The judge had made a joke, warning her not to go into labour. It had set the scene at the trial, showing everybody clearly whose side he was on.

I wrapped my arms around my stomach, but the pain was bearable. I hadn't seen these photos for many years. There had been a moment, after my husband and I had got divorced and I was going through my belongings to see what I was going to take with me, when I had held the envelope and considered throwing away the photos. What had stopped me? Not the possibility that they might be important as evidence in a murder case. That had never even crossed my mind. Then what? This selection of photos had always seemed to highlight what had happened. I had kept them in my scrapbook for a while to make sure that I stuck to the commitment I'd made to myself. If I didn't interfere where I could, this was what could happen. Maybe that was the reason I'd hung onto them.

There was only one photo with Dennis and Angela in it. Dennis had been allowed to attend the trial, but was accompanied by a guard. It had taken four months for the case to come to court. He looked angry but was smartly dressed. He'd also had a haircut. In this photo, his hair was short again, not quite as short as it had been in the footage of the birthday party, but it could easily have grown to this length in four months. Remco sat in the row behind them. He was already separate.

Useless photos.

I took my scrapbook out. I looked at the empty pages. I thought back to Remco telling me that I'd saved him. That by making sure that Ruud Klaver was found guilty, by locking him away, I'd saved all of them.

I undid the plastic that covered the sticky side of the page and slowly put the photos of Ruud Klaver's trial back where they belonged.

I returned my scrapbook to its place in the cupboard, then went into my study and looked at my drawing of the case. I now understood why Ruud Klaver had confessed to Carlo's murder. We'd had forensic evidence and a witness, so he must have been sure he was going to get convicted for that murder anyway. But Nancy's lie had given him the opportunity to claim that it had just been the result of a stupid fight. He must have been worried that we were going to find out he had also killed Maarten Hageman. His sentence would have been much longer if we had realised he'd murdered two people and was involved in organised crime. Who knows what else had been hidden in his past. Did he kill Carlo because he'd found out about Maarten's murder? Had Carlo seen Klaver and Maarten together, maybe? He had worked on the nights that Maarten came to the restaurant. If Maarten had been keeping more than his share of the money that was laundered through his restaurants and Carlo had been in the kitchen when Ruud had come to take him to task about it, that was absolutely a motive for murder.

Ruud's lawyer had probably advised him to confess to this one murder, for a lesser motive, as our evidence was such that he wouldn't get away with it anyway. I completely understood all the actions from the past.

What had happened more recently was a different story. It must have been soul-destroying for Dennis and Angela when they found out that Ruud had been guilty all along. That he had lied to them all these years. Especially for Dennis, who had spent his youth, his entire life really, defending his father, researching his past and piecing everything together. I didn't think he had gone to school after high school. He had devoted himself to proving his father's innocence, only to find he had killed two people.

His father hadn't been at his birthday party because he was in Arnhem murdering someone.

That must have hurt.

Had it hurt enough to kill him? To hit him with a car?

And now Remco had literally fled from his family.

He had made the right choice, I acknowledged to myself. I had no evidence for anything. I couldn't even prove that the birthday-party alibi was fake. The only thing I could do was to get someone to admit what had happened.

There were three people who knew the truth. One was on a plane right now and wasn't going to tell me anything because he thought his life was in danger. One had had his life destroyed by his father's lies.

The obvious choice was to start with Angela.

On my fourth visit to the Klavers' house, I was no less uncomfortable. Unlike last time, at least today Angela opened the door and let me in. She didn't say a word, but turned round and went up the stairs, certain that I would follow her. She sat down on the sofa, crossed her arms, crossed her legs, but still didn't say anything. She wasn't going to offer me a cup of tea. There were no pleasantries.

That worked for me.

'Remco's left,' I said. I picked my words carefully. 'He's safely on his way back to Dubai.' I looked at her face to see if my choice sparked something in her, but her features seemed frozen.

'I know,' she said. 'I dropped him off at the airport.'

'Do you remember the night I came here and arrested your husband?'

A surprised gasp escaped her lips. 'Do I remember? Of course I remember.'

'I remember it too. I remember it really clearly. In fact, I can close my eyes and see it all in front of me again, like an old movie.'

'Are you here to apologise for what you did?'

'Apologise?' So that was why she had let me in this time. That was what she thought I was here for. I smiled. She couldn't be more wrong. 'Of course not. I'm here to tell you that I know.'

'Know?' Her eyebrows pulled together in a frown. 'Know what?'

'It's that stabbing that makes my memories of Dennis so crystal-clear. I still know exactly what he looked like. I know, for example, that he wore green pyjamas. He was barefoot.' I watched Angela closely. 'And he had shoulder-length hair.'

'So?' She paled a bit under her make-up.

'So this.' I placed the photo of the birthday party in the

291

middle of the table and turned it so that it was facing her. 'This is fake. Or no, not fake, but it's of another year.' I tapped on Dennis's face in the photo. 'He's got short hair. This wasn't taken three weeks before I arrested your husband. My guess is that this photo is from the previous year. Is that right?'

Angela pursed her lips but stayed silent.

'Even if I have to contact every parent of every child in these photos, I will find someone who has evidence of what year this was. A parent with a photo with a date stamp shouldn't be too hard to find. Or maybe with a birthday card with an age on it. Happy eleventh birthday. That must be in a photo somewhere. Or perhaps there's one taken from such an angle that I can count the candles on the cake.' I took the photo back. 'This was the party for when Dennis turned eleven, not twelve.'

'You bitch.' Angela's hands were gripping the edge of her seat.

'Where were you on the evening of the tenth of October?' That was the evening that Ruud had got hit by that car.

'I was here. With Dennis,' she added quickly.

'With Dennis,' I repeated. Of course she was going to give her son an alibi; Angela Klaver was the queen of the false alibi, after all. This would be the third one she'd supplied. 'I don't even know why I bothered to ask. Are you sure you don't want to just tell me what happened? After Sandra told Dennis that she had information about a second murder, did Dennis break into her house? That gave you a couple of hours' warning, didn't it? Time enough to fabricate an alibi.

But I'm really curious.' I put the photo back in my hand-bag. 'Did you tell your husband? Did you tell him that you now finally knew that he'd been guilty? Or had you known all along?' I leaned forward. 'Maybe it was only Dennis who believed in his father's innocence. Maybe he was the only one who felt betrayed. Because you'd known all along.'

Angela stood up from the sofa. 'Leave this house right now.' She moved to grab my arm, but I pulled away from her grip.

'I'll go. For now. I'll come back once I have the evidence.'

She put a hand on my back and gave me a shove towards the door. 'Leave! Now! I'll call our lawyer!'

I went down the stairs before she could push me down. I paused at the bottom. 'I just feel sorry for your son,' I said. 'For Remco, I mean. Your other son. I can't imagine what it must have felt like to have his own family attempt to murder him.'

'He tried to commit suicide.'

'Okay, you keep telling yourself that. Good luck with it.'

Chapter 36

It wasn't far to cycle to Dennis's flat. I would just have this one chat and then I would go and liberate my car.

I paused outside the door. Maybe I shouldn't have come here by myself. That I had my gun with me was only a small reassurance. I remembered Sandra saying that she had suddenly been scared after she realised she was dealing with a potential double murderer. I had met plenty of murderers before, but that didn't mean I was entirely comfortable stepping into the lion's den. I texted Charlie the address, and asked him to join me there urgently. Sometimes you needed extra muscle. I waited until he replied that he was on his way over, and double-checked that my gun was loaded before I rang the doorbell.

I wasn't sure what to expect, but I was surprised when Dennis opened the door and invited me in. I had been sure that he would leave me standing on the doorstep. Had his mother not called to warn him? I was hesitant about entering the flat, but set my phone to record our conversation and then joined him inside.

His flat was still a shrine to his father. I had half expected him to have dismantled it and taken all the photos down, but Ruud Klaver's face was still smiling at me from a golden picture frame. Did his son not feel any guilt over what he'd done? That surprised me even more than the fact that Dennis had let me in.

I stayed standing in the middle of the room, wanting to be ready to act if I needed to. I didn't particularly want to needle him – this was, after all, the man who had most likely hit his father in a stream of red mist – but I also knew that I might well be a trigger. He was much more likely to lose control and admit what he'd done if I was here by myself.

He looked at me with a smirk on his face. 'Are you here to admit it?' he asked.

I narrowed my eyes. 'Admit what?'

The smile disappeared. 'I've withdrawn my complaint. Now admit that you were wrong.'

'Wrong about what exactly?' I pushed my hands into my pockets.

'My father was innocent! Admit it.' His face was serious, as if he truly believed it. Was that possible? Had he pushed the truth down so deep that he had convinced himself with his own lies?

I frowned. 'You don't have to act in front of me,' I said. 'I know what happened. Your father killed Maarten Hageman and Carlo Sondervelt.'

'What?'

'You burgled Sandra Ngo's house and you and your mother fabricated that alibi together.'

'You're unbelievable! Even now you can't admit the truth.

Everybody knows my father was innocent. It was on *Right to Justice.*'

There was something about the angry desperation in his voice that pulled me up. Even though I was still on my guard, I was no longer as nervous as I had been when I first stepped into the flat. All I needed to do was to stay calm, keep him calm and get him to accept what had happened. Because I now believed he still didn't know. He still thought his father had been innocent. That was why his photos were still on the wall. That was why he was still asking me to admit that I'd been wrong. I would have time later to work out what that actually meant, but I also knew that here was my opportunity.

'Do you remember the night of your father's arrest?' I said in the tone of voice I would use with a scared child.

Dennis shook his head. 'Don't change the subject.'

'Do you remember your twelfth birthday party?'

He laughed on a single exhalation. 'You've seen the photos.'

'I'm not talking about what's in the photos. Do you remember the party itself? What did you do?'

He looked surprised at the question. He was probably so taken aback by it that he answered without thinking. 'We went bowling,' he said. 'We always did.'

I nodded. 'When I was a kid, we did the same thing every year. I even had the same classmates. Did you?'

'I guess so.'

'It's hard to tell what happened in which year. I sometimes know because of the clothes I was wearing.'

'Right.'

'This,' I held out the photo, 'this wasn't your twelfth birthday party. It was your eleventh.' My voice was calm. He'd been a kid at the time. What had he known about what his parents did? What had he known about the effect of stabbing someone? 'Do you remember?'

'Mum said . . .' He bit his lip and scratched his chin through his beard.

'Sandra Ngo called you first when she had evidence that showed that maybe your father was guilty. Did you tell your mother about that?'

'Of course I did.'

'Where were you on the evening of the tenth of October?'

'The tenth? I was at home.'

'By yourself?'

'Yes.'

His mother had said that he'd been with her. She had given him a false alibi. But then immediately it struck me that maybe she had given herself a false alibi. What if she hadn't lied on behalf of Dennis, but for herself?

Dennis looked at the photo. He studied it closely, as if he was seeing it for the first time. 'I think I turned twelve here. I really do.'

'You don't remember the birthday party where your father didn't show up?'

Dennis shook his head. 'He was never there. He never showed up. I remember this one because he did. I was twelve.'

'Look at your haircut,' I said. 'Didn't you have it longer later? Don't you remember that it was almost down to your shoulders?'

'I don't know. I don't know.' For the first time, he sounded lost and unsure of himself.

'Where were you when your brother tried to kill himself?'

'I was at work. I know that because my mother called me. She said I had to come to the hospital.'

'All day?'

'Well, all morning, until she called. Then I left.'

'And you've got witnesses to that, right?'

'Oh yeah, my colleagues can tell you.'

'Thanks, Dennis,' I said. 'Thank you for your time.' I looked around me again, at the photos of his father, at the files on the shelves. 'I'm sorry,' I said. Such a wasted youth. 'I'm sorry for what happened to you.'

'You see,' he said, 'that wasn't so hard.' The smirk was back on his face.

He hadn't listened to my words. He'd only heard what he wanted to hear.

I didn't correct him. 'I spoke to Barry Hoog the other day,' I said instead. 'He said that if you ever wanted to talk to him, he'd be happy to meet.'

All the blood drained from Dennis's face. 'You bitch.' He balled his fists.

'Don't misunderstand me. I didn't say it to attack you,' I said kindly. 'Barry's doing well. I think he really would like to talk to you. Think about it. Call me and I'll arrange it.'

I left him staring at the photo of his birthday party.

I called Charlie as soon as I was outside. 'Sorry,' I said. 'False alarm.'

'I'm nearly there now,' he responded, and I could hear the disappointment in his voice.

'I'll see you back at the police station.' I got back on my bike. I needed some time to gather my thoughts, because my assumptions had been wrong.

The wind gusted at my back and pushed me towards a crossing with a main road. There was no other traffic, and my light was green. If I pedalled hard, I would make it through the light before it turned red. On the other side of the street, a man on foot was going in the same direction. To my right, the bookshop on the corner was closed and all the lights were off.

Suddenly a loud clunk came from my left. Had the wind brought down a tree? It hadn't sounded loud enough for that. It had sounded like something insubstantial getting hit.

I thought all of this in a second, and that gave me the chance to veer sharply to the right. But before I could reach the pavement and get off my bike, I was struck from behind. The impact threw me forward over the handlebars. I flung my hands out to break my fall, but I couldn't stop my own momentum. I hit the ground. I must have sounded insubstantial too.

The car stopped a few metres in front of me. It was a dark Mercedes. I was pretty sure I'd seen that car before. I blinked to get everything back into focus so that I could read the number plate.

But before I could memorise the digits, I saw the tail lights come on.

The Mercedes was reversing towards me.

Chapter 37

I scrambled back as quickly as I could, on hands and knees, to get to the safety of the pavement, but I was still on the ground, and more worryingly still, in the road, when I heard the engine of another car coming up behind me. It pulled in right in front of me, effectively blocking me from the Mercedes. The Mercedes' tail lights went out and its engine roared, and I watched as it disappeared into the distance. Then I realised that I should have tried to get out of the way, because the right-hand door of the other car opened and a man got out.

I sat up and readied myself to make a run for it. The world spun for a few seconds and went black as all the blood rushed from my head. I had to put a hand on the ground to steady myself, and as pain shot through it, my vision came back and I recognised the man.

It was Charlie.

My breathing slowed and I dropped my head forward and laughed. I'd never been so pleased to see him before.

He stared at the tail lights of the disappearing car, then turned and looked at me with open concern. 'Jesus, you nearly gave me a heart attack,' he said. 'I hadn't even realised it was you at first. I just saw that there'd been a crash. Look at the state of your bike.'

'What are you doing? Go after that car.'

He ignored me and knelt by my side. 'Are you okay?' He put a hand on my shoulder.

'We need to get that car.' I was happy that my voice didn't wobble at all.

'It's gone. But don't worry, I've got most of the number plate. We'll find it. I'm more worried about you right now. Are you injured anywhere?'

'I think I'm in one piece.' The worst of the pain was in my hands, which had taken the brunt of the impact. They felt as if they were on fire. I carefully turned them palm upwards. Where there had been skin, there was now a mixture of grit and blood. It was nasty and painful, but not serious. I carefully moved the various parts of my body, my arms, my legs, and was relieved when they all did what I wanted them to do. There was a large gash in my jeans and I could see a cut in my leg where the pedal of my bike had hit me. That wasn't too bad either. It wasn't even deep enough to need stitching. 'Just tore my jeans and lost some skin on my hands.' I quickly turned them over again so that I wouldn't have to see them. My left wrist was painful – I had probably sprained it breaking my fall – but it was bearable and I could move it. 'The bike got the worst of it.'

That was an understatement. The bike was a write-off. The front wheel was folded double and I thought that maybe the Mercedes had driven over it.

'Let me have a look at your hands.'

I held them out to him.

He carefully turned them over and grimaced. 'Let's go to the hospital. Get those cleaned up.' He wrapped his arm around my shoulder and helped me upright. 'I'll drive you.'

'The hospital? Are you kidding me? We don't have time for that.'

Two other cyclists came by and stopped. 'Are you okay?' one of them said. 'Did this guy hit you with his car? Do you need help?'

'I'm fine,' I said. 'It wasn't him. He stopped to help me. The car that drove into me took off. It's long gone.'

After various exclamations of disgust, they got back on their bikes and cycled away.

'Did you see who was driving?' Charlie said.

'I'm pretty sure I know who it was.' I plastered a fake smile on my face. 'Do you want to come with me and arrest her?' Of course I was shaken up after having come off my bike, but adrenaline would keep me going. I didn't want to think about what could have happened if Charlie hadn't arrived just in time.

'Did it hit you on purpose?'

I remembered those tail lights coming on. 'She would have reversed into me if you hadn't turned up.'

'Are you sure you won't go to the hospital?'

'And give her time to get rid of her car? Let's go.'

'You keep saying *her*. It wasn't Dennis Klaver, then? I thought that maybe he'd followed you after you left there.'

'No, I'm pretty sure it was his mother. Angela.'

'What about your bike?'

I stared at the useless lump of metal. 'Let's leave it here. If someone wants it, they're welcome to it.'

Charlie dragged it out of the road. Then he changed his mind, popped the car boot open and swung the bike's skeleton inside. He opened the car door for me, and I even had to ask him to do my seat belt up because my hands refused to cooperate.

'Where are we going?' he asked.

I gave him the address. As we sped through Amsterdam's streets, I called for backup. 'You were really lucky,' Charlie said after I'd disconnected the call.

'I know. I heard her hit something before she clipped me. I managed to get out of the way. She must have waited for me outside Dennis's flat.'

'Do you think she killed her husband?'

'Yes, I think she did. Stop here.' From where we sat in the car, we had a perfect view of Angela Klaver's front door. 'We'll keep an eye out, but we'll wait for backup.'

A dark Mercedes was parked outside. It was the same car that I'd pulled Remco's unconscious body out of. A large scratch ran along the hood on the right-hand side. It was from either the handlebar of my bike or maybe the pedal. The house was dark. There were no lights on.

'I don't think she's here,' Charlie said.

'That's the car that hit me.'

Charlie got out and I followed him. He studied the scratch, careful not to touch it. 'With a bit of luck, we can match that up with your bike. And you were going to leave it behind to get stolen. That's important evidence. It's a good thing I was there.'

'I'll make sure I have a traffic cop with me every time I get into an accident,' I said.

Just then, another car pulled up in front of the house and Dennis Klaver got out. He looked up at the dark window, then took a set of keys out of his pocket.

I thought that he looked back at me as he opened the front door to his mother's house.

Chapter 38

'What do you want to do?' Charlie whispered.

'Mum!' I could hear Dennis shouting. The lights on the first floor came on.

'Are you armed?' I asked Charlie.

'No. What are you thinking?'

I looked at my hands. I had my gun but I didn't think I'd be able to use it. I could see that the front door was still open. Dennis had looked back at me. He'd left the door ajar on purpose, I was pretty sure of that. If this situation had come up a couple of days ago, I would definitely have stayed outside and waited, because I'd been convinced that Dennis and his mother were in it together. I would have suspected that she'd called him after she'd failed to kill me, and that I was going to walk into some kind of trap.

Now I wasn't so sure.

I felt more secure for having Charlie here to back me up, but I would have felt even better if I'd been able to hold my gun.

Did Dennis understand that his mother had been lying to him? Did he now know that his father hadn't been innocent? Should I be worried for his mother's life? But then why had he left the door open?

Was I supposed to stop him, as I should have stopped him ten years ago?

At that thought, it was no longer possible for me to stay outside. I walked up the path at the side of the house and approached the open front door.

I heard shouting as soon as I got into the house. Hand on my gun, because it made me feel safe even if I wouldn't be able to aim it, I went up those stairs again.

Angela Klaver was cowering in the corner of the sofa. Dennis loomed over her, imposing like a bear raised on its hind legs. I was about to get in between them, but instead I paused, giving myself a few seconds to read the situation.

'Why didn't you tell me?' he screamed. 'You let me believe that he was innocent. And he was guilty all along.' He made a visceral roaring noise and punched a cushion that rested on the side of the sofa. It was not so close to his mother as to make me want to interfere, but it felt as if things could tip at any minute. My muscles were tensed and I was ready to jump in as soon as it was needed. I had to be careful, though. This woman had tried to kill me earlier, but I shouldn't let that cloud my judgement about what I was going to allow her son to do. If anything, I should err on the side of caution.

But I also wanted to let this play out. I wanted to hear what these two people were going to say to each other.

I was aware of Charlie behind me, and I motioned to him to stay back and keep quiet. He could act as my safety valve. He would let me take the lead on this, but if at any point he thought that my assessment of the situation was off, I expected him to say something. Do something even.

'Dennis.' Angela spoke calmly, as if this display of anger wasn't unusual. Her voice belied her body language, though, because she hadn't moved from her seat in the corner. Her feet were off the floor and she held her knees to her body. Was she worried he'd kick out?

'It was my eleventh birthday? Not my twelfth?' His voice was confused and childlike, as if he had been transported back to that age.

'I will make it up to you,' she said.

'What? You're going to make up for all those years I campaigned for him?'

'I didn't know.' She unwrapped her arms from around her knees. 'I didn't know either. That's why I got so angry at him. He lied to me all this time as well.'

We knew, I wanted to say, but I stayed quiet and let the scene play itself out.

'Remco knew, didn't he? Why didn't we listen to him?' Dennis visibly deflated.

Angela's head came up sharply. 'Why do you say that?'

'He once tried to tell me, when I saw him in Dubai a few years ago.' He lowered his arms until they were dangling by his sides. 'I wouldn't listen. I thought he just hated Dad.'

I thought Remco would be happy to hear that his brother had remembered that discussion. That thought reminded me of the time Remco had recorded our conversation. I took my phone out. With Charlie here, I had a witness to whatever Dennis and Angela were going to say, but I wanted recorded evidence to back it up.

'He's a coward,' Angela said. 'If he was going to tell me, he should have done it years ago. Not days ago.'

'What happened? Did you tell him that? Did that upset him? He said we should do some stuff together, and then he tried to kill himself.'

Angela shook her head. 'I only scared him a bit. Then the police turned up and ruined the garage door.'

'You're quite something,' he said. 'No wonder he left the country. I wondered about that. It never seemed right. I can't believe you did that.'

'He was going to talk to that police detective. I tried to reason with him.'

'Your own son.' Dennis sat down heavily on the seat opposite his mother. 'You're crazy.'

'I was at home the whole time. I would never have let anything happen to him.'

She'd been in the house when Sandra and I turned up and rescued Remco? I hadn't spoken to the doctors about exactly how long it would take someone to die from carbon monoxide poisoning, but I didn't think he'd have had much longer. Angela could tell herself that she'd never wanted to harm Remco, but I wasn't certain she wouldn't have.

'I wanted to protect you,' she said. 'I wanted to make sure you never found out.'

'Never found out about what?' Dennis's voice was suddenly sharper. 'About Dad? Or about you killing him.'

'He lied to us all these years. He ruined our lives. When he first went to prison, he told me that confession was worthless. That he'd done it to get a reduced sentence. He swore to me that he'd lied under oath. That the girl, Nancy Kluft, had been making it up all along.' She laughed. It was a bitter sound.

I wrapped my arms around my waist. Of course, Ruud had been right about one thing: Nancy had lied. She had lied under oath about the motive for murder.

'And then Sandra Ngo found that proof and all he could say was that I'd misunderstood him.' Angela's voice grew louder, as if she had to force the sound through suppressed tears. 'That he'd never claimed he was innocent but that he'd wanted me to know that he hadn't tried to chat that girl up. That he hadn't killed Carlo Sondervelt over a girl. As if that was what mattered. As if it was important *why* he'd shot the guy.'

Dennis shook his head. 'So why go on *Right to Justice*?'

'He said he didn't want to let us down. That it was too late to change his story. He made it sound as if it was all our fault. It made me so angry. So when I saw him . . .' She shook her head. 'There was hardly even a dent. Only the front light had shattered. It was just as if it had never happened.'

'Turns out that both my parents were murderers,' Dennis said. 'That's enough, isn't it?' he added softly.

I knew he was speaking to me. 'Yes,' I said. 'It's enough.'

He got up from his seat without saying a word. I put my hand on his arm as he went past me to go down the stairs. 'Think about it,' I said. 'What I mentioned earlier. Call me.'

He nodded and I watched him leave.

I allowed Charlie to arrest Angela Klaver for the murder of her husband. I told myself that it was because my hands hurt too much to put the cuffs on her, and that it wasn't about giving Charlie this moment of glory and closure. I paid close attention as he read her her rights, but he followed the procedure correctly. It wasn't as if he'd never arrested anybody before.

I hoped Dennis wouldn't live to regret what he'd done here. Maybe this was another time that I should have stopped him. But I'd let him do it, and I hadn't interfered, because it felt important to let him take responsibility for this moment. As if it would allow him to take responsibility for the rest of his life. I hated that his mother had said she'd done it all for him. She'd done it for herself and I hoped he understood that. I also hoped that he would be able to lead a normal life and make up for all the years he'd lost misguidedly campaigning for his father's release from prison.

Chapter 39

A few weeks later, I went back to the Turkish café. The waitress gave me a menu that I didn't need, because I knew what I was going to have: some of that garlicky yoghurt dip with lots of bread. Still, I pretended to study it, because that would give me something to look at while I was waiting.

Barry arrived a few minutes later. He opened the door with the button to the side and wheeled himself in. As he'd said, this place was wheelchair-friendly. He was wearing a shirt and tie. It was very different to what he'd worn last time, and it showed either that he was taking this meeting very seriously, or that he was nervous and had dressed up especially, using his clothes as armour. I could understand both of those reasons.

Before I could get up and take the chair opposite me away, the waitress came and did it for him. He was clearly a regular here.

I hadn't been sure how I'd feel when I saw him next, but in the end, I was just really glad. 'Good to see you, Barry,' I said, and I meant it. I gave him my menu. 'Here, have this. I'm going to order that thing you had last time.'

'I thought you didn't like garlic?'

'It's not that I don't like it; I just try to be considerate towards my colleagues. Today it doesn't matter because it's my day off. Did I tell you that I had to go into a meeting with the Commissaris right after eating that last time? I'm sure my breath stank.'

'Was it a good meeting?'

'Nope, I got told off for passing on information to *Right to Justice*.' I scrutinised his face. 'But it was you, wasn't it?'

Barry studied the menu. 'Did she tell you?'

'I had it figured out already anyway.' I grinned. 'Did you forget what I do for a living? I'm good at finding things out.'

'I didn't mean to harm you. That's not why I did it.'

'I know.'

'She came to me early on, maybe a few days after Dennis had been in touch with her, and asked me if I thought there was a possibility.'

'That there had been something wrong?'

'That Ruud Klaver had been innocent.' He put the menu down. 'I thought there was. I knew you'd done your best – I didn't doubt you as such – but I never liked that case. I never liked that confession.'

'And you were right, of course. There was a reason why Klaver confessed: it was to stop us investigating further.' I looked at my watch. 'He's late,' I said. Ten minutes late, to be precise. 'Do you want to order?'

'Let's wait a bit longer. He'll come.'

'How much information did you give her?'

'I helped her run some queries. I still have a couple of friends in the force, and they gave me access to the database.'

'I should have done that, shouldn't I? I don't mean give her access; I should have found that second murder.'

'Yeah, we should have found it.'

I appreciated that 'we'. 'I think I've got better at the job over the years.'

'You've done some crazy things.'

Maybe so. Ruud Klaver's case had taught me how I didn't want to behave, and perhaps I'd gone too far over to the other side. I knew how awful it was when you felt guilty for not stopping something. What Barry thought were crazy things, I'd done because I now found it hard not to interfere in a potentially violent situation. I was actually proud of myself that I hadn't stepped in when Dennis talked to his mother.

'Getting crashed into while I was cycling wasn't too bad, all things considered.'

'Is that what you're going to do Angela Klaver for? Causing a cycling accident?'

'The prosecutor is looking at it right now. Remco is still in Dubai, refusing to testify to anything. Sandra did that podcast to apologise and set the record straight about Ruud's guilt.'

'Yes, I heard that. At least you've now closed Maarten Hageman's murder case too.'

'That's true. But in the end, Angela will probably get done for two hit-and-run incidents.'

'Not attempted murder?'

'It's all about what we can prove. We have to be realistic. Of course the prosecutor will make it clear that she hit her husband with her car in a fit of anger. She will get a jail sentence.'

At that moment, the door opened again. Even though I'd been expecting him, it took me a few seconds before I recognised the man entering the restaurant. It made me smile that he was dressed so similarly to Barry. He'd also made an effort and wore a shirt and tie. Now that he'd shaved off his beard, I could finally see his face. I could finally see how young he really was.

He sat down between Barry and me. I passed him a menu.

'It's good to see you, Dennis,' Barry said. 'Thanks for coming.'

Turn the page for a sneak peek at the next
Lotte Meerman story . . .

A DEATH AT THE HOTEL MONDRIAN

I

The Liar

Chapter 1

The only reason that I was in the Lange Niezel on the edge of Amsterdam's red-light district at 5.52 a.m. was because I was doing Detective Ingrid Ries a favour. She'd sounded in a panic when she called. You had to love a job where helping out a friend led to standing at a crime scene at this ungodly hour of the morning. It was neither raining nor below zero, but I was glad I'd grabbed my woollen hat on the way out. It was late November, and winter didn't feel that far away. The lingering darkness made it seem as if the night had hit snooze on the alarm clock and had settled in for at least the next hour and a half, wrapped in a duvet of thick grey clouds.

Two seagulls were strolling down the silent alley as if they owned it, picking up thrown-away fries on their morning patrol. Twenty minutes ago, when I'd first got here, there had been the noise and bustle of an ambulance crew and some of my uniformed colleagues. Now the assault victim had been taken to hospital and the others had gone. I shivered in my thick coat and hopped from one foot to the other to reduce the time that my boots made contact with the ground. The flapping of a shop awning dominated the otherwise silent street. A street cleaner and I were the only people here. I checked my watch: what was keeping Ingrid? Sure, I lived closer to the crime scene than she did, but if she'd called me out of bed to fill in for her boyfriend, the least she could do was not leave me here by myself.

The street cleaner was still waiting patiently, because nobody had told him to leave. He was one of those anonymous people who kept the city tidy. He was African; I would guess Somalian. His head was too small compared to his body, which was bulked out by an enormous thick coat. He glanced around him. I showed him my badge, but that did nothing to reassure him. A gust of wind pushed a McDonald's wrapper down the road and lifted it in the air as if to taunt the man. His eyes followed it regretfully. His back was bent over the bin on wheels that he pushed all day. Clearly he would much prefer to chase the wrapper than talk to me. I didn't take it personally.

'When did you first see him?' I asked. I shivered and wrapped my coat around me. The autumn air was thick with moisture.

'First? Maybe four thirty?' The man's Dutch was basic and heavily accented.

'Four thirty? You called us at . . .' I looked at my phone, 'five minutes past five.' I thought about switching to English, but he seemed to understand me as long as I spoke slowly and articulated carefully. The victim, still unconscious and unidentified but at least now in the hospital, had been found slumped in the doorway of a coffee shop with his face turned towards the wall and half hidden by the facade. I had seen him as he was being loaded into the back of the ambulance. People must have noticed him but assumed he was drunk or drugged up, and sleeping it off, and would have hurried past.

'He hadn't moved.' The African's voice was halting and soft and I had to concentrate to hear him over the sound of the wind.

'How many times did you come past?'

'Four times. Four circles.'

Circuits, I corrected automatically in my head, but I knew what he meant. 'He was already here when you started work?'

The cleaner nodded.

'Did you see anything? Did you see someone punch him?' The victim's face had been severely battered. I'd had a chance to swap a few words with the paramedics before they carted him off. They suspected a broken cheekbone and nose, in addition to a number of broken ribs, judging by the severe bruising around his torso. 'Did anybody kick him?'

The man shook his head. 'No, no fights tonight. Just the man.'

The fight must have taken place before the cleaner got here.

'Can I take your name, please?'

'I have a passport. I have a job.'

I smiled to allay his fears. 'I know. But just in case we have any further questions.' Depending on where this man originated from, it was quite possible that he'd had a bad experience with police en route to the Netherlands. To be honest, he could have had a bad experience with the police here. 'And I'm sure the victim will be grateful to you for calling an ambulance.' I spoke very clearly. 'Thank you for that.' Especially since you're scared of the police and just want to keep your head down and the street clean. He'd been the Good Samaritan who'd done what plenty of tourists and people out drinking in the early hours of the morning hadn't.

The man shivered. He had two scarves tied around his neck. One looked like a football scarf, but I couldn't identify the team. The other was dark blue, the same colour as his coat. Maybe it had been provided by the council.

'Can I buy you a coffee?' I said.

'Can I go? Please?'

I asked for his name and telephone number again. This time he gave me the details without arguing. After I'd written them down, I wished him a pleasant rest of the day and let him go. He seemed more grateful for being allowed to leave than for my thanks or my offer of a coffee.

The glow from a streetlight exposed the early-morning aftermath of a night filled with too much fun, empties and cigarette butts littering the places the cleaner hadn't yet got to. A deadly silence hung around the area. In the evening it would be swarming with punters, tourists and people out drinking, but now there were just the two of us: a police detective and a street cleaner. He reached the McDonald's wrapper and speared it with a pointed stick, then shivered again. It wasn't even real winter yet. On an impulse, I pulled the hat from my head, rushed after him and gave it to him. He pulled it on, stretching it far enough to fit him, and thanked me four times before moving on. I watched him as he made his way carefully down the street, sweeping up cigarette butts and crisp packets.

When he turned the corner, I started to focus on the walls of the buildings along the street, looking for CCTV cameras.

I hadn't found any by the time Ingrid finally joined me. As she walked over to me, she was stuffing the last of a croissant into her mouth. Flakes of pastry fell on the front of her coat. I was always surprised how she managed to stay so skinny. The bumps of her wrists were visible where the sleeves of her jacket didn't cover them perfectly. She'd once told me that it was hard to find clothes that fitted because her arms and legs were so long. Her short blonde hair was brushed up into spikes.

'Thanks for helping me out, Lotte,' she said. 'I should have called Bauer or someone else from the team, but I wasn't thinking straight.'

Bauer was her boss. I understood why she hadn't called him. 'It's not a problem,' I said. 'How's Tim now?' Tim was her boyfriend. They worked together in the serious crime squad. Ingrid had been on my team before moving to join him a month ago.

'He's better now that we know what it is. He has to have his appendix out.' She rubbed her eyes. 'We were at the hospital for most of the night. They're keeping him in until the surgery.' She walked towards the coffee shop where the victim had been found. 'Was there any ID on the guy?'

'No, nothing. His pockets had been cleared out. No wallet, no phone, no car keys, not even a public transport card.'

'It's the fifth violent mugging around here in two weeks,' she said.

'Weren't the others a bit closer to Centraal station?'

'True, but I wouldn't rule out the possibility that they were all done by the same lot. They probably just spread their net a bit wider.' She bent down to examine a scuff mark on the door that could have been there for weeks. There would be little forensic evidence available to us. If he'd been punched and kicked, there wouldn't even be a weapon.

'Our only hope is CCTV footage,' I said. 'There's got to be a security camera around here somewhere.'

But most of the shops along the Lange Niezel still had their shutters down. Early morning was the red-light district's equivalent of the middle of the night. It would be worth coming back once they'd opened again. One of them might have caught something on their internal security cameras.

'Did you talk to the guy who called it in?'

'Yeah, the street cleaner. He didn't see anything; just the guy slumped in the doorway.'

As Ingrid continued to examine the coffee shop doorway, a man approached me.

'Are you the police?' He wore a woollen trench coat, a green and white checked scarf wrapped around his neck. He was smartly dressed for this time of the morning. Probably on his way to work.

'Yes, I'm Detective Lotte Meerman.'

'Great,' the man said. He was wearing glasses, and his dark hair and beard were shot through with grey.

I could feel a smile growing on my face. It was possible that he'd witnessed the assault. He looked like the kind of person who would come forward if he had. The kind of person who thought it was his duty to society to report what he'd seen.

'I thought it was important,' he said, 'to let you know that I'm not dead.'

Ingrid grinned at me. Her mobile rang and she quickly walked away.

I pushed my hair off my face. 'Of course you're not.' I tried to keep the disappointment out of my voice. There was no reason not to be polite. After twenty years in the police force, I'd seen my share of delusional people. Early on in my career, an elderly woman came to the station every week to tell us that her neighbour had killed her cat. When I went to her house after her second or third visit, I found the cat very much alive, but also very overweight. The surprisingly understanding neighbour told me the row had started because he'd told the cat's owner that she was feeding the animal too often. Since then, she'd got it into her mind that he was trying to kill it.

The man standing opposite me this morning was at least two decades younger than that elderly lady – probably in his late forties. At first glance there was nothing to indicate that he was mentally disturbed. His eyes were focused as he looked at me. But his hands were so tightly folded together in front of him that it looked as if his fingers were strangling each other. There was a bruise on his left cheekbone. It appeared to be recent.

'When I saw you,' he said, 'I felt I should at least tell you that I hadn't died.'

There was something odd about his speech. His Dutch wasn't the basic and accented version that the street cleaner had used earlier on, but it was halting. Almost as if he hadn't spoken for years.

He swallowed. 'I . . .' he started, then fell silent again.

'Take your time,' I said, glancing at my watch. 'Have you been ill?' Maybe he'd had a stroke. I scrutinised his face, but there were no signs of it.

He shook his head.

'Is someone saying you're dead?' A celebrity's obituary had been mistakenly released the other month. Maybe something like that had happened to this man too.

I shot Ingrid a glance that would hopefully tell her I wouldn't mind being interrupted, but she was still on the phone. 'What happened to you?' I pointed to his bruise.

'Nothing. That's nothing.' He seemed to come to a conclusion. 'I'm Andre Nieuwkerk,' he said. 'Andre Martin Nieuwkerk.'

The name took my breath away, and it was a second before I could answer. He was the right age.

Or at least the age Andre Martin Nieuwkerk would have been if he hadn't been murdered as a teenager thirty years ago.

'You can't be,' I said.

Colour flared up on the man's face. 'I'm at the Hotel Mondrian for another day.' He rearranged his scarf with deliberate care. 'People should know,' he said, 'that I'm not dead.'

Ingrid ended her call and came over. 'That was the hospital,' she said. 'Our victim has woken up and named his attacker.'

The man in the long coat turned and walked away. I thought about calling him back.

'We can speak to him now,' Ingrid said, more urgently this time.

Even though I could see the excitement in her eyes, because this was the first solid lead in this series of assaults, she sounded exhausted and looked frazzled. She hadn't slept all night because she'd been at the hospital with her boyfriend. Tired people didn't always ask the right questions.

'Okay, let's go,' I said as I watched the man cross the bridge.

Acknowledgements

It's hard to believe that this is already my fourth Lotte Meerman novel. I feel incredibly fortunate to have readers who like reading my books as much as I love writing them.

I know that I'm even more fortunate to have a supportive group of people around me who make my books shine. In Allan Guthrie from The North Literary Agency, I have a fantastic writer as my agent. My editor Krystyna Green, Amanda Keats and all at Constable and Little, Brown have helped me make this book the best it could possibly be. Working with you is an absolute pleasure.

Finally, special thanks go to Anne Patterson, Chris Williams, Jean Hyland, Joel Kosminsky and Kathy Searle in my writing group who continue to give me constructive feedback, no matter how many different versions of the same chapter they have to read.